GW00469504

OPENED GROUND
The St Jude's Hauntings

Vicky Fox

ISBN:979-8-5979-5342-7

DEDICATION

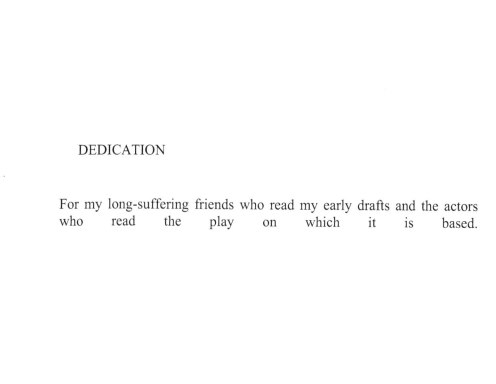

For my long-suffering friends who read my early drafts and the actors who read the play on which it is based.

Contents

ACKNOWLEDGMENTS

To Suzanne Bartlett for information in her book on the life of Licoricia of Winchester 'Marriage, Motherhood and Murder in the Medieval Anglo-Jewish   Community'

Prologue 1275

John the Smith and Wat the Thatcher, being the senior free men of the village, went to each cottage to rouse folk to search for the boy. He had been missing for half a day and last seen when his brothers had been playing with him in the grounds of their father's hall that morning.

The master had told all his tied men to abandon their labour and focus on the outlying woods and hedges. The remaining villagers were to concentrate on their own little gardens and piggeries in case he had taken shelter in one of them. Even the earth closets were to be searched, lest he had fallen in, and new layers of the midden would be examined.

Most of the villagers said they wouldn't recognise the child that had been lost. They had hardly seen him; he was kept at home with his brothers and taken to the church by a private entrance and seated in the family pews away from common folk.

Wat joked with Goodwife Wendle that she should check her brood of ragged brats to see if he had crept in amongst them and been treated like one of her own.

'How many have you got these days?' he said 'Have you counted them lately?'

She said she thought she had at least nine alive now, including her dead sister's. She knew as much from her fingers and thumbs; but their ages varied so much, she wouldn't notice a small one when the pottage was being dished out.

'He is a small 'un' said John, 'according to the master's servants, he's a tiny lad who's being trained in book learning and kept to his studies most of the day.' He thought one day the child would have to take over the running of the master's estates, being the eldest.

'Maybe he's going to be a courtier to the new King Edward,' said Wat 'And they be teaching him dancing and courtly skills that the likes of us don't need to see.'

Sounds a lot easier than labouring as a serf or scratching a living as a free man, John thought, wondering why he'd run away. Unless someone's took him, or he really has met with an accident.

The other boys were younger and didn't remember how their older brother had gone missing; they seemed genuinely upset and had cried until their father had shouted at them. They were probably crying because their mother was sobbing uncontrollably, so that eventually the wet nurse took the youngest and female servants scooped up the other two.

John and Wat knew that they had to look in the church and the churchyard, and make sure the old priest didn't have the little lad cleaning out his stables, mistaken for a village boy.

It was quite a walk to the church on the hill and they went via the cleric's cottage; the housekeeper there had heard of the troubles and searched the place already. The priest was away visiting a dying man in the next valley, and a quick look in the stables found nothing but a thin ginger-haired youth polishing a bridle and stirrup leathers. They carried on over to the churchyard.

The darkness under the ancient yew trees gave the place a sense of otherness, so different from the sheep-cropped downland that it was like entering a sacred place even before you got to the little church. John reminded himself that this was an ancient sacred place, from pagan times before there were Christians in the land.

They took their staffs and prodded aside tall clumps of grass and weeds. Wat searched every corner inside the church and John searched the tidy graveyard with its plethora of little crosses marking the passing of so many children and infants. How can some have so many children when he and his wife could produce none? She had started and lost a few and wept bitter tears that there was not even a grave to visit.

He joined his friend at the church, and they steeled themselves to enter the crypt where the bones of the dead were stored. Priests, and those above, were treated differently even in death and kept within the church away from common folk. Neither man relished disturbing them, but they moved aside the heavy door and took candles with them calling his name in a whisper and praying that there was no response from the souls that might still linger near their bones waiting for judgement day.

They watched where they stepped, afraid of vermin and human remains alike, and when they had descended fully, they lifted their candles to take in the sight of rows of skulls and long bones laid out on the shelves. It was nowhere near full and they gaped in astonishment at the huge stones embedded in the walls. John was the first to notice the smaller dish-shaped stone set to one side and stained reddish brown.

They had both done enough slaughtering of animals to recognise that stain and the smell of blood. Without speaking they turned and mounted the steps, trying not to think what might be behind them in the darkness. In the churchyard John asked Wat if he had heard the story of a stone kept for sacrifice. They agreed not to speak of it again. The boy was not there; they had done their search.

He was about to ask him whether he thought it was human blood in the stone, when there was a shout from the west side of the churchyard. The ginger-haired youth was at the church well looking at something he had caught in his bucket. It was a child's shoe.

Wat ran to the village and brought as many men as he could find, abandoning whatever they were doing. Plenty of women and children hurried along with them and watched the unfortunate youth being lowered against his will into the deep well, with an extra rope to fish out what lay there. His complaints about not being able to swim had been batted aside and, being the lightest, he was chosen to journey into that dank hole in the chalk until he reached the water, some fifty feet below.

It was high entertainment for the villagers. His groans were greeted with a ripple of satisfied chatter and he was instructed to tie the rope about the child's corpse, and they would haul it up. One wag shouted that they might even deign to bring up the youth too, but he was hissed at by the women. The small body was hauled up quickly and he was laid on a grassy grave.

It was John that carried him from the well and laid him on the grass and, not being used to carrying a small child, was slow to realise that the body was strange. The women noticed it first, and a low murmur of horror arose as they saw that his arms and legs had been broken. Not just in a few places, but as though he had been wrung out. His face was white and angelic, unmarked in death, but his throat had been cut.

They stood gawping until John said: 'Someone get the master quick. Now. Tell him we've found William.'

Chapter One –30 October present

It had been raining for days. Positively apocalyptic, thought Eleanor as she turned the old Land Rover into the Stansham community centre car park. It felt as if she had been living in wellingtons and waterproof coats; and even with the aga running all the time nothing ever seemed really dry. Mud had been tracked from fields onto the roads, and the footpaths were so drowned in puddles that it was hard to see the edge of the road in some places.

Eleanor was meeting Clayton Winters from the parish council to discuss the 'situation' with the churchyard. Her cottage was closest to the church of St Jude and she regularly walked the perimeter of the hill. She had watched as the new farm road on the east side of the hill became covered in dirt and chalk deposits. Now there had been a development that anyone would consider horrific; part of the churchyard had collapsed and this had exposed the coffins, some of them fairly recent. Although the church had been deconsecrated more than eight years ago, families in the village and surrounding area still visited occasionally to pay their respects.

The church of St Jude had been built in the middle ages and was on the highest hill in the area about three quarters of a mile from the village so it should not have been badly affected by flooding. It seemed that the new road had somehow destabilized the underlying chalk. Most of the older graves near the building were intact but some of the soil from around the tower had been washed away, exposing stones that had never been visible before.

Eleanor slid out of the car and picked her way through puddles to the community centre's electronic door. It didn't open. She knocked and Clayton appeared, unlocked it and let her in. He was a retired solicitor and had not been in the village long, only about fourteen years; still a newcomer thought Eleanor, without irony.

'Sorry Eleanor, the automatic mechanism is playing up. Damp must have got in.' They made their way into one of the offices leaving her wet coat in the lobby.

'I've been in touch with the Church about the graves' he said. 'Undertakers have been on site this afternoon to remove the most badly affected ones, you know, where the coffins are exposed. The footpaths and bridleways will be closed as well. We don't want any embarrassing incidents.'

Eleanor accepted a mug of steaming coffee. She thought how everything seems to steam in this weather.

She said 'Have you seen the weather forecast? This storm should be the last for a while. It will probably blow itself out sometime this evening'. She sipped her coffee and then wiped her spectacles on a clean tissue that she carefully removed from a little packet. 'You know those archaeologists will be turning up too? From the university.'

'I think that might have been a bit premature of you Eleanor, inviting them so early. They could have come in after the dust had settled, as it were.'

'But Clayton, everything is changing so quickly around the church. Every day reveals something new. I think the structure of the building is sound but it looks quite different now that the foundations are exposed. At the very least they can give us an assessment of the situation.' She paused 'Anyway, it's been agreed with the Church authority and they own the property. They seemed quite happy someone was taking an interest in it. It's been seven years since they took it off the market. This might be an opportunity to fully assess the site and get something moving.'

'Are these archaeologists aware of its history?' Clayton looked concerned.

'I set it all out in this email' Eleanor opened her bag, pulled out a sheet of A4 and showed it to Clayton.

'I see you've addressed it from the Stansham History Society.' He shuffled in his seat but said after a pause: 'Do they know it's just you now?'

She shrugged. 'They know what they need to. I've told them the approximate date of the church's construction - Norman, that there was an Anglo-Saxon predecessor and that there are other local monuments including some that we believe to be from the Neolithic period.'

Clayton neatly dunked his biscuit into his coffee 'I suppose they're aware of the magic and mystery aspects of Stansham? Whatever they find will attract a lot of interest on social media.'

'If they've done any research on the internet, they could hardly avoid it. The most commercial aspects of the village these days are known to be druids, wiccans and ley lines' She almost added that otherwise it was only a dormitory for Winchester and London containing overpriced properties. She continued 'Anyway, they're specialists in Anglo-Saxon history and the leader is a professor with plenty of published studies of the south of England so I expect he'll have a no-nonsense attitude to the fantasy aspects.'

He was about to hand back the email, then remembered something, and said enthusiastically 'It's Adam Glover! I saw that TV programme he was in. He was very good at describing the bloody battles that happened hereabout. Lots of stuff about gruesome Anglo-Saxon and Viking customs too. Goodness knows where they got that information; before Alfred it wasn't called the dark ages for nothing.'

'Exactly, Clayton, he's another attractive, youngish academic catering to the masses' appetite for stories about the origins of England. And because he is well known and has had a taste of fame, there should be less chance of him slinking off without fully exploring St Jude's and 'its history' as you call it.' He will not be able to resist the media attention if he finds something here, she thought.

'He's got quite a following, you know. The ladies think he's very attractive. For a professor' he added when she did not respond.

'Well he can't count me amongst his groupies, despite his sexy voice and tight jeans.' Eleanor straightened her glasses 'Anyway, they should be going directly to the pub in the village and tomorrow the weather will be clearing so they'll have an interesting day ahead of them.'

They finished their coffee and began to tidy up. Eleanor noticed that the fridge was well stocked with milk and that there were several new boxes of cereals in the cupboards.

'Are you arranging a breakfast club?'

Clayton groaned and said 'I hope we won't need all that, but with the amber flood warning there's a danger that the Nib's Down culvert may not be able to cope with additional rain. If it can't we need to be prepared for the old streams to find the easiest way off the hills. That usually means along the roads and if that happens, we'll be cut off. Some houses may be flooded, so the community centre has to be prepared.'

Eleanor thought about the archaeologists and whether the pub would be affected. There was little she could do about it now and the landlord would have a plan of evacuation if needed. Her cottage should be safe as it was halfway up a hill adjacent to St Jude's.

Clayton was thinking the same and wondering how many extra he might have to cater for: 'Staying at the pub, are they, these archaeologists? How many are you expecting?'

'Apart from Dr Glover there's an assistant who is another academic, and this morning they informed me that there will be a younger, student type to help with the grunt work. They'll probably call-in specialists when they've assessed the situation' Eleanor scanned her phone 'I should have heard something by now. They must be on their way.'

'And they're all staying at the pub? No one will decide to go to the church and work through the night or anything stupid?' Clayton chewed the skin on the sides of his fingers, a bad habit he was trying to kick but he always reverted to when he was worried. Eleanor tutted and he stopped.

'You'll make them bleed. Look, I know why you're worried, but this is too good an opportunity to miss. They're self-funded, serious academics, and we need to know more about the church and the things that have been happening since it was deconsecrated.'

Clayton shook his head sadly 'Well the last vicar was quite happy to see the back of it.' He studied her but she did not react so he continued 'Are you sure that this is not about the effects that place has had on your family? The other site investigators were professionals too, Eleanor. You're the only person who regularly visits the church now, apart from the occasional thrill seeker. And the fact that your cottage looks directly onto the hill must make it difficult to move on.'

'Especially since all that business when Peter left, you mean?'

Clayton looked embarrassed. Eleanor stuffed the email back into her bag and faced him resignedly 'I admit it has been difficult for me in this village since he left me for that woman. I thought things couldn't get any worse.'

She paused and Clayton said 'I'm sorry ...'

'As you know they did get a lot worse but none of it was my fault. All the people in the village who knew what was going on but just tittle tattled in secret, they were more responsible for what happened than I was, and they have to live with that.'

'Nobody blames you. Although they were surprised when you moved into your aunt's old cottage.'

'There was no point keeping our family home, and this way Peter and Lauren can get as far away as possible. Canada is the latest plan I hear.'

Clayton thought for a moment and then said 'It's quite a struggle keeping the magic and mystery visitors away from the church. This interminable rain has helped.'

'Well it's locked and the windows are boarded' said Eleanor 'though when they hear about the graves opening it will be like Whitby in 1890 and full of unsavoury people.'

'We're not expecting a visitation by Count Dracula, I hope' said Clayton.

'I wouldn't be surprised. There are some very odd types that turn up around here. Especially when they read about the child that was murdered in the thirteenth century and found in the church's well.'

Clayton put up his hands 'Eleanor you know that the parish council have done all we can to deter visitors. We and the Church have kept up the pretence that it isn't safe and we can't allow anyone inside...'

'It isn't safe' she interrupted.

Clayton continued 'But I understand that it is structurally sound. You know, I was sceptical at first when you said that being a consecrated church helped to, somehow, keep a check on the bad luck that has dogged it. But now I do believe there is something in the suggestion.'

'Bad luck?' Eleanor stared at him 'It's a malign influence. It delights in suffering and misery.'

Clayton blinked and resumed nibbling his fingers.

She went on 'It wasn't just a coincidence that they and Angus were all working in the church when Peter and Lauren's affair started. I believe something in that church caused them to behave as they did.'

He shifted in his seat, uncomfortable at being privy to the feelings of an abandoned older woman.

'I know you don't see it Clayton, you think I'm bitter and looking for an external cause when, in fact, he just didn't love me anymore and had fallen for a younger woman; call it lust or love, whatever. But to run off as they did and then for that terrible, awful thing to happen. I think something evil exists in that place and it delights in misery.'

'Now come on Eleanor, it was a tragic sequence of events. It's people, not places, that cause tragedies.' He knew where this was going, they had had this conversation before.

'Don't forget that my Dad never got over what he saw in that church seven years ago. I'm going to get to the bottom of it.' She had taken on complete responsibility as caretaker of St Jude's. No one else wanted the job.

'Please be careful. There must have been a good reason why the Church decided not to sell it, after all the initial interest.' Clayton was worried, he knew that it had been offered to the parish at a peppercorn rent if they would maintain it and put it to good use. The parish council regularly discussed the future of the St Jude's, yet they were unable to accept such a generous offer. The place brought with it the paralysis of a whispered fear, and the parish council could decide nothing.

'I was born and bred here Clayton; my family have lived here for centuries but it's as though I don't fit in anymore. When I heard what had happened to the children, I went up to the church and stood in the centre of that shell of a building with its bare walls and boarded up windows and I screamed my defiance. I said to whatever exists in the dark spaces of that church: you have broken my heart but you haven't broken my spirit. I'm going to find you and expose whatever you are!'

Clayton waited for her to continue. 'Did, did you see ……?'

'Nothing, just a fluttering of pigeons and a slight scuttering of leaves.' She looked at him intensely and whispered, 'But I knew the evil thing was listening, and I knew that it had heard.' He shivered, not sure what frightened him more, the thing or Eleanor. He would not venture into the church or the churchyard at night for any reason.

She started slightly as her phone pinged. After reading the message, she sighed and stood up.

'Oh no, the fools are intending to go straight to the church. That was Dr Glover at a petrol station, they're almost here. It'll be dark soon and the weather is terrible. I'll have to go up and check that they're ok. Goodbye Clayton. I hope it goes well later, let me know if you need any help from me tonight.'

She would go back to her cottage via the village shop and ensure there was plenty of food and drink if they became cut off. The rain was still coming down in steady sheets and the wind was gusting unpredictably. She might be tempted to stay home and let them cope with the storm and the church, but she had sent for these people and she was responsible for them. She pulled up her hood and went out into the late afternoon.

Behind her Clayton watched the old Land Rover emit a cloud of exhaust, and he had a strong temptation to cross himself.

When Adam's battered Volvo estate had pulled up outside her flat Sarah had been packed and waiting for about forty minutes. He was always late; she knew this from experience and yet she dared not delay her own preparation because on the one occasion that she did he would show up on time and no doubt pay back the criticism that she had levelled at him over the years.

Five years they had been lovers, and he a married man. Did she want more? She was not certain and now she would have to decide, because things were going to change, and this was the weekend that matters must come to ahead. She had been rehearsing and planning what she would say. Adam was late for things because he could never decide what he wanted, but whatever it was it had to be just out of reach.

Leaving preparations for a journey to the last minute meant he was always late; everything was a rush so that he did not need to think about it too hard. It became exciting for him, she thought. It was stressful for everyone else. His wife had left him at home one year when heading off to the airport because she did not want to risk missing the flight. They now always stayed at an airport hotel and managed to muddle along. Jane was meticulous and the absolute opposite of her husband.

Sarah was sure she knew about the affair but did not seem to mind and they had got on well whenever they met socially. Adam was in his element at social events. His Eton education had equipped him with the ability to talk to anyone with confidence and he loved to relate anecdotes about the digs he had run and the extraordinary archaeology he had discovered. He was witty and handsome and despite never seeming to spend time on his physical appearance he had firm muscles and broad shoulders that always made her melt. She particularly like his forearms when he rolled up his sleeves.

She sighed. A long weekend in the country investigating a disused church and staying at cosy pub with a log fire and good food. It would be difficult to give this up, but she was getting older; thirty-four next birthday. Perhaps she could enjoy the weekend first and tell him as they were leaving to come home. That wouldn't be using him, really. The car swung into her car park and someone got out of the passenger seat. Oh hell, she thought, it's Chris, Adam's nephew, and he didn't look happy as he got into the back seat. Adam looked bad tempered as he slammed the door and came to the entrance to call for her.

Sarah swore. It looked as though things were going to be even more complicated than she had expected.

☩   ☩   ☩

Chris sat in the back of the Volvo estate. The windscreen wipers were working at their hardest and visibility was intermittent as the rain moved in shoals across the landscape. He was squeezed against the overnight bags of his uncle and Sarah, his 'assistant'. Chris always thought of that title in apostrophes because he knew what was going on between them and had done for years. Not that he didn't like her, she was attractive with shoulder-length blonde hair and a ready smile, but he couldn't understand why his Aunt Jane would put up with their affair for so long.

If he had asked his Aunt Jane, she would have told him that with Sarah she knew where her husband was. Up to his armpits in old pottery, bones and dirt and fully occupied with his work. It didn't matter to Jane; she had a career as a director of a venture capital company and enjoyed her independence. A lauded academic husband with a burgeoning TV career just added to her kudos at social gatherings. His 'bit on the side' was a small price to pay; and they were discreet.

Chris was missing his own girlfriend. She was back at university, but he didn't want to return to study accountancy despite his parents' pressure and financial bribes. He wanted to study history and archaeology like his uncle. He knew this trip had been arranged to put him off and to convince him that it was hard and uncomfortable work. But he was determined to show them that he was more suited to a life outdoors with a physically demanding, practical job than looking at figures and seated all day at a desk.

Well, he was certainly uncomfortable now; in more ways than one. He thought about asking are we there yet? He felt like a child on an adult holiday, but he would show them how responsible he was and .... his thoughts were interrupted by a massive jolt and the car stopped.

'Damn and blast. I didn't see that pothole - the surface water conceals everything under it. This road's rubbish. I suppose it's been eroded by the rain.' Adam was famously short tempered, and nothing was ever his fault.

'Is the car okay? Do you want me to get out and have a look?' Trust Sarah to volunteer.

'I'll drive forward slowly and see if we can hear anything. Open your window and listen. You too Chris'.

They opened the windows, flinching at the sudden onslaught of wind and rain. The car moved forward and lurched over rocks and gravel.

'Sounds all right Adam and it doesn't sound as though you've got a flat tyre.'

They slowly carried on and Chris realised how bleak the landscape had become. The well-tended gardens of the outlying villages of Winchester had been replaced by the wide empty fields and ditches of the chalk downs. Clusters of trees were being punished by the wind and chalky water ran down the single-track road.

They were going uphill now and he could see an old-fashioned sign at a junction that pointed to a road off to the left; it said Stansham ½ mile. He was about to point this out when Sarah said:

'Aren't we going to the village first Adam?'

'I thought we'd have a quick look at the church, get an idea of what we've got to look forward to and it might give me some ideas for additional research online when we get to the pub'.

Chris brightened at this. Something to see. He was looking at the sheeting rain over the pale fields and was startled when they entered a dark tunnel of yew trees. Adam turned on the lights. The sides of the road were steep and the trees, bearing a heavy load of water, leaned close to the car.

'This road should lead directly to St Jude's and nowhere else.' Adam said, 'Since the church was deconsecrated there probably haven't been very many visitors.'

'This isn't the road that has led to the collapse of the graveyard?'

'No. I believe that was a new farm access track on the other side of the hill.' He looked at Chris's anxious face in the rear-view mirror and laughed 'Don't worry Chris the undertakers should have finished removing the decomposed bodies and the open coffins by now, at least according to the 'history society' lady.'

'Why don't they remove all the graves after a church has been deconsecrated? asked Chris.

'I suppose most of the graves are incredibly old and it would be a futile task. To my mind if you buy a church to convert it into a house then you should expect its history to remain in place.'

Chris decided to ask a question that had bothered him for ages. 'Why do they put graveyards and cemeteries on the top of a hill? Surely they must be polluting the water table that runs from the hill that way?'

'That's a very good point Chris' said Sarah.

'But in early Christian times it was more important to be able to rise at the second coming without ...' started Adam

'Getting wet feet' finished Chris. Sarah laughed, and he realised it was the first time he had heard that laugh for a while.

Adam grunted, then the car turned a sharp corner and stopped, Sarah and Chris bounced against their seat belts.

'Watch out' said Chris. 'Why did you stop?'

Then he caught his breath.

They were silent as they looked at the small square church, it seemed out of place, inside its circle of ancient yews. It was built on a small hill so that the graveyard fell away from it. It had unremarkable blank sides with small windows, a few buttresses and a tower at the western end that faced them. Part way along the church there was a porch which must be the main entrance thought Chris, and it had a moss-covered tiled roof. The gutters overflowed and the tower appeared to sit up oddly on a low plinth. It was surrounded by old tablet-shaped headstones, overgrown and stained dark by the years and by neglect. Adam drove on into a rough car park with a horse trough at the end.

Chris's excitement at being involved in a real archaeological dig seemed to drain from him and was replaced by a feeling of dread. The yews were frantically whipping themselves in the powerful wind but the church crouched like a cornered animal so that his first impression was that it was quietly malevolent. Between it and them lay a boundary wall and a lychgate that looked unsafe. A more recent square building was set back inside the graveyard wall. He was disappointed by his feeling of dislike for the place when this was his first real dig, and Sarah obviously felt something similar. She said, 'The church looks unwelcoming, and that gate is moving in the wind.'

Adam laughed 'It's exciting, isn't it Chris? It's been unused for eight years, so it's bound to look abandoned.' He was genuinely delighted with the scene and the wildness of it.

'I just didn't expect it to look so ugly' Chris said, 'How old is it?'

'Norman over a Saxon original.' He pointed to the side of the church 'Look at that massive yew tree on the other side of the tower. It's so close to the building, and probably extremely old. Some of the oldest trees in the country are yews.'

Sarah was still not convinced that it was safe. 'There are a lot of old trees up here Adam, and this wind is really stressing them. Perhaps we should go to the village before it gets dark.'

'Nonsense Sarah. Let's go and have a look around at least. The history society woman told me where they hide the key so we can explore inside if you don't want to get wet. Chris, grab some of the boxes from the boot and follow us.'

They struggled into their waterproofs inside the car, and then out into the rain and a fitful wind, despite the shelter that the trees offered. Chris dutifully carried as many of the kit boxes as he could manage, and Adam led them through the lychgate and amongst the older graves. He reminded himself that the newer graves were on the other side of the church where the farm road had caused a landslide and opened the resting places of the more recent interments. He found the idea of this macabre but exciting. An adventure to tell his friends. Perhaps it wasn't going to be such a bad week after all. If his hands weren't so full, he would have taken a few photos to Instagram them; maybe he'd get time later.

When he turned back from his examination of the lychgate and the sodden canopy of yews, Chris found that Adam and Sarah had disappeared into the church. Great, he thought, I'll put these things in the porch and take a few shots before they miss me. He dropped them on a bench in the porch and went back into the rain. He couldn't resist having a closer look at the large yew tree on the other side of the tower. It was hollow, you could climb right into it. He had read somewhere that it made yews difficult to age because you couldn't count the tree rings.

With cold wet fingers he managed to find the camera on his phone and scanned the scene. As usual he was distracted by incoming messages that had arrived whilst they were travelling, but he noticed zero bars on his reception. So he couldn't send anything, but he could take some photos. He carried on around the church and noted the modern vestry added to the north side opposite the porch. There was a brief lull in the wind and he shivered, looking up at the building. He knew it was fanciful but he could have sworn the church knew he was studying it, it was waiting. For a few seconds he felt light-headed and that same feeling of dread that he had experienced when he first saw it returned and made him shudder.

All the windows were boarded, he supposed to prevent vandals from breaking them. The blind old church and the yew tree seemed to lean into each other. Even ivy that had started up the walls had given up and withered on the stem. He retraced his steps to the western end of the building and the gravel path, standing between the gate and the porch.

The scene was colourless, the darkening rain-washed sky, distant and neutral, was reflected in the grass as though in water, so that the porch looked inviting. Oh God, he thought, I must be mad standing out here; he felt cold chills on his neck and realised that rain was seeping through his hood. He fled to the darkness of the porch as Adam shouted for him; and outside the yews continued to slap against the wind with dark fingered branches.

Adam found the key where the local history woman had

said it was, and opened the door, he went inside as Sarah hung back. The interior of the church was calm and still, and very dark. All the windows had been boarded up, including the three large east windows, two with white boards and one with something darker. Adam thought perhaps they didn't have enough white board but the more he looked at it the more it seemed to him that a dark mould had discoloured the boards on the right. He supposed the stained glass had been sold to raise money and also to prevent it from being damaged during a long period of disuse.

Most of the interior decoration and practical paraphernalia of a church had also been removed. Only a few permanent stone features remained. There were a few grotesque, roughly executed carvings near the roof, and he noted that it was showing signs of dampness. And some of the wooden pews were still there, arranged haphazardly in the small space. They would have to use their phone flashlights until the torches were unpacked from the kit boxes.

'It looks as though the electricity is off, is it sensible to come in here? Shouldn't we be heading to the pub? It'll be getting dark soon and the road is just going to get worse' Sarah said from the doorway.

He didn't reply; he was engrossed in his own thoughts. In academic circles he still had a sound reputation, and now an independent TV company that had begun shooting history and archaeology programmes had given him a trial and were interested in him as a presenter. He was just young enough to appeal to the buying public that financed the programmes, but he brought some gravitas and was building a reputation that he hoped would drive his career to new heights. He had always taken pride in his appearance but underneath his confident, almost arrogant, exterior he was concerned that every year bright young men and women were being produced by the universities. At some time, possibly soon, his marketability and intellectual clout would begin to decline. That was why he was keen for this investigation to produce something significant and why he felt so committed to it.

Wings flapped above them.

'Pigeons' said Sarah.

'Or bats' he teased.

She was always the cautious one, whereas he still liked some danger and he could feel the usual keen anticipation when facing a new challenge. Since his recent success on TV he thought the academic world had become rather sniffy. He knew that it was mainly jealousy but he could not afford to be a one hit wonder. He needed to find another exciting subject for a series that would cement his reputation and ensure that he had plenty of consultancy and presentation work for years to come.

There was no point relying on his agent, he had to get out and find the subjects that would capture the imagination of the viewing public. He remembered the rather visceral expression a local TV pundit had used: 'In this business you eat what you kill.' He was, he realised, quite excited that this opportunity had dropped into his lap. The history society woman must be a fan, he thought. There would be massive public and academic interest and he was keyed up at the chance to explore a church that had been the source of so much speculation in a village famous for its connection to the supernatural.

His senses seemed unnaturally keen, so he closed his eyes and smelled the air like an animal. The odour was unusual, not unpleasant but familiar, like many of the old libraries he had studied in over the years. It evoked a different time and for a moment he experienced the thrill of memory of a younger more optimistic version of himself when anything was possible, and he hadn't tasted disappointment or failure. He kept his eyes closed and listened, but instead of the hushed murmur of a tranquil library he heard only the wind and rain battering the roof.

'It smells sort of familiar in here, don't you think Sarah? It brings back memories of old libraries and books; you know, the nice musty smell of vellum and parchment and the heady odour of ink.' Sarah smiled at that idea, she had taken her jacket off and was shaking the rainwater out of the door; she seemed reluctant to come all the way in. Adam thought she may be unhappy to have Chris foisted on them when they had planned to be alone.

'And did you see the exposure of stone under the tower?'

he continued trying to arouse her interest 'I reckon we might still have some Saxon structures under the Norman building.' Adam closed the door, after shouting to Chris to get a move on and bring the equipment into the church. They could not leave it in the porch overnight.

Sarah turned as if to help him but Adam caught her arm, pulling her towards him. The idea of Chris being close by excited him and he wanted her to reciprocate.

He whispered in her ear 'I know we should have been here all alone, just the two of us staying at the charming little village pub. What's it called?'

'The Devil's Finger; very romantic.' Sarah's face was close and she didn't pull back; but she was still being cool. Then a noise in the porch caused him to move away, grinning and wagging a finger at her. 'Devil' she whispered smiling.

He smoothly changed the subject 'I'm surprised they've left so many pews here, but I suppose if a buyer was going to convert this into a house they could 'repurpose' them in some way, perhaps as floorboards or in the garden.'

'It's hardly a garden, Adam. It's still very much a graveyard.' She used her phone to light up the walls. 'Did you notice that the church seems to sit upon its own little hillock? And the damage caused by the rain is having the effect of leaving only the monuments and gravestones sticking out, like bones. There isn't a lot of evidence of visitors, no flowers or tributes; but even so it does seem disrespectful just to abandon the graves.'

Chris shouldered the door open and blundered in dripping rain across the stone slabs.

'Let me help you' said Sarah taking some of the boxes and stacking them on the nearest pews.

'You can make a start emptying the boxes Chris, and Sarah will make sure that nothing has been damaged by the rain. What took you so long?' Without waiting for a reply Adam strode into the vestry on the opposite side of the small church. 'I'll just have a look in here.'

The vestry was a small room with warm wooden panelling and orange walls. There was a series of hooks along one wall, presumably for vestments. The shelves were mostly empty and dusty, but there were some old pamphlets. A couple of pews had been brought in and set against the walls. The effect was quite different to the church. He realised it had the slightly sanitised smell of public lavatories and sure enough beyond a glass panelled door were a small kitchen and a toilet.

Adam was puzzled. In the church he had experienced nostalgia and euphoria, powerful emotions he had not felt for years. Now he faced again the middle-aged man's tedium of ordinary life, with predictability stretching all the way to the grave. He supposed that was the reason he liked to conduct extra marital affairs. It wasn't the sex but the secrecy. He did love Sarah; she was fun and funny and they enjoyed their time together. She was also confident and impressive in many ways, plus she did not expect too much or show any jealousy of Jane. In fact, the two of them got on very well and he had contemplated suggesting a threesome, if only in his fantasies.

However, a little rational thought revealed that they would both be so caustic in their responses that he would never recover his current position of power. He relished being the holder of the secret, the giver of the favours. If only it were that simple. Jane made it clear that she did not need him. He was a social asset; and recently Sarah, with her softer more loving nature had started to pull away from him. He stood behind the door looking at her through the gap and deliberately listened to the conversation in the church.

Sarah had begun opening the kit and, looking at the bedraggled young man, said 'I think it's great that you've come along at such short notice. But shouldn't you be starting back at college?'

'I should have gone back in September but I'm not sure it's what I really want to do.' Chris went on 'Dad insists on me doing either accountancy or law because he's paying for everything.'

'I sympathise' said Sarah. 'What would you prefer to be studying?'

'Oh, history definitely, or archaeology. Maybe ancient languages.'

'I expect you've been told umpteen times but it's hard to make a living from the past.'

'You and Uncle Adam do.'

Sarah agreed but said 'I was lucky enough to have inherited money when my father died. He and my mother were divorced and he never remarried. Your parents are hale and hearty I hope?'

'Yeah …. I'm sorry, I shouldn't be ungrateful. But Uncle Adam does ok.'

'You know that your Aunt Jane has a very good job in the City.' Adam flinched at that, although it was true.

He became aware of an awkward silence as Sarah continued to unpack kit and check the inventory. Then Chris said 'He seems quite happy.' Adam could only see Sarah and she looked briefly at Chris before she blushed and continued to unpack. Adam felt a stab of jealousy and realised that his hostility to Chris was that of an older man confronted by a young challenger. How ridiculous it all is he thought, as Chris walked off around the church, partly to cover his embarrassment and partly to warm up.

The rain continued to pelt on the roof and Sarah finished her work. She said 'What's taking Adam so long? We don't want to get stuck here.'

Before Chris could reach the vestry door Adam reappeared 'Well everything is quite sound in the vestry, if a little uninteresting. The extension is more recent, but this plain rectangle is exactly what I'd expect from a medieval church. It doesn't seem to have had the usual Victorian upgrade.'

'Adam, I still think we should be heading down to the village. The road was barely passable on the way here.' Sarah stood up and was about to continue when she stopped. 'Did you hear that?'

Adam looked blank but Chris said 'Yes I heard it. Like the sound of something rubbing or dragging, it was faint but didn't sound like wind or rain.'

Sarah turned to Adam 'It might have been that tree. It's right up against the building.'

'I heard nothing' said Adam as he continued to explore the church. He knew they should be leaving but the smells and memories of a simpler time were anchoring him again and he was reluctant to go out into the storm. I could be perfectly happy in this place he thought. 'I suppose we should be heading off.'

He turned startled as the door opened and a middle-aged female entered, clutching an over-sized handbag and a briefcase. She looked around short-sighted and dried her glasses on her scarf. Why do these middle-aged, middle-class women always have bobbed hair and wear scarves like a uniform, he thought, disgruntled. Waxed jacket and wellingtons brigade and with an attaché case to set it off.

'I'm afraid you won't be going anywhere this evening. I've been sent to tell you that the culvert has become blocked, local roads are not safe, and all the village accommodation is being used for local people. To be honest I don't think we could make it anyway. My Land Rover only just got up here.'

'And you would be?'

'Sorry, I'm Eleanor. I run the local history society and it was I who contacted your university about the damage to St Jude's and the, erm, exposed graves, when they started to show.'

Adam arranged his face into a genial smile and warmly shook her hand.

'Delighted to meet you Eleanor. I'm Dr Adam Glover. This is .....'

'Sarah Madeley' offered Sarah, shaking hands and smiling.

'And Chris.' Chris offered a wave.

Smoothly Adam said 'We owe you a debt of gratitude Eleanor. This could be a very unusual source of archaeological material.' He paused 'But are we really cut off? Well I'd better phone my wife.' He scrabbled in his pockets 'Sarah, where's my phone?'

'You won't get a signal' started Chris as Sarah handed him a rucksack. They both avoided Chris's accusing stare. Damn it, Adam thought, he must suspect something, as he found the phone and walked out of the church.

Outside it was almost dark. He thought of Thomas Hardy's observation that the crepuscular light of dawn and dusk differs in that the light particles are more active in the dawn and the dark particles are more active at night. This dusk was full of active darkness, as though the blackness under the lychgate was absorbing the colourless grass and creeping towards the church. He reluctantly turned to the phone.

✠   ✠   ✠

'I don't suppose you brought any food with you?' Chris asked Eleanor.

That's a very good point thought Sarah. She hadn't even considered it, by now she had expected to be sitting next to a cosy fire in a village pub with Adam. In fact, she was starving.

'Actually, I did' said Eleanor 'I thought we might get cut off so I grabbed as much as I could from the village shop and from home; it's just chocolate and crisps and some fruit cartons. Oh, and some cheese and rolls and a flask of coffee; it's in the car. If this lovely young man would give me a hand, we could bring them in.'

Sarah was amazed at how relieved she felt and her regard increased for this funny, fussy woman with her Hermes scarf and attaché case. She had been disappointed at not being alone with Adam, but if she was going to be stranded on St Jude's hill in a creepy disused church, she preferred to be in company.

She was pleased when Chris pecked the woman on the cheek with 'What a godsend you are Mrs ….'

'Eleanor, please' she continued with some hesitation 'and … I brought my booklet on the church and the village which you might be interested in …' Eleanor began to unpack her briefcase.

Adam interrupted her by bursting through the door with 'Bloody hell! There is no signal at all.'

'Oh dear no' said Eleanor 'It's usually pretty bad up here, but I understand that the storm has taken out a mast I'm afraid.'

Sarah was about to say that they'd have to make the best of it and was surprised when Adam burst out 'I was counting on this evening to do some research on the village.'

Chris and Sarah were embarrassed, but Eleanor blithely handed out a slim A5 volume to each of them. 'I thought you might be interested in my booklet, er draft booklet, here are some copies – one each.'

Sarah was not quick enough to stop Adam saying in his most patronising tone.

'Yes, thank you ... well, perhaps as background. But I doubt you have much on the pre-Norman period and my speciality is the Anglo- Saxons. I doubt there is much written about this area before the Domesday Book.'

Eleanor looked slightly downcast and explained that the present church was built in around 1100 and was about to continue when Adam cut her off.

'Yes, that is obvious from the design and construction.'

Before she could react, Sarah said 'Thank you Eleanor, I'd love to have a look at it.' And Chris added 'Me too'.

Eleanor smiled and said warmly 'We were just about to fetch in some food from the car but if you prefer you could all come over to Hare Cottage. It's not far, though it would mean a drenching, but it should be reachable on foot.'

That was truly kind of her thought Sarah and even Adam seemed a bit embarrassed at his lack of grace. He thanked her and then announced that they could not impose upon her hospitality and would be happy to stay at the church. Eleanor looked briefly at Sarah and Chris before returning her appraising gaze at Adam. Then she smiled and took Chris out to her Land Rover.

While they were gone Sarah asked Adam why he was being so obnoxious. The woman had invited him to an interesting site and was trying to help. He made an excuse about feeling oddly sensitive and said that perhaps he was coming down with something, a chill, or a headache. He wanted to know if Sarah had felt anything strange about the church, and he tried to explain his reaction to the odours and the sharp memories they conjured. Sometimes he felt like this before a migraine.

Chris and Eleanor returned with armfuls of carrier bags and they made a square sitting area with four of the wooden pews so that they could sit together, pool their lights, and keep their kit in one place. Eleanor dug out lanterns, matches, and candles from one of her carrier bags and altogether they had a reasonably well-lit area of the church. They would need plenty of light if they ended up spending the night there.

Sarah said 'Perhaps you could show us around. Are there loos and some water?' Reassured that water was still available as well as basic facilities, she found the torches in the kit bags and Chris and Sarah followed Eleanor into the vestry.

There was something reassuring about Eleanor's common sense, Sarah decided, and she was glad that she didn't have to spend the night acting as peacemaker between Chris and his uncle. The presence of a third party should take the edge off that. She had been annoyed when Adam turned up with Chris and announced that he would be joining them on this trip. She was used having a close relationship with him, cemented by their common love of archaeology and history, and of each other.

She was counting on being alone with him and there was a good reason for that, she had something important to tell him. The recent version of Adam, the TV version, tended to play to a crowd and was not the one she had fallen in love with. She was concerned that if his TV career took off, the serious enthusiastic man she had known for five years might soon be gone forever.

When they returned bringing the lights they had taken with them, Adam jumped up and stared about. His face ashen.

'Did you hear that dragging sound?' he asked, 'My light failed.'

When they said they had heard nothing and all stopped and listened intently he seemed embarrassed but covered it by laughing and said 'That got you. This torch must have been made in the dark ages.'

Chris rolled his eyes Eleanor laughed politely, and said: 'It can be a frightening place' adding 'The vestry is relatively modern and quite cosy. We could sleep in there.'

'I shall sleep in here' Adam said quickly.

Sarah was surprised. She wondered why he seemed so drawn to the building. What had he said? A familiar smell. She felt a twinge of jealousy, he looked younger somehow, as though caught up in some memory that he hadn't shared with her.

Eleanor started to speak 'Sleep in here? Oh, I wouldn't if I were you.... there are rumours .... '

Chris perked up 'Rumours? That it's haunted? Fantastic. Well I bag to sleep in here. I've never slept in a haunted building before.'

Adam scoffed. 'We're scientists Chris. And we are dealing with the dead every day. I've handled more bones than I care to remember. We don't spook easily.' To his irritation Chris laughed as though he had meant to make a joke.

Sarah said 'Well I'm for the vestry. It may be a deconsecrated church, but it was a church for a very long time, and there's no point in waking the dead. They've been disturbed enough as it is.' As she prepared to take her bag into the vestry, she heard Chris say:

'Eleanor, what sort of rumours were they? Will you tell us some of the stories? I don't mind hearing about the gory details.'

They really didn't need an uncomfortable night compounded with what passes for entertainment to a 20-year-old, thought Sarah. She looked at Adam hoping that he would nip it in the bud, but he seemed not to be listening. He looked as though he was in a trance, with his eyes closed and fingertips pressed together as though trying to remember something elusive.

Sarah said 'Yes, that's right Chris, all we need is a ghost story before settling down for a night in a disused church.'

Chris couldn't resist 'And corpses floating, literally, down the new farm road.' Eleanor looked at him quickly, but he was on a roll. 'It sounds like the Night of the Living Dead that was a classic tale of zombies'. He looked delighted and prepared to take some photos of the church to impress his friends. He turned the camera on Eleanor who was pouring coffee and she looked directly at him. The expression on her face sobered him immediately.

'Have some coffee' she said.

Feeling more chastised by her look than any tongue lashing he had ever received from his parents or Adam, Chris accepted a cup and also a piece of chocolate. They sat on the pews and drank the hot liquid gratefully. There was a short awkward silence then Sarah asked:

'Have you known Stansham long, Eleanor?'

'All my life. I used to come to Sunday school up here and was confirmed in this church. I was married here. My mother was buried here.' She broke off as Chris choked on his chocolate.

'I'm sorry, this must be very disturbing for you' said Sarah.

'Not anymore. The congregation of St Jude's had dwindled to virtually nothing by the time it closed, and we'd been sharing a vicar with two other parishes for a long time. It wasn't worth her coming over in the end. I stopped attending services a long time ago.' Eleanor seemed quite relaxed about the fate of the old church. To make conversation, Sarah asked her if she still lived in the village.

'Oh yes. The cottage I live in now has been in my family for generations. I was born in it. It's just across from the church on the other side of the valley. You would have seen it if the weather had been better.'

'It's always been your family home?'

'No, I moved in after my aunt died and my husband had left me.'

'Oh, I'm sorry,' said Sarah.

Eleanor showed no emotion but continued. 'The Mortons are one of the oldest families in the village. Especially now, with incomers and the steep rise in prices, young people can't afford to buy property in the area.'

'That's a common complaint in rural areas. At least there won't be too many second homes here, you can commute to London.' She thought about it 'But I suppose commuters are absent most of the time at work.' Sarah continued 'And how often does the history society meet Eleanor? Do you have any other current projects ongoing, apart from the Stansham booklet, that is?'

She hesitated for a few seconds and the wind gusted causing the roof tiles to rattle and a draft chilled their feet from the door. Eleanor took a deep breath.

'Actually, I am now the only remaining member of the

Stansham history society.'

That even got Adam's attention. He asked, 'What happened to the others?'

She paused but evidently decided to tell all. 'My husband started it four years ago after I gave him a metal detector for his birthday.'

Adam rolled his eyes but Sarah said, 'Some amazing finds have resulted from detectorists locating caches buried in times of conflict, especially Anglo-Saxon.'

'Peter was very enthusiastic and there were quite a few detectorists in the area who joined the society, so that at its peak, three years ago, there were seven of us. And the booklet I gave you is only an initial draft, but I was going to use it to attract other people to the society. I was hoping you might uncover some Anglo-Saxon pottery and maybe build a picture of the settlement to add to the later medieval information that I've been looking into. I've collected quite a few copies of documents.'

Chris couldn't resist asking 'What happened to the other members? Was there a big falling out in the group, did they form a rival society?'

Sarah felt a bit guilty, but she had the feeling that Eleanor might be the friendless oddball of the village and that they were stuck with her. Yet she did not have the air of a difficult person, rather of pragmatism and practicality. Then she surprised them.

'My husband left with the wife of one of the other detectorists.'

Neither Adam nor Sarah reacted, and Chris suppressed a nervous giggle.

She continued 'The group had been working on the history of the church and its association with the other local ancient monuments. They were researching stories, commonly held but unsubstantiated, that had been rife in the village for years. I had no idea what was going on until they ran off together.'

'Sorry' Chris said and looked mortified. Adam and Sarah said nothing.

'I woke up one morning to find my raspberry canes had been dug up.'

They managed not to laugh at this and looked sympathetically at Eleanor, waiting for her to continue.

'One of my neighbours thought I wouldn't be needing them I suppose; perhaps an abandoned woman doesn't need such luxuries. It was a typically small-minded mark of disrespect. As if, because I hadn't managed to keep him at home, somehow it was my fault as much as theirs. I suspect that a lot of the villagers had known about the affair before me.

'He and his new woman had gone to the Maldives on holiday,' she cleaned her glasses. 'It was something Peter and I had always promised we'd do one day. He took his car, some clothes and his passport, expecting to send for everything else.'

There was an awkward silence; no one knew what to say.

'In the event he didn't ask for them' Eleanor continued; ominously, thought Sarah.

'Eaten by a shark?' said Chris.

'Chris!' said Adam.

'I am so sorry' Sarah said sensing that something must have happened to him. 'Did you know her well? You must have been devastated.'

'It was harder for her husband; he worshipped her and they had two little girls. He was very distressed; he took the children to Scotland before she could seek custody of them.'

That must have been terribly difficult, thought Sarah and there was another awkward pause until Chris said:

'Was he a Scot? I could understand him wanting to take his kids before she got custody and made it difficult for him to see them. Did she get them back?'

'She never got them back' said Eleanor simply and without emotion, 'they died.'

'How dreadful' Sarah said, and she knew that Chris wanted to know the details, and so did she but she could not bring herself to ask.

Eleanor looked at nothing in particular 'He drove them, in the family car, off a pier into a loch, and they all drowned. No one knew if it was an accident or deliberate, and whether it was planned or a spur of the moment decision. He may have regretted it as soon as he put his foot on the accelerator.'

Their mother must have been destroyed thought Sarah. Even Adam looked shaken. Eleanor continued:

'My husband had been his best friend, we lived next door to each other and went on holiday together, and I often baby-sat the girls. Lauren was quite glamorous, much younger than the rest of us, but things started to fall apart when her husband was made redundant from a local business in Winchester. It wasn't his fault, I'm sure it was just a strategic decision. He would have found another job, though it might have meant commuting to London. She obviously didn't want the uncertainty and financial insecurity.'

She paused 'No, I shouldn't say that; I don't know what was going through their minds, but it didn't take long for them to make their plans and elope. Then, when they were due to return, Angus did' she hesitated 'what he did. The whole horrible thing was too much for the village though. It was in turmoil and has never really recovered. Some people even moved away to try and forget the tragedy. Luckily the outsiders coming in are relatively free of that taint.'

The villagers knew about the affair and condoned it, thought Sarah, now they have to live with it. She asked, 'Are they still together, your husband and the children's mother?' She was thinking; how could they ever be happy again?

'I believe so; Peter and I have made a clean break.'

Sarah desperately tried to think of something appropriate to say but there was nothing and she was relieved to hear Adam change the subject.

'So, you've been researching medieval history in the archives Eleanor?'

As though waiting for the opportunity to leave that story behind she immediately brightened and explained that the parish records were now held in Winchester. Medieval court cases were usually in French and the clerical documents in Latin which would have a been a difficulty for research as she was not familiar with either Latin or Norman French. She had been relieved to find that the village and the church had attracted a lot of interest from Victorian archaeologists who had carried out excavations of the ancient sites and reported in the Archaeological Journal or The Gentleman's Magazine.

There were also local journalists who had covered them for newspapers. She had found a number of first-hand accounts that she intended to incorporate into the booklet on St Jude's.

'Actually Eleanor' Adam continued 'I am surprised that this church hasn't been acquired for redevelopment. I should have thought that it would be a very attractive property, with its proximity to Winchester. Lord knows the Church of England could use the money. It was deconsecrated what, eight years ago? That's a long time for a valuable property to remain empty, especially in this area.'

'There was a lot of interest initially. Mainly wealthy people from London. They'd turn up in expensive cars for a viewing; occasionally they'd commission an architect to draw up plans for renovation. Surveyors would start investigating ...' She looked at them curiously 'then something would happen, and they never came back. As I said, there are rumours.'

'What sort of thing?' asked Chris eagerly. 'I mean, they wouldn't have stayed in the church overnight, like us?'

'Oh, it would happen in broad daylight.' The silence in the church seemed palpable to Sarah, the howling of the wind and rain briefly stilled.

'Some were just aware of a presence, maybe a sudden chill in the air and a reluctance to remain here. Others simply refused to discuss it. Now the only people who come up here are those with relatives in the newer part of the graveyard. And there are fewer and fewer of them and they don't usually come inside the building.'

Chris was curious 'Have you ever seen a ghost Eleanor?'

'I never have, as it happens.'

'You must have suspicions though, don't you?' Chris pressed her 'Please, tell us what you think the surveyors and architects saw.'

Eleanor hesitated and looked around at the dark stained window boards.

'I know that one man said he was taking measurements near the altar. He was a local and had worshipped here for years when it was a church, so he didn't expect to be frightened by anything he might encounter. He thought he was alone, then he realised with a shock that something was standing just behind him. He could see a man perfectly clearly when he turned his head with his peripheral vision and by moving his eyes.'

'It was a ghost?' Sarah and Chris said at the same time.

'Did he recognise the man?' asked Adam 'Or could he identify the dress or period in which he had supposedly lived?'

'He was filthy and half-naked with long hair and a beard.'

'A half-naked man? That's a new one on me.'

'The man exuded a stench of despair. That's how he described it.'

'Sounds like a tramp or hysteria. That's all it takes for rumours to start.' Adam smiled.

'Anyway, the Church sent their own people to investigate … then they took the property off the market. I think you'll agree Dr Glover that they wouldn't have done that if they thought it was hysteria.'

Nice one, thought Sarah. Then she asked 'How do you know so much about it? Did you interview the man who saw it?'

'He was my father.' She turned to Adam. 'He wasn't given to hysteria Dr Glover, I can assure you. Dad used to be a chippy, a carpenter, and someone had asked him to take a look at the possibility of re-using the pews and inspect the wainscoting for damp.' There was a pause as they waited for her to continue. 'He's dead now. Whatever he saw, and felt, it terrified him. He refused to come up here after that even though my mum was buried here. He never visited her grave again.'

'Is your mum still here?' asked Chris nervously, thinking of his earlier remarks.

'Oh, she's not here now' Eleanor replied. 'I had her reburied. She and dad are buried together in a cemetery near Winchester. This churchyard was not a peaceful place, even without the collapse of the graves.'

Sarah was torn between the sad story of the family ripped apart by infidelity and betrayal, and the chilling story of Eleanor's father and a ghostly presence. She felt sympathy for the woman. Did Eleanor feel cursed? The effect of each account was compounded by being told in this dismal cold place, the abandoned shell of a church; but she could not shake the sense that they were being watched, and she didn't like it. Chris felt it too, she was sure, but Adam seemed comfortable in the place. He had been moved by Eleanor's story about the children, but he still seemed quite happy about the thought of spending a night here. She said:

'I am so sorry to hear that Eleanor. It must have taken a lot of courage to come up here after us with daylight fading.'

Eleanor was quite phlegmatic in her response. 'Oh, it doesn't worry me. I knew you would need my help; you know, something to eat and drink. The locals all reckoned that Dad must have been tipsy or starting to go senile or something. I've never had any bad experiences up here.'

They sat for a while in silence finishing their coffee and tidying away wrappers and crumbs. Chris said: 'I can't imagine living here, like in a house.'

Adam boasted that he would love to live there, with modernisation, perhaps a tasteful extension and a mezzanine floor; cut down some of the yews to open up the view. Yes, thought Sarah, you'd love to be lord of the manor on St Jude's hill, entertaining and impressing your friends with a detailed account of its history and a few ghost stories for seasoning.

Fortunately, Chris couldn't help bursting the bubble and pointed out what a torment it would be for children whose school friends would ask 'Have you seen the ghosts yet?' What a nightmare they'd be to put to bed.

'Mum, can I play with Grandad? No, you've dug him up twice already this week.' Nobody laughed and Adam, rightly thought Sarah, chastised his nephew who apologised to Eleanor. But she just smiled and pointed out that any new owners would have to ensure that relatives could have access to any remains of their ancestors on the property.

'But there can't be any remains still inside the church itself surely?' asked Sarah.

'That isn't at all clear, I'm afraid. It proved quite difficult to investigate as thoroughly as the Church would have liked. In recent years services were held sporadically and the little congregation just used the main church building and the vestry, they never stayed here any longer than was absolutely necessary. So far as I know no one has thoroughly explored the deeper recesses of the building, and there have always been rumours that a crypt once existed.

Sarah knew that would be catnip to Adam and Chris straightway said, 'Is that where they kept bodies and bones?'

'I suppose it might have been an ossuary where they kept bones when the graveyard became full. A crypt tended to be a later addition to larger monasteries, and they often didn't keep the whole skeleton as just the skull and thighbones were considered enough to allow resurrection.' Adam said 'Eleanor it would be quite unusual for a church of this size to have a crypt, I would be very surprised if there was one under St Jude's.'

Both he and Sarah were amazed when Eleanor said: 'But we know there was an anchorite.'

'Really? Are you sure?' They were surprised by this information because it was such a small church, and Chris said he didn't know what an anchorite was.

Eleanor dug out her booklet on the village and St Jude's church.

'Look my husband, Peter, discovered quite a lot of information about the middle ages. And I have found some additional information in the archives which I've brought with me. They are photocopied documents to enable further research.'

Adam stood and began looking more intensely at the church. 'Do you know whether the anchorite was resident in the building and where he was kept?'

Eleanor referred to the booklet.

'Let me see ...' she read '*An anchorite is believed to have been walled into a cell at St Jude's church sometime between 1290 and 1305*'. She had not seen a contemporary account of the anchorite but a Victorian text on the diocese did mention a Hugh Critchley. Adam started pacing around the church looking at the walls and the floor.

'I wonder where the cell was ... '

Eleanor continued '*Together with the shrine of Little William he attracted many pilgrims and visitors and this brought great financial benefit to the local community and to the church.'*

'Who was Little William?' asked Chris 'and why did he have a shrine? And what is an anchorite?'

'Little William was a young boy who was found murdered in a well in the graveyard at St Jude's church. The nature of his death was such that the local people treated him as a martyr and made pilgrimage to his grave to ask for help and intercession with the afterlife,' said Eleanor.

'Of course!' said Adam 'The Winchester to Canterbury pilgrim road was not far from here. They'd get two saints on one journey. You're on your way to see Thomas á Becket and you can make a detour to Little William, staying at the local inn, making donations to the church. Bit of a gravy train for the locals.'

'But Little William was never a saint. He wasn't canonised, and any rumours of miracles were never authenticated.' Eleanor stressed.

'Still, an anchorite and a shrine, at a time when a splinter from the true cross would have been housed in a jewelled casket … it would have been big business.' Adam continued 'It doesn't mean that there could be treasure here Chris. Anchorites took a vow of poverty and were kept apart from everyone else. They were like hermits who had given up the secular life and were effectively dead to the world. In fact, sometimes a form of funeral would be held when they were walled up. They were fed and their bodily needs were taken care of, but they had no human contact. Did you make any progress in locating the cell Eleanor?'

'We never found the crypt or a cell. He might have lived in a cell above ground that has now been destroyed. So we concluded that the crypt was just a rumour.'

'Anchorites are really interesting Chris' Sarah continued 'They had some human contact when members of the community sought their advice on spiritual matters; then they could talk to them through a grill. Anchorites or anchoresses were considered to be holy men or women because they had nothing to distract them in their communication with God. Some even had miracles associated with them. They were deemed to be 'living saints'; able to intercede with God.' She wondered how such a small church had found itself with such attractions as an anchorite and a martyr and she was surprised by Adam's excitement. This was not his period. 'Eleanor, what can you tell us about Little William? Do you have a date for his martyrdom and do you know what happened?'

Eleanor referred to the booklet again and read '*His throat had been cut and his body mutilated.*' It also says*: 'the village had benefitted from the resulting trials of six Jews in Winchester and their deaths by hanging.* There isn't any more in the booklet, but there is further detail in the Victorian papers.'

Adam turned to look at Sarah 'I'm guessing it was a blood libel.' He was interrupted by a vibration from the stones beneath them. 'Did you feel that?' They all stood and looked at each other as it was followed by a sound of something being dragged. 'What was that?'

'Something's on the roof' said Chris looking up.

'I don't think so, it seems to be coming from the ground beneath us' Sarah looked at the floor and at the remains of coffee in her cup that still moved slightly.

Adam walked to the panelling at the front of the church and to the right of where the altar would have stood. 'The sound seemed to be coming from this area. It looks like a relatively new piece of panelling here.'

Eleanor quietly said 'It was put in during the 1950s. It's the area my father was looking at when he saw …' she stopped. 'He saw the anchorite didn't he? Long hair and beard, filthy …'

A rasping sounded, stone on stone, perhaps, almost a sigh.

Chris said 'Is this place safe? It's not going to fall down on us?'

They listened to the fading storm then Adam said 'Don't worry Chris. It's been here for 900 years. I daresay it moves a bit when it dries out and then gets wet again.'

Sarah pointed out 'If there is a crypt all this rain may have caused subsidence.'

'Maybe I should have a look around outside. I want to see the stones exposed under the tower.'

'But it's still windy and raining Adam. Surely it can wait.'

Sarah objected, but seeing that he was determined and might be reckless 'It's dark and you're not familiar with the layout of the churchyard.'

'But I am' said Eleanor 'I can show you around Dr Glover. If you'd like?'

They agreed that a quick look should be safe and Sarah made him promise to come straight back if he saw anything to suggest the building might collapse. She was glad that Chris remained, and her fear was not just of physical danger. She was aware of a growing sense of unease since Eleanor told them the story of the family and the deaths of the children. She knew why she had no interest in exploring the churchyard at night in the middle of a storm and had to admit that she was less brave than she used to be, more careful of what she did and ate and drank.

Eleanor and Adam pulled on their waterproof outer clothes and as they reached the door Adam turned and asked Sarah to explain to Chris about the blood libel and the medieval treatment of the Jews.

She said, 'That can wait surely?' She thought: we don't need more stories of murdered children and terrible consequences.

But Chris pleaded 'Oh, please Sarah. I am woefully ignorant about the thirteenth century; it would give me a much better idea of the period you are all talking about. And it's relevant to Little William and the church we are investigating.'

Chris's enthusiasm persuaded her, so as Adam and Eleanor left through the porch door, she began the story with which she was so familiar. Sarah had a Jewish grandmother, so it was part of her own heritage and something she had become aware of when quite young.

'As far as we know Jews were originally brought to England by William the Conqueror in 1066. The Norman conquest involved a massive reorganisation of English life. I daresay he wanted them to establish financial systems and to lend money for building projects as well as for their skills as craftsmen. The activity of lending for interest was forbidden to Christians by the usury laws of the time, and kings found Jewish bankers useful for financing their frequent wars.'

Chris interrupted with 'I know that they were expelled at some time.'

'Yes. In 1290 by order of Edward I after a turbulent century and increasing persecution, instigated by the Church in the main. During the thirteenth century there were not many Jews in England, but some were very influential. Through their networking they provided a type of national and probably international banking system when nothing like that existed. In an age when finance was unsophisticated they were able to furnish the king with an important source of tax and provide secured loans to asset-rich knights and aristocrats.

'Prejudice against any faith other than Christianity was commonplace among all classes, and these were the days of the crusades against heretic Christians as well as Islam. You probably haven't heard of the Fourth Lateran Council - that was a big meeting in Rome in 1213, and it started a period of severe restrictions on non-Christians. In England the king had to take responsibility for Jews in order to keep them, and they were known as the King's Jews.

'That didn't mean they were slaves exactly, but they had a duty to the king in the same way that serfs still had a duty to a landowner at that time. They couldn't move around freely and, in most cases, could only hold land for a year and a day. This worked in the king's favour because if a borrower defaulted on a loan secured on property, the Jew who had loaned the money and now owned the property had to sell it on pretty quickly. The king could prevail upon the Jew to sell it on favourable terms to someone he wanted to reward or compensate.'

Chris interrupted 'This was the century when barons and knights were rebelling against the king, wasn't it? They had property, castles and power and he expected them to fund his wars. King John and so on.' He cursed his patchy knowledge of the medieval period. Everybody knew about Richard the Lionheart and bad King John, but he knew next to nothing about his son Henry III, and only a little about Henry's son Edward I.

Sarah continued 'The three sources of power in that century were the king, the barons and the Church and all were hungry for money. The Jewish money brokers worked for the king and initially had done well in terms of wealth and power, and of course they had influence. They were a rich source of income for the crown, a sort of intermediate tax collecting system. If the king wanted money, he taxed the Jews who in turn called in their debts and it was the gentry and trading classes who paid up. There were few other ways for the landed classes to raise capital but mortgage their assets to Jewish moneylenders.'

She added 'One way to make money was by waging war. Most warfare consisted of besieging castles and if you won you kept the property and ransomed your noble captives. If you lost, someone had to raise money to buy your freedom.

'There were a lot of knights who ended up owing money to Jewish moneylenders and it was in their interest to destroy any documents that could prove the debt existed. Outbreaks of violence became increasingly widespread; there were instances of genocide. As the Jewish community was expelled from more towns and therefore more places of business, they had to build their communities in a dwindling number of key cities.

'Winchester was an important centre. If Jews were attacked by the populace during periods of unrest, they could shelter in the castle. There's still a Jewry Street in Winchester today.'

'And the blood libel?' asked Chris.

'I'll come to that. But you must understand that throughout the thirteenth century their lives got harder, many converted to Christianity, the rest were forced to wear a yellow badge. No, not the Star of David exactly, but a stone tablet shape representing the ten commandments. Eventually they were not even allowed to lend money and their use to the exchequer vanished; then in 1290 Edward I expelled them.'

'And Oliver Cromwell let them back in the 1650s after the English Civil War.'

'That's right' said Sarah. 'Was that your A Level period?'

'I've always been interested in the civil war. But I never followed up on why Cromwell let them back. I daresay he needed them to bring their banking skills. They were allowed to stay after that. So, tell me about the blood libel.'

'The best way is probably to tell you the story of little Sir

Hugh of Lincoln. It is well documented through a contemporary account in 1250 by Matthew Paris, although he puts it in the most racist terms. He became a martyr in the same way as William. Accusations of the ritual murder of Christian children by Jews had become increasingly common during the previous century, and this was all over the country. It's called the 'blood libel' because the stories alleged that Christian children's blood was used to make Passover bread. There was a massive trial of Jewish men and multiple hangings. One poor Jew confessed but if you torture someone enough, they'll admit to anything; and implicate others. There was never any proof that Jews were responsible for children being killed.'

'So it was a witch hunt?'

'Exactly. Ritual gatherings meant that any number of Jews would come together for ceremonies and they could be implicated if a local child was murdered. It was always profitable to someone in power because a convicted Jew's property became forfeit to the crown.'

Adam and Eleanor came through the door at that moment and he added: 'And the king sold that property to powerful local men. It was in the interest of people to blame the Jews for murdered children and the Church did very well out of child martyrs, as we know. There were supposed miracles and resulting pilgrimages and donations.'

He seemed invigorated from the fresh air, thought Sarah, perhaps they all needed to take a walk outside. She asked about the state of the building and he reassured her that it was fine, the noise they heard had probably been a shifting of soil magnified by the emptiness of the church. They took off their outer garments and hung them up. His hair was wet, and he combed it back with his fingers like a preening animal she thought, feeling a flash of physical desire. He almost strutted up to the altar space and looked up. Eleanor was watching him with a bemused smile.

Sarah continued explaining to Chris 'Little Sir Hugh of Lincoln wasn't canonised either, though he soon acquired the title of 'Little Saint Hugh'.' She turned to Eleanor 'It's possible something similar happened here at Stansham.'

Eleanor said 'Apart from what we have in the booklet there is mention of an archaeological investigation during the Victorian period, and some trouble at that time involving local people, and a mysterious death. I think there may be more detail in the documents I've brought with me.'

She went on to explain that William's grave was to the left of the altar, in the floor. Adam walked to the spot and looked around.

She continued 'There was a William brass, it was worn almost smooth by people who collect brass rubbings, but they took away all the brasses when they deconsecrated the church. It was a horrible time, the villagers rarely attended church, but they were not happy about the deconsecration.'

'The church and the church hall are usually a focal point for village life' said Sarah.

'I don't think this church has fulfilled that function for some time. I daresay you'll be sceptical but some of the more superstitious villagers have always believed that the church was built so far from the village and not in its centre because this hill has a curse on it. You can see that St Jude's was a hill fort at some point in the past.'

'I didn't notice the earthworks as we drove up here, though that may have been because of the poor visibility' said Adam.

Eleanor continued 'There were rumours that a curse would fall on the village if the church was not protected by Christian faith. Anything prehistoric still has the aura of the supernatural, you know, the older races that lived here, their henges and stone monuments and the magic. It's big business around here.'

Sarah looked at the others. Adam was smiling and Chris was looking around, Eleanor was watching them; she had an odd inclination to laugh and a similar urge to see if there was anything hidden in the many shadows listening.

'I think the new vicar was glad to be rid of the responsibility. She was quite a young woman with plenty to occupy her in other parishes and she wasn't here long. In fact, she avoided coming whenever she could, and a very old member of the lay clergy would often take what services were held. No one wanted to get married in such a gloomy place and very few wanted to visit their deceased relatives here, so burials, or more often cremations, took place at the municipal facilities' said Eleanor.

'You mentioned a curse. Do you have any idea what might have been the basis for that rumour, there is usually a story passed from one generation to the next, or was it a pseudo explanation for bad luck, a recent conspiracy theory? I am aware that the area is famous for its association with magic but I assumed it was locals cashing in on tragedy' said Adam, not unkindly.

'Well,' she said, 'we have local ley lines and the Devils Finger and the Devil's Dyke.'

'And you think that these might be a Neolithic standing stone and earthworks. It is likely that there was an iron age settlement as several have been found locally. But New Age thrill seekers are always attracted to any idea of the devil' Adam said 'I would expect that, like most of the south of England, there would have been extensive habitation in stone age times but often there is little visible evidence, probably as a result of farming and the destruction of monuments by locals in search of building materials. Also, the Victorian archaeologists were often no more than treasure hunters and their predecessors had a habit of excavating round barrows rather robustly. This allowed the farmer to take the opportunity to flatten the mound once the damage had been started.' Adam continued to walk around the altar site, as the others sat together.

'What do you believe Eleanor? Do you believe that something evil was released on the day they deconsecrated the church?' asked Sarah.

Eleanor thought for a moment 'On the whole I think I do. Terrible things have happened since that time. I know that it might have been just coincidence, but I am not prepared to dismiss it as such. And the devil has ways of sweetening a deal: commercially, the village is doing well now. There are gift shops selling wiccan items and souvenirs. It's on the tourist trail with bed and breakfast business in houses and farms, and good roads to London and a nearby train station in Winchester.'

'This church would be great for ghost hunters' said Chris. 'The creepy yew trees and the atmosphere of the churchyard would be thrilling, why not encourage them and charge them to spend the night in the church?

'Apart from being disrespectful and provocative to the ancestors?' Eleanor said. She was straight-faced. 'The villagers try not to draw attention to the church. We point out that the standing stone is on the other side of the village, although I daresay that will change as the older families move away. Though I can't see city commuters wanting too many visitors in their rural paradise.'

She continued 'We occasionally get tourists who specifically want to visit the churchyard, but this is discouraged and the church is locked. To deter them we have recently claimed that the building is unsafe. The country is full of marvelous old churches. Most people don't come to look at the church.'

'Are local people really so superstitious that they ignore a significant site because of evil spirits?' Adam said.

Reluctantly Eleanor said 'There is often increased interest in the well whenever the local press republishes William's gruesome story, but that has been enclosed in a secure building, so no one can see the place where his body was found. The main attraction of the area is to mystics and fantasy fans, so the pub has changed its name from The Star to The Devil's Finger. There's more money to be made from stories of hauntings and ghosts than historical facts.'

'Yet you invited us to carry out a preliminary survey of the church, and you have prepared a booklet' Sarah said.

Eleanor hesitated before responding. 'Call it intuition or superstition, but I know in my bones that something significant is going to be revealed tomorrow.'

'It's Hallowe'en tomorrow' said Chris. 'Do you think the souls of the dead are going to walk? They say that the barrier between life and death is at its thinnest on 31st October.'

'Don't be ridiculous' Adam was now lying on his back where the altar had been, looking up at the roof of the church.

'Things that can't be explained have been seen here,' said Eleanor 'but I was pretty sure you wouldn't be put off by the supernatural and would enjoy examining the archaeology and the archive.'

'Victorians loved a ghost story' Adam muttered but he then conceded that there might be some traces of Anglo-Saxon Stansham if they did some digging.

'I haven't found much in the documents, although there are plenty of rumours and speculation. Winchester is close and that meant that Alfred's court was in the vicinity and there was supposedly a great victory over the Vikings locally, possibly on St Jude's hill' said Eleanor. 'It is mentioned in the Anglo Saxon Chronicle but the actual site is vague so it could have been somewhere else. The story is that a wooden church was built immediately afterwards, and the yew trees were planted in commemoration of the battle.'

More violence thought Sarah. How many lives have been lost in this place and what is the darkness that resides here? Is it the cause of the violence or a result of it? She realised that she was not thinking in her usual analytical way but something about this night would be a turning point and she was unsure whether to welcome or fear it.

Eleanor continued 'There might be more information from the Victorian papers. I really do need help; together we might find something relevant.'

Adam sat up 'What do you say Sarah?'

Sarah agreed readily and Eleanor produced a sheaf of photocopied documents from her case that had already been divided into sections: newspaper reports, court cases and scientific journals. Chris was given the newspaper reports, took them to a quiet corner and set about studying them with interest. Sarah chose the court cases and Adam was left with the journals, which he split with Eleanor.

They gathered their papers and lights and prepared for a period of study. Sarah and Adam sat together as they usually did, and she asked him quietly what he had found outside and if there really was no danger from the building.

'I think it's the old yew tree that grows so close to the building. It has been moving about in the wind and I wouldn't be surprised if the roots were becoming mobile and rubbing against the stones. It seems quite stable so isn't likely to fall on us.' He frowned and put a hand to his forehead as if in pain.

'You're very pale Adam, are you okay?' Sarah said 'Is it a migraine?' They usually occurred when he was relaxing after a stressful period and she hadn't had to deal with many of them.

'It's a visual disturbance, lights and swirls and I feel sick. I don't think I can read' he explained. 'I need a dark quiet room and my medication.' He took his backpack and papers and went into the vestry.

'Poor chap' said Eleanor.

'Yes. I don't know what has brought it on but the migraine drugs should help' Sarah closed her eyes and thought of the things she must do this week. At some time, she would have to get Adam alone and have a serious talk with him. It was going to be an odd few days. She sensed the presence of another person and opened her eyes and gasped. Eleanor was looming over her.

She looked over at Chris who was reading with his ear buds in, cutting him off from their conversation. She looked at Eleanor, and the older woman reached over and took her hands kneeling in front of her. She put her face uncomfortably close to Sarah's and spoke quietly.

'You know that there is something unholy here, don't you? You can sense it. Not everyone can.' Sarah nodded. 'We think that we have control over our lives, but we are just flotsam in the great scheme of things. The old ones used to call upon the earth and the stones to help them in their struggle for survival. We don't do that now, we have technology, and we feel safe. But it's just a veneer, a varnish on the unknowable spirit. Women know how little control we really have over our bodies.'

Sarah felt uncomfortable. She didn't want to be rude and pull away, but the woman was intrusive.

Eleanor moved closer to Sarah and dropped her voice. 'Look I am sure you think I'm being superstitious, but I want you to be aware …. it's not straightforward here. There is a primeval force in the earth that has acquired a taste for blood.'

Sarah shook her head and tried to break away but Eleanor was strong and leaned in closer so that her mouth was next to her ear. To Sarah it smelled of stone overlaid with the slightly sour flavour of the coffee they had drunk. 'It's becoming stronger now that the constraints of Christianity have gone, and some people feel those carnal urges more than others. Would you say Dr Glover was behaving normally?'

Sarah sat back feeling nausea, and was about to argue with Eleanor, but the woman continued 'There is another soul with us. One that can't be seen yet, a presence that clings precariously to this world.'

Her eyes were now closed and her face impassive, and she had dropped Sarah's hands. They sat in silence listening to the faint sounds of the wind but there was nothing else, except the thudding of Sarah's heart that was so violent she thought it must be visible. Was Eleanor a witch?

There were no birds or bats or mice or rats to hear. The candle flames burned brightly and steadily, the shadows in the little church remained still. Chris saw them listening and it seemed to him that the two women had an understanding and had become allies. He briefly turned his phone light up to the roof space and scanned the church, causing little ripples in the shadows, but it was quite normal, if not quite benign. Rather as if it was waiting for something to happen and was capable of being very patient.

Sarah slowly got up and moved away from Eleanor who remained still, with closed eyes. She took with her the bundle of papers. But she felt so disturbed that she could not focus on the court archives, so she decided to finish reading the booklet about Stansham and St Jude's history. Eleanor had confirmed that there was some information about the Reformation, the Civil War and Victorian eras. They each set out their papers, spread around the little church and settled down to work.

Chapter Two – the Booklet *draft*

Stansham and the Parish of St Jude's

By Peter and Eleanor Davies

Overview

Welcome to Stansham, a village near Winchester in Hampshire within the western boundary of the South Downs National Park. According to our Wikipedia entry, mentions of Stansham or Stayns Ham were recorded as early as 963 AD. Stansham is within the boundaries of Winchester City Council, and of course Hampshire County Council, as well as being under the South Downs National Park Authority.

The village has a variety of facilities as well as shops and pubs. The Community Centre (formerly the Parish Hall) is the venue for a number of groups and is also available for hire. The village green, owned and run by the Community Centre, has a duckpond fed by a stream from Nib's Down, a cricket pitch and football pitch bookable via the Community Centre, as well as a playground.

Shops & Pubs

Stansham has an excellent pub – The Devil's Finger - serving food and local ales. It gets its name from a single tall standing stone on a hill adjacent to the village. At the heart of the village is the Stansham Post Office & Stores, with the Witchery Tea rooms set behind it.

Souvenirs and books on wiccan practices can be purchased in one of several gift shops and at the local museum. The Old Forge in Green Lane is a museum of witchcraft and sets out the history of this practice, providing private parties with a large function room that is available for hire.

Where to stay

Accommodation and traditional food may be found in the Devil's Finger Pub and several local farms and houses offer Bed and Breakfast. Ridgedown Farm off the B247 allows camping by arrangement. The most up to date list of accommodation is kept at the Community Centre where there is a free car park.

St Jude's Church (now deconsecrated)

St Jude's was deconsecrated in 2011 following a decline in population numbers and the local congregation now worships in St Mary's Church in the neighbouring village of East Wellsley. Details of the work of the church, clergy and services at St Mary's can be found on their website.

The church of St Jude's can be visited by following Church Lane out of the village for about three quarters of a mile. It is a fascinating building having been built in around 1100 on the site of an Anglo-Saxon church that is mentioned in the Domesday Book of 1086.

An anchorite is believed to have been walled into a cell at St Jude's church sometime between 1290 and 1305. Together with the shrine of Little William he attracted many pilgrims and visitors which was of financial benefit to the local community and to the Church.

A brief history of Stansham

The earthworks that surround Stansham were largely ignored until the nineteenth century. As the site currently exists, much of the great henge that surrounds St Jude's hill has been broken down by local farmers to facilitate cultivation of the land. Its size and significance can only be appreciated from the air where it can be seen to consist of a grass-covered, chalk-stone bank that is 839 feet in diameter (256 metres). It still stands 11 feet high (3 metres) in places, and must have been an impressive landscape feature in its heyday. There is one main entrance point, near the church.

There are three round barrows on St Jude's hill which may be bronze age or considerably older. They were investigated by archaeologists during Victorian times and have been seriously eroded by farming practices.

The remaining standing stone, known locally as the Devil's Finger, stands as a single sentinel to the north of the village and has attracted wiccans and followers of old-style religions, such as druids to the area. In the same vein the round barrows are known locally as the Devil's Humps and the ditch as the Devil's Dyke. Followers of ley line theories have also recognised the Stansham phenomena as significant in the web of lines criss-crossing Southern England.

The chalk ridge of the South Downs was an ideal transport route during prehistoric times and is marked by the ancient tumuli and evidence of iron age settlements. Christianity was brought to Britain during the Roman period but in the fifth century the Saxons settled and brought their pagan religions. A further period of Christian conversion took place in the seventh century when St Wilfred built churches in the local areas of Sussex and Hampshire.

We do not know when St Jude's was originally constructed but it existed at the time of the Norman conquest and is valued in the Domesday Book at 6 shillings. It was probably built as part of the consolidation of Wessex under the reign of Alfred the Great. There is very little documentary evidence from this time but there is a rumour that a battle between Saxons and Vikings was fought on St Jude's hill. In commemoration of the victory the Saxons planted yew trees and these now surround the church.

One of the many rumours about the Anglo-Saxon church was that Harold Godwin had worshipped here when travelling between the major boroughs of his short-lived kingdom, before the battle of Hastings. His adds another brushstroke of colour to the picture of Stansham through the ages and another attraction for the tourists. Sadly the Anglo-Saxon church is now gone, demolished by the Normans and replaced by a stone and flint building but roughly the same size and orientation on the footprint of the old St Jude's.

The road from Winchester (Venta Belgarum) to Silchester (Calleva Atrebatum) passed close by what we call Stansham in Roman Britain. Almost the same route was followed by pilgrims in the Middle Ages when travelling from Winchester to Canterbury to visit the shrine of Thomas á Becket.

The church was a place of pilgrimage in the Middle Ages as it housed the remains of a martyred child, Little William, and for some seventeen years housed the cell of an anchorite, Sir Hugh Critchley. An anchorite was a man (or woman) who gave up their secular life to dedicate themselves to communion with God. They were treated as living saints and their advice frequently sought by visitors.

Little William was a young boy who was found murdered in a well in the graveyard at St Jude's church. His throat had been cut and his body mutilated. The rumour soon spread that it was a religious blood rite, that he was kidnapped, fed on sweet food and crucified or bled until he died. Stansham had also benefitted from the resulting trials of six Jews in Winchester and their deaths by hanging.

The village thrived on the back of wool production for almost a century until the Black Death in 1348 when approximately two thirds of the people perished. After that the little community never reached more than about 100.

There was rumoured to be a manor house of considerable size just to the south of the village, constructed in the Middle Ages. Stories have been passed from one generation to another that a plague or fire destroyed the inhabitants and the building. No trace could be found in the Victorian excavations but aerial photography during drought has revealed the footprint of a substantial building in that area. Geo physics investigations were carried out on behalf of Channel Four for a possible documentary but the economic recession meant that the project was cancelled.

Probably due to its reduced size and impoverishment the village did not attract much attention during the upheavals of the next few hundred years. It was largely unscathed by the

Reformation when Protestantism was foisted onto the largely unwilling and uneducated populace. The priest became a vicar and married and brought up his family in the vicarage, a cottage on an adjacent hill.

Stansham was also little affected by the English Civil war which wrought so much destruction on the mother church in Winchester. There was a witchcraft trial during the war and the witch executed by suffocation.

In Victorian times the new interest in archaeology and the Middle Ages gave rise to investigations into the local tumuli and into the history of the church itself. A stained-glass window was added at this time as a gift from a charitable foundation in Winchester. This is no longer to be seen as the fragile items have been removed from the now disused church and either sold or housed in the Winchester Museum.

Until its deconsecration the church contained several brasses that were very popular with collectors of brass rubbings, including that of Little William, the martyred child. Copies of these rubbings can be obtained in the church for a donation.

Chapter Three

Sarah was surprised and excited to find that there might be images of the old brasses at the church. They should help to add depth to the back story of Stansham. She quietly asked Eleanor if they were still here. The other woman was back to her pleasant, helpful self and offered to look for them in the vestry where she supposed they might be. She could check on Dr Glover and she might be able to find some additional medicine if he still had the migraine. Chris said that as they were going to disturb Adam, he would avail himself of the loos.

They left Sarah in the quiet of the church with the flickering shadows and her mind filled with the suggestion made by Eleanor that something evil was waiting. She thought of the abandoned graves of people who had been loved, and of the weddings, christenings and funerals that had been celebrated in this church.

She felt exhausted and could barely keep her eyes open so she decided to lie down on one of the benches, on her most comfortable side and closed her eyes for a few minutes relaxation; it was going to be a long night. The wind had dropped and the church was almost silent. To prevent herself from listening for creaking and rustling she focussed on her favourite image: that of a warm spring day and birdsong.

She felt an overwhelming rush of fatigue and surrendered herself to the luxury of the half world between waking and sleeping. It was an unfocussed space where unreal things seemed real and she usually felt safe. Sarah had been an only child with an absent father and she had an imaginary friend called George. That imaginary friend still occasionally appeared in her dreams. He had grown older and was now a man who always seemed to wear suits; he was bespectacled and bookish, with brown hair and sideburns.

The frequency of his appearance coincided with periods of stress, when she was studying, or had difficult decisions to make. His presence was so vivid that sometimes she felt her waking life to be a pale shadow of her sleeping one and wondered if she should seek professional help. In the end she had decided that he was a creation of her subconscious mind and was not only harmless but useful in assisting it in processing important information.

As she relaxed towards sleep Sarah became aware of his presence near her. Then she saw him, and he was in St Jude's church, but the church was different. Sun was pouring through the windows. It was a bright day in spring, she could hear the songs of blackbirds and thrushes. George was in shirt sleeves and kneeling near the altar at the eastern end of the building which was lit by a small stained-glass window. It was quite simple and not especially colourful but the church was light and there were several brasses on the walls. There was a pulpit and a very small choir stall, a tiny organ at the front and a stone font near the door. Behind her the Norman tower loomed like an unseen presence and she could not turn to look at it.

George was looking at a brass rubbing that he had just made. His hands were black from the wax ball and papers were strewn about him. The brass was of a child holding a lamb. Unusually, he was not aware of Sarah's presence and made no attempt to communicate with her. He had another brass rubbing that she could not see. She had the feeling that he was somehow horrified by what was on the second paper, but he was fascinated by both images. As she tried to focus her eyes on the brass rubbings the church melted away and she was in a small study with walls lined with books and an old-fashioned desk on which the images were now laid out side by side. There was an oil lamp and the remnants of candles; this must be another time, she thought perhaps another century.

She wanted him to speak to her and willed him to turn, but a small slim woman appeared at his side and Sarah was puzzled. The woman was wearing a tabard over another dress, with an elaborately decorated girdle and she was fully veiled although her grey hair fell below the veil to her waist. This was not Victorian dress; her clothes were exotic and from an earlier time.

The man she knew as George was startled when he noticed the woman. He looked around the room as though seeking an explanation for her presence, then he drew back in horror and looked, she thought, as though he had seen a ghost. He appeared to be thinner than she remembered, and Sarah saw that his face was pale with dark shadows under his eyes.

The mysterious woman beckoned him to approach her and Sarah was disappointed that she would not hear what was being said, but dreams, even benign ones, are not always within the control of the dreamer. The woman took George's face in old hands adorned with heavily jewelled rings, and drew him towards her veil.

No, thought Sarah, pull away. But he seemed unable to move and then his face was covered by the light veil that hid all within it and she feared for his safety. After what seemed a long time the woman dissolved into a fine mist that began to dissipate around the darkening room; he staggered, fell back and collapsed. As he sprawled on the floor the last remnants of the mist hovered above his face. He sat up violently with wide eyes. Crawling forwards he reached for the papers and looked at them in horror. She briefly glimpsed the other rubbing, dark and disturbing.

George shook his head, obviously in distress. This emotion filled Sarah as though it were her own experience. She called out to him and tried to reach him but found the light growing dimmer and the floating sensation she had experienced as she fell asleep became a falling one. She woke violently with a start.

She was sweating and hot and knew that she was going to be sick. Damn - not now, she thought. She pushed herself upright and started to walk to the door, if she was going to be sick it would be outside. Her legs gave way and she sat down on the nearest pew, put her head down and slipped into unconsciousness.

The church was dark and quiet, the wind not much more than an occasional gust against the shuttered windows as Chris entered. He wondered vaguely where Sarah was then saw her apparently sleeping on a bench near the door so he made an effort not to wake her as he relit the candles that they had placed earlier. He thought she looked pale but everything seemed colourless in this light. He walked to the area where the altar would have stood and tried to imagine what it might have been like with people and music.

From a long way away, Sarah heard hissing as neurons fired in her brain. A small voice said, 'I'm Sarah Madeley', as though she might not know who she was. As the white noise faded, she saw shadows and light and had to fight the desire to scream but began to ground herself as she felt the hard bench under her cheek and smelled the old brown varnish and the cold damp of the church. She moved.

'You're still with us then? I thought you would be the last person to fall asleep in a haunted church.'

'Chris, oh thank God. I fainted, I felt so sick.'

He'd seen people pass out through drink but not like this. She looked ill and was very pale so he put a hand on her shoulder and suggested a fruit juice, for the sugar. She looked at him wide eyed and he saw that her pupils were dilated.

'I saw something.'

'Really! Was it a ghost?'

'Not a ghost exactly; it was more like a dream' she replied.

Chris was disappointed, but he fetched her a fruit drink and sat next to her.

'What did you see Sarah?'

'I am sure that there was a ghost in it but it happened to someone else a long time ago.'

She told him what she had seen and heard, as precisely as she could, knowing that dreams are apt to fade. She was able to describe the church and then the old-fashioned room in detail. The ghostly presence of a veiled woman intrigued them both but it was just a dream so what could be the significance? Sarah felt better and they agreed not to mention it to Adam yet, not until they had more understanding of the relevance. She was grateful to Chris for listening without judging and it was refreshing to be with someone who was young and open to all ideas.

'Did Eleanor find the brass-rubbing images? She has been a long time looking for them.'

'Yes, but when I came out Adam had latched on to them and they were looking through them' said Chris.

'He must be feeling better' said Sarah.

'Eleanor gave him some more coffee and I saw her put something in it. Whatever it was, it worked quickly and when I left she was giving him a neck and shoulder massage.'

They sat in silence as Sarah absorbed this. Perhaps she was a witch, she giggled, 'Really, a massage?'

'I know. And he was smiling. It's weird.'

After a few minutes Adam appeared from the vestry with a handful of printed pages and Eleanor followed him. He seemed relaxed, his headache gone, and he handed the prints of the old brasses to Sarah with the comment that, apart from the William brass, they were as expected from a country church. There were Tudor ladies and gentlemen and the oldest ones were members of the Critchley family, but none of the anchorite Sir Hugh Critchley.

As Sarah looked at the image of a child holding a lamb, she felt her body tingle. She had seen that brass rubbing in George's hands. On an impulse Sarah asked 'Eleanor, what was the church like when they held services here?'

Eleanor frowned and tried to remember; she had not been a regular churchgoer for some time. She described the altar that Sarah had seen. Then Sarah described the pulpit and the font with uncanny accuracy and said to Eleanor 'What about the windows at the altar?'

'They were very large Victorian stained glass affairs as you can see from the size of the boards, and must have been colourful with three separate pictures, at least originally. In the centre was a Christ figure, and St Jude was on his right; the window on the left side of Jesus had been boarded up for as long as I can remember. I supposed it must have been broken and they couldn't afford to replace it. You can see that those boards are darker than the white boards of the other two windows. I've been looking for a photo of the original three-part window to go in my booklet about the village.'

Sarah described the window she had seen but Eleanor shook her head. She looked at Chris. 'That's not the window I saw. Perhaps it wasn't this church.'

Sarah was disappointed, but then Chris asked: 'When was that window installed?'

'About the middle of the nineteenth century.'

Chris turned to Sarah and said, 'It just means that your dream must have been of an earlier time.'

Adam sighed 'Sarah is famous for her dreams and her vivid recall of them. I am sure she lives an extra life in the dreams she has.'

All three looked at Sarah who tried to downplay its significance, but Eleanor asked her to recount it in as much detail as possible.

She described the dream, recalling the purity of the air in the church, its sweetness, and the silence broken only by birdsong.

'It was late afternoon and I know that the church was decorated, there was a white cloth and candles on the altar, a rail, and a lot of spring flowers. I am sure there was no wainscoting as there is now, but there had been brasses on the walls, and smaller plaques. I saw a brass-rubbing of William holding a lamb. I suppose that would be the symbol of a sacrifice. The man doing the brass rubbing had another paper, but I can't recall the image, just that it was horrible, shocking somehow.'

'That wouldn't be the same man you are always dreaming about?' Adam said wearily.

'Yes, it was' Sarah said by way of explanation to the others. 'He's not in every dream, but quite a few and I feel as though I know him. Anyway that pleasant scene faded into a book-lined room that definitely seemed Victorian. The air was close and smoky; I had another glimpse of the frightening brass rubbing but I still can't remember in any details. It must have been a brass of the anchorite. Don't you think Eleanor?'

Eleanor could not remember seeing it.

Sarah continued 'The man's dress was early Victorian, I'm sure and he was worried. Then a veiled woman materialized; she must have been a ghost, and she told the man something that distressed him even more. She faded into him and then disappeared like smoke. But also she was different, more exotic and not from the same period. Do you think this is a message from beyond the grave? Perhaps it relates to our investigation into St Jude's.'

Chris and Eleanor were silent but Adam's reaction was

immediate.

'Sarah I can't believe you expect us to take that seriously. It's ridiculous to waste time on a dream when they are simply manifestations of anxieties chewed up with bits of information.' He turned to Eleanor. 'If you don't remember seeing a brass of the anchorite then either it was removed some time earlier or it was boarded up and that means it might not have been taken away. It may still be here.' He began to walk around the perimeter of the room scrutinising and tapping the walls.

Chris made a sympathetic face at Sarah and said 'It would be great to find his tomb but I don't understand why a member of a wealthy family like Sir Hugh would have become an anchorite in the first place when he presumably had wealth and power.'

'Perhaps he had something to atone for' said Sarah 'Christians of the middle ages believed in heaven and were terrified of hell. It wasn't possible to purchase indulgences until much later so he would have to make an act of contrition to atone for his sin. What were a few years of penance compared to everlasting life?'

Adam chipped in 'In fact, you had to be wealthy to enter holy orders or have all your bodily needs taken care of at that time. The last thing the Church wanted was the undeserving poor avoiding their allotted toil to be fed and watered at its expense.'

Sarah continued 'It was a time of great superstition and faith; people may have behaved violently and venally but they really believed that their souls were at risk, and the clergy were immensely powerful. The Church was a state as powerful as Europe's secular states, it formed alliances and waged wars, sent out papal legates to promote its ambitions. It had the ultimate power of excommunication to exercise control over kings and nobles if it was thwarted.'

'It's likely that Hugh Critchley gave property to the Church to facilitate his incarceration. Do we know much about him and his family? Perhaps we can piece it together' said Adam.

They joined Adam at the front of the church where Eleanor had indicated the William brass had been, and stood in silence as they looked at William's grave. They listened to the remnants of the storm, much quieter now. The bare interior of St Jude's was oppressive. There were no brasses or other adornments except the cobwebs and dust that moved in the light of their lamps and candles.

'Do you think he's still under those slabs?' Sarah asked. She looked at the small photocopy of a brass rubbing of William holding a lamb and the words 'blood sacrifice' would not leave her mind. She thought she heard a scraping sound again and glanced at Eleanor who seemed not to have heard it. Then she caught Chris's eye and he definitely had. She thought he looked afraid.

'Did you hear that sound?' he said.

It increased in volume and Adam backed away from the group. A slate slid from the roof and hit the vestry. The scraping sound stopped.

'It was a roof slate. I thought William was trying to get out' said Chris laughing nervously.

Eleanor dropped to her knees and began brushing the dust off the stones; such a gentle movement, like a mother smoothing her child's bed clothes thought Sarah.

As though telling a bedtime story Eleanor spoke as she continued to brush the old worn stones of the grave. 'I don't know for sure but I think he may have been disinterred in the nineteenth century. There was a story that my grandmother used to tell me when I was a child. If a baby was born illegitimate, or if it died unbaptised, the priest might refuse to bury it in consecrated ground, but a parent sometimes buried the body secretly in a corner of the graveyard. Stillborn infants also might be found there. She said there was a rumour that at Stansham the practice had extended to burying them in the grave of Little William in the hope that the 'saint' would intercede on their behalf in heaven.'

Chris went back to his papers and began searching through them.

'Well, it's an interesting tale' said Adam dismissively. He was still searching the walls and moving pews aside to look into dark corners. The others were wrapped in their own thoughts; when a vixen screamed and they all jumped. Eleanor stood up quickly and hurried away to the nave.

'Found it. I knew I had seen something on that' Chris was excited, as he waved some papers aloft.

They were relieved to have an excuse to gather again in the square of pews and the pool of light. He said to Eleanor:

'You know you said they began to carry out investigations into old sites in Victorian times? Well, I've found a newspaper article with pictures about an excavation of Little William's grave in …' he consulted his papers. 'October 1847.'

He found the paper and read from it.

'Right, it says *and so it happened that when the body of Little William was uncovered by Dr Macey, the eminent archaeologist, a quantity of other bones was uncovered*' Chris looked around significantly '*of tiny babies. On being interviewed by the magistrate, the highly respected historian could not account for the extra sixteen or so skeletons found in the grave but suggested that it may have been used as an ossuary.*'

Eleanor gasped but Adam scoffed 'That's very unlikely, he must have lied. Let me see it.'

Sarah reeled slightly, trying not to show her feelings. The babies' skeletons placed in a medieval grave shocked her but more significantly the name Macey meant something to her. She had found his name in her ancestry investigations, although she knew nothing about that branch of the family.

Adam read '*The bones were removed and, amongst much wailing from the common women of the village, were taken to be housed in a place of scientific enquiry where they may be seen by the curious at tuppence a time.* Typical *The reason for the opening of Little William's grave was for historical study and to ensure that the remains were safe, particularly in view of the looseness of the brass. This is now in place and firmly screwed down. Our artist Mr McKinley has made a drawing of the skeleton of the child martyr who now lies alone in his grave, devoid of the company of those sad little souls.*'

'Good god' said Chris 'They dug him up and found a load of babies.'

Sarah shuddered. Had it become colder in the church or had someone walked on her grave?

No one spoke until Adam said

'It seems reasonable. You have a miscarriage or your baby is stillborn and can't be baptised, or the priest refuses to baptise it because it is born out of wedlock. You don't want to just throw it on the midden, do you? Who better than a child saint to take care of it? I don't see the connection with your gentleman brass-rubber Sarah, if he ever existed. In any event such practices were quite common at the time, though not usually in the church itself. This Dr Macey must have been familiar with that. The ossuary story was just to cover the embarrassment of the vicar. He must have been mortified and was probably castigated by his superiors.'

Sarah was silent. She knew that the children of paupers were not valued. She thought about the plight of unwanted and orphaned children in Victorian times. Their lives were cheap, they became chimney sweeps, coal miners, anywhere you might want someone small and expendable. Baby farming was common to enable poor women to continue to work, and infant mortality rates were high. But the village women would not have wept and wailed at the removal of the skeletons if they hadn't meant something to them. Why did Macey disinter Little William? Did he have any connection to the haunted man she had seen in her dream?

Adam continued reading '*However, our reporter heard that a rumour has gained ground in Stansham that the churchyard of St Jude's is haunted. A spectre in a dirty grey shroud has been seen to glide to and fro and various speculations were afloat concerning the portent. Was it the murdered child, affronted at his disinterment, missing his child companions, or something viler and more malicious? No maid can be found hardy enough to carry her water can to the church well after dusk. Even men having occasion to take the short cut from the fields will linger at the lychgate until they are joined by others.*'

'You mentioned a picture?' Sarah said and Chris continued to rifle through his papers.

Dr Macey, the archaeologist, Sarah thought, is he the man I have been dreaming about? She thought about the shock on his face and how the lighting had changed and she knew why she had had that dream and why she had felt afraid.

Chris gave a whoop of triumph. 'Look in the papers from the following year there's a drawing of Dr George Macey by his friend Robert McKinley. It's really good.' He handed the page to Sarah who stared at a pencil sketch of a young man in wire glasses, clean shaven with straight hair and sideburns. It was the man who so frequently appeared in dreams, and this was a shock. Her mind had not invented him, he had existed. The rational explanation for his appearance in her subconscious was mistaken. How could such a thing happen? Was he an ancestor? She had to know more about him. She turned to Adam and with a calmness she did not feel said:

'This is the man I saw in that dream.'

Adam looked at her for a long moment. At first she felt their attraction to each other as always, but then saw him pull away and close part of himself to her. The connection had gone.

'Sarah, I'm not sure whether I'm convinced you experienced a ghostly manifestation of something that happened in the past, but I can accept that the coincidences are strong. Do you have any idea what might have prompted Dr Macey to excavate William's remains? And who was the mysterious woman who appeared in your dream?'

She told them she did not know the veiled woman but that her dress seemed medieval not Victorian. She had told Adam her dreams on many occasions, and he often teased her about them, but she did not think he would now connect Macey with George. Sarah was torn between wanting to know more about Macey and finding a way to identify the woman as Adam suggested. She decided to research Macey on her own, she would not tell them that she felt she had known him her entire life.

She turned away from Adam and glanced at Eleanor and found the woman staring at her as though she knew there was more to the dream. Sarah made an excuse and went into the vestry to collect her thoughts. She went to the toilet and, as she washed her hands, stared at the hollow-eyed woman in the tarnished mirror illuminated by a makeshift light.

As she thought how the last few hours had turned her world

on its head, she heard the faint sobbing of a child. It was coming from outside the vestry. She shook the water from her hands and picked up the torch; the sound was coming closer and something was being dragged along the ground. There was an outer door in the vestry but it was locked. She struggled with it and heard the thing move past her and on towards the tower along the side of the church.

Sarah followed the sound to the corner of the kitchen then went back into the vestry as Chris burst through the door.

'Are you ok?' he said, 'we heard a strange noise.'

'Not from me. I heard something being dragged along the side of the church, and a child crying.'

They looked around the vestry, kitchen and toilet and found nothing unusual. Adam called out to them, irritation in his voice.

'What are you two playing at? Come back in here.'

Puzzled by his aggression, Sarah asked Adam and Eleanor if they had heard the child crying and a dragging sound.

'We heard a scream, which I assume was you' said Adam 'stop messing about Sarah. You have misled us with your ridiculous dream.'

Sarah turned her face away and fought back tears at the unreasonable attack. She was shaken by the ghostly sounds outside but more disturbed by Adam's words. He was being unfair, surprising Chris but not Eleanor, who sat apart and had been silent since her shock at the revelation about the babies. Her hands were crossed in her lap as she watched them. She's quite inscrutable thought Sarah, like a cat with a group of mice. She decided to ignore Adam, took a deep breath, and spoke to her.

'Eleanor, I think you may know more about the child burials than you've told us. If they were just an illegal way of keeping them in sacred ground then why did the veiled woman appear and what did she say to make Dr Macey so horrified?

She must have told him. That must have prompted him to disinter William and make the discovery of the others in his grave. Look, I don't know if she was real or a ghost from the past but burying the bodies of babies in William's grave wasn't doing any harm so why did she interfere? Please tell us what you know, even if it is only unsubstantiated rumour or myth.'

Eleanor shook her head.

Chris had heard more of their previous conversation than she thought. He said 'Please Eleanor, I know you believe there is something ancient here and that it has acquired a thirst for blood.'

Adam snorted with derision and was about to speak when there was a gust of wind and another tile slid off the roof and smashed against a gravestone causing them to jump. Eleanor relented. She stood and walked up to the grave of Little William and started speaking. Her face was thrown into sinister relief by the lamps and torches.

'It's nonsense, I'm sure, but you have asked so I will tell you. When we were children, we used to tell stories in the school yard and in secret places where we played. It was only a playground story, but many nursery rhymes have their roots in some historical event. You see, children from Stansham go to school in East Wellsley, a neighbouring village, and we were largely ostracised by the other children, you know what kids are like, we belonged to a tainted parish, so we were fair game I suppose.

'Anyway, they both disliked and feared us, so we used to tell stories when we wanted to scare them and sometimes if we wanted to frighten each other. There was one story that had been handed down by generations of Stansham children, and I daresay the adults had heard it but refused to either confirm or deny it.'

She closed her eyes and drew her fleece closer around her and adjusted her scarf as though she was cold. 'The story was that every year a small child was chosen from those who had been naughty and taken to St Jude's church on Samhain's Eve. His, or her, parents would then say a prayer to Little Saint William for his soul and they would leave him in the church overnight. They would return in the morning to see if the child was still there.'

'And if the child was not there?' asked Chris.

'Why, a monster had come from under the church and had carried them off. Possibly they had been eaten, but in any event, they were never seen again.' She said this without a smile.

Adam laughed, and Chris looked between him and the women, unable to decide how to respond. He did not laugh.

Adam said, 'How many children did this happen to in your childhood, Eleanor?'

'A few years a child might be lost to illness, an accident or taken by a parent who moved away. We knew that this was just a cover story. They had really been kept somewhere to be sacrificed as a tithe to hell at Samhain.' Her face was so straight that neither Sarah nor Chris could tell if she was joking. They desperately wanted her to burst out laughing.

Adam was losing his temper.

'So, they were sacrificed to a pagan god at Hallowe'en? The great ancient evil that you believe resides in this place and has been unfettered by the deconsecration of the church?'

'Yes, the church was built here to keep that evil in check.'

'You believe that don't you? You stupid woman. It's people like you that give us a bad name, you and your superstitious nonsense.'

'Other cultures have creatures who punish children, such as Krampus and Black Peter' said Sarah but Adam just turned away. Anxious to change the subject she continued 'In addition to the William brass, Macey had another brass-rubbing that I couldn't see clearly. It might have been the anchorite brass and as it might still be here, we could try and locate it.'

Eleanor shrugged and shook her head. She was staring at Adam with a hostile and watchful expression, so Sarah turned again to the prints of the brasses that he had brought from the vestry. She looked through them, the oldest were a child and man in armour from the relevant period and an image for two children and a woman. There were only three others and they were unremarkable and showing matrons or gentlemen in early Tudor dress.

She said 'I can't remember the image but I know that it horrified me. Please Eleanor, have a look at these and tell me if any are missing.' She handed them to her.

Eleanor said 'These were the ones I planned to use in the booklet, if it ever got it printed.'

'I'm sure there must have been another brass rubbing,' said Sarah urgently 'we must find it. If it is of the anchorite Hugh Critchley it may be a something to do with the hauntings.'

Adam was incredulous. 'I can't believe you are connecting the anchorite with ghosts, Sarah. He was a holy man and was more likely to have been the victim of evil than the cause. For years people revered him; he dedicated his life to religion while remaining in a cell.'

'You mean he was buried alive, don't you?' Sarah insisted 'There was probably a reason for that. Eleanor's father saw his restless spirit here and he haunts the church.'

'Really Sarah! Ghosts! What are you thinking?' Adam shook his head 'I agree the story is sinister but we're scientists and we will find the answers to these questions through a scientific approach.' He passed his hands over his face and closed his eyes, he was never going to accept that a paranormal event might occur, thought Sarah, but she was now beginning to believe in the supernatural.

Eleanor looked at their faces and then said 'Honestly, I can't remember ever seeing a brass like that in the church .... but Dad told me about the wainscotting installed in the 1950s and when he came back seven years ago, he was doing something to this wood panelling here, on the opposite side of the altar from William's grave. I suppose and that was why he saw the ghost and that it must have been the anchorite.'

'The panelling was used to hide an ugly brass?' Adam said.

'My Dad knew all about it; I think he was an apprentice when it was installed. Anyway, it was generally rumoured to have been commissioned to cover up something that the villagers had found unacceptable .... I don't know - difficult to stomach.'

'Why not just remove it?' asked Adam.

'Superstition I suppose. It must have been important at one

time and they didn't want to just take it out. Perhaps it frightened them, nobody wanted to remove it so they covered it up. I don't know much more than that, and I can only guess where it was.'

'It might still be here' Adam was excited by the prospect of finding this trophy. 'Where did you say it was?'

When she did not react, he felt obliged to apologise for his earlier outburst. 'I'm sorry I called you a stupid woman, there are things here I have never encountered before. Please forgive my clumsiness; we do appreciate your help Eleanor.'

Eleanor had the upper hand and made Adam listen to her story in full. 'I remember my parents refusing to sit on the right-hand side of the church, at the front, there were always spaces there. They always walked me to and from Sunday school when I was little and didn't like me playing here. That was impossible because we lived so close the churchyard was my playground. I was popular because everyone wanted to play at our cottage. All the village children loved the chance to run around the graves and find poison ivy and deadly nightshade and pretend to cast spells on anyone they didn't like.

'My parents would say that the well was dangerous and the well-house door was never locked in those days, but the drop had been covered by a grate as long as I could remember. Still, the well was very deep and even with the grate it was an irresistible dare to walk over it. If you dropped in a stone it took ages to splash into the water below. Me and my friends thrilled at the thought of a goblin living in it who would climb up the walls and reach its poisonous fingers to clutch at a child's leg.

'It's likely that mum and dad's caution was not rooted in practical concerns. I was a sensible child and I knew there was something they refused to tell me.'

Hesitantly she said: 'I expect my father did see the original anchorite brass when it was being covered in the 1950s. You know what young men are like, he wouldn't have been able to resist having a look, assuming he hadn't already seen it during services. My parents never talked about it. People didn't talk about upsetting things in those days. They just tried to forget about them. Like their experiences in the war.' She walked up to the same area of wainscoting and turned to look at them.

To Sarah it seemed that something had changed in that area of the church, but she could not quite see it. She turned to the others. 'Is it my imagination or does there appear to be a stain on the wall underneath the darker window panel. It's just above the wainscoting that Eleanor is standing near.'

Adam thought it had always been there, and Chris was not sure. It was definitely there though, perhaps the power of their torches was failing and the light not so bright.

Sarah saw a fluttering shadow quickly scale the window mullion. 'Did you see that? The shadow that went up the wall?'

Chris said that he thought he might have seen something from the corner of his eye. Eleanor had seen nothing; the movement had been behind her. Adam had definitely seen it but he just shrugged and gruffly suggested they were all becoming paranoid; he went to stand next to Eleanor looking down at the wainscoting. Sarah joined them and was surprised at the complexity of the patterning on the wood. She said:

'The wood is beautiful. Such cloud-like shapes and whorls. It could be a piece of walnut. What do you think?'

She was surprised when Eleanor said, 'It just looks like the brush-stained varnish effect that was so common at the time, nothing expensive.'

Adam said 'Don't be stupid Sarah. It is totally plain, no pattern at all.'

Chris joined them and stared at the panel. He thought he could see a face in all the swirls of dark varnish, and he wanted to side with Sarah because Adam was being so abusive. Then it faded and all he could see was the old-fashioned dark varnish. 'Ugly brown wood' he said, not wanting to seem too fanciful.

Adam continued to stare at the wood. 'Why don't you girls go and powder your noses before a ghost frightens you.'

'Adam! Don't be ridiculous. If you insist, we will leave you to it.'

How rude, Sarah thought. It might be the effects of the drugs taken for his migraine. He really ought to get some sleep. She and the others went towards the vestry leaving Adam alone at the panel.

Taking their torches and lanterns meant that he was in darkness and for the first time in his life he felt a visceral fear. Not like the excitement of skiing a black run or riding a horse at a gallop but a fear like suffocation that you only feel in nightmares.

Perhaps he could see a pattern after all. The thought that Sarah was right enraged him and he closed his eyes against a fit of anger. He fought a desire to smash something and controlled himself with difficulty. He would take a closer look at this and he knelt down in front of the wainscot under the dark boarded window.

When he reopened his eyes the light had gone and he could hear a man whimpering. Someone was over at Little William's grave and it was open; he could smell decay. 'No, please, leave me alone' a rough voice said. 'Don't come any closer, I've got this here, and I'll cut you. No, please…' there was the sound of heavy boots on the flagstones and a struggle. A short scream then the sound of running feet. The man was leaving the church.

He heard a sigh of satisfaction close to him. It was more terrifying than the scream; then Chris's voice brought him to the present. He was furious.

'You really are a dick sometimes. You know that?' Chris whispered to him. The women had left the church.

'It wasn't me. I didn't …' Adam started to say.

The tree roots moved against the church stones and it sounded like the groan of a man in pain. Adam felt the world turn and to stop himself from falling he grabbed at the wooden wainscot for support. His fingernails scratched deep gouges in the softened varnish as though the surface welcomed his embrace.

'That wasn't me.' He intended to be reassuring but his voice was rasping as though he had not used it for years. 'We must get out, the darkness, the deaths.'

If Chris expected a fight, he wasn't going to get it. Adam sounded terrified. 'What's the matter?'

He tried to prise his hands from the panel 'I can't get my

fingers off the panel!' A sob burst from him, the pain of his fingers coursed up to his temples and burst into a full-blown migraine. The exploding stains of light made him blind, and for a second his aching head felt so heavy that he almost rested it against the panel for the coolness. Horrified he realised that he would be stuck like a fly in the web of a spider. He was sweating and tears streamed from his eyes.

Chris watched his uncle crumble in pain and incomprehension.

'Chris, help me' he breathed.

To cover his fear Adam pretended to wrestle with the wooden panel, kicking it and cursing as though he was trying to remove it. 'Help me with this Chris. Let's see what monster lies under here! Get one of the crowbars.' To his relief Chris immediately disappeared to the back of the church and began rummaging in the kit bags.

With torturous slowness Adam peeled his fingers off the panel; he could have screamed with the pain. Relieved to be free, he sat against a pew and cradled his ruined finger tips. What a fool he was to have touched the thing, but how could he have known that it was dangerous? There must be something in what that witch of a woman had said.

When Chris brought up the tool, he told him not to touch the panel and showed him his hands. The remains of his skin and the bloody smudges left behind on the wood shocked the younger man. The pain was excruciating and the relief of being free had been replaced by burning and throbbing. He had to get some more painkillers, perhaps Eleanor would have something he hadn't already taken. But he needed Chris.

'Will you help me Chris, I can't see. The migraine.'

Chris helped him to his feet, took his arm and they walked down towards the vestry, Adam nursing his hands, tears streaming.

Adam was the first to feel it, a terrible cold and the dread of inevitability that spread from the corner of the church they had just left. He stopped and the younger man stumbled, cursing and apologising at the same time.

'Chris. Can you smell it?'

Chris looked back at the panelled area, now in darkness,

that bore his uncle's skin and blood. The silence was overwhelming. Adam should get his hands attended to, but he was transfixed. He could smell something. Incense. Sweet and cloying like the rituals of death, almost covering the horror of it. He grabbed Adam by the shoulder.

'We mustn't stay here, it's dangerous.'

He couldn't move then, he was held in the terror, and they heard a voice as the light settled around them and the front of the church became a black mass. A man's voice, not much more than a murmur, seemed to be saying the prayer for the dead.

'Requiem æternam dona ei. Domine, Et lux perpetua luceat ei : Requiescat in pace.'

Chris was so close to Adam that he could hear his uncle's heart beating. He could tell that he was still blind. Chris had to take charge of this.

'Who are you and how did you get in here?' He didn't expect a reply but the man in the shadow said:

'Pater.' The voice was rasping and it might have been Adam's, Chris turned to look at him but he shook his head. Chris continued:

'Are you a priest? What are you doing here?'

'Filius meus.'

Chris felt relieved 'So you are a priest.'

The man said nothing and Chris felt perhaps the priest would require an explanation for them being there. As his uncle was blind and in pain, he had to try and explain.

'Then you know that the graves have to be opened when this sort of environmental disaster happens. I am sure that the undertakers have been very respectful.' There was no response 'Just to clarify, we're not undertakers … we're archaeologists …'.

Adam whispered 'Please no more ….'

But Chris continued 'We are investigating the Anglo-Saxon church and we will be respectful but of course the church had been deconsecrated. Adam grabbed his arm, wincing with pain 'Please, this isn't ….'

Chris continued 'The storm has exposed old stones below the church.'

Adam said more urgently 'Chris … no …'

Chris looked at him and was about to shake off his hand when the man said something in an echoing whisper.

Adam collapsed onto his knees and tried to pray with as much faith as he could find that the thing would go.

'Chris, leave it, please, I can't stand any more. It's not human.'

'No – don't be silly, I heard him. He's here. Give me a light, I'll show you.' Chris took the lamp and walked up to the front of the church. There was no one there. The marks of Adam's fingers on the panelling were dark and the stain leaked down from the darkened panelling over the window.

'There must be a concealed door' Chris insisted.

Adam stayed at the back of the church.

'It wants a blood sacrifice' he said.

'No' insisted Chris 'He said we should save our souls.'

'Save yourselves. We've got to get out of here.'

Chris stopped and listened; he heard nothing 'It's the pain affecting you Adam. It must have been some old priest with dementia that wandered in …. I'm not sure how he got out but I'll have look around.'

He walked back to the porch door then he stopped and looked at Adam slumped on the pew. 'It was just some old man. We won't tell the others; we don't want to upset them. We'll just go and sort out your hands. I'll come back in case anybody else comes in.'

He led Adam to the vestry but Chris sounded braver than he felt, and when the vestry door closed, he stayed pressed against it for a few minutes. The church was quiet and gradually his confidence returned. Well, he thought, I wanted to see a ghost, now I might have heard one at least; and it wasn't pleasant, but it didn't hurt me. What happened to his uncle's hands? He could not imagine the pain that he must have been in, and he had kept calm only because he wanted to reassure Adam, he had never seen him in such a state. Broken down, old.

He was becoming more confident as he walked about the nave. He did not believe that ghosts could hurt the living and reflected that there is so much history everywhere in this country, I bet there are ghosts all over the place. He looked in the kit bags and shone his lamp around the church, swivelling suddenly and pointing it like a gun as though to catch out any spirit that might be too slow to avoid being seen. He was puffed up with pride at being able to protect his uncle, the professor, and he was keen to see a ghost. Of course, no one would believe him without a photograph so he set up his phone camera and tried to anticipate where it might appear.

The light cast shadows from the stone mullions. They seemed like little faces and arms that moved in the corners of his eye. The church was still and quiet, and infinitely more patient than he was. His strutting and jaunty confidence faded so that when it happened, he was entirely unprepared. He was standing looking at Little William's grave thinking of small skeletons as the candles at the back of the church went out one by one.

He rushed down to re-light them. As he struck the match, he heard a child's voice

'Papa'

It was behind him in the Norman tower, and he was overwhelmed by a feeling of sadness and bewilderment that drifted from the back of the church. He knew that something was starting to form. It seemed such an effort for something small and weak.

'Papa. My legs'

No, he thought, please don't let it be a child. Not a dead child. I wasn't expecting this.

'Papa please'

He turned slowly and reluctantly to see it, him, expecting a small boy. To his horror it was the skeleton of a child in a shroud, a faint and luminous thing huddled in the corner of the tower. Chris forgot about raising his phone towards the apparition. He was still some distance from the child and almost burned his fingers on the forgotten match. As he dropped it the child spirit faded. He thought, it's gone; do I look for it? What did it want? He shone his phone light at the area where it had appeared. There was nothing. He turned and reached again for the matches and a lantern.

A sensation of dread crept over him as the air behind him

became cold. He did not want to turn and look but inevitably curiosity would overcome his terror. Sweat had broken out on his brow, and his hands were shaking. He was afraid to close his eyes and he felt that he must strike another match, which he managed to do while holding the lantern in one hand. As he turned the light to look behind him, he staggered back. The thing was so close to him. Impossibly, the skeletal child was next to him and looking up at him, holding out his arms to be picked up. How long he remained like that he did not know. The match was extinguished, and Chris blacked out and fell between the pews.

Chapter Four

The storm had passed; but for the gutters on the church and the dripping trees the churchyard was now as silent as the empty sky. There was a waxing crescent moon and enough light to give shadows to the graves. Small animals darted about keeping as hidden as possible, but never coming too close to the grey implacable walls. Outside there was calm and a sense of resignation, or perhaps anticipation. Animals ate and were eaten. A bat lingered at a window ledge a moment too long and something silent landed on it. A dark stream flowed down the silver-grey wall.

Adam was hiding in the vestry nursing his bandaged fingers; Chris had recovered from his blackout but was convinced that there was someone else in the vicinity of the church and that there were hidden doors. It was more comfortable in the vestry; the dark orange walls and wooden panels made it feel homely. Chris was there too, and his hand was heavily bandaged and seeping the bright red of blood. Eleanor was sweeping up glass in the church from Chris's smashed lantern and Sarah went to help her.

She opened the door and walked to the centre of the church but could not see Eleanor. Sarah stopped and listened, fearing that the woman had been attacked by something or perhaps had abandoned them to their fate. In a moment bordering on panic, she turned back to the door and Eleanor popped up from behind a nearby pew.

'For God's sake you made me jump!'

'I'm sorry. I thought the broken glass would be dangerous as it's quite dark between the pews. The young man has a really nasty cut on his hand. Has it stopped bleeding?'

'I'm hoping he won't need stitches. The first aid bag has plenty of wound closure strips and they should hold the skin together. I've cleaned it and we've all had up to date tetanus shots. To be honest I'm more worried about the damage to Adam's fingers. I've never seen anything like it. The outer skin has peeled off, and fingers are full of nerve endings, so

God knows what sort of pain he's in.'

She stopped and wiped away a few tears of sympathy and blew her nose. Eleanor said nothing. Sarah continued 'But it's not just that, he seems to have broken down and he said he went blind. He can see again now so it might have been panic; Chris had to look after him, he just didn't know what they should do next. What could have affected him in this way?'

Eleanor shrugged so Sarah took a torch and went to look at the front of the church where the wooden wainscoting lay. Eleanor did not accompany her and Sarah had to admit the darkness seemed darker there than anywhere else. Chris and Adam had heard a man's voice from that corner so there might be a secret entrance and some psychopath was waiting to pick them off one by one.

'That young man shouldn't really be here' said Eleanor.

'Yes, he didn't like the sight of so much blood. He's lying down and keeping his hand up. He was very brave; I suppose the shock of seeing such a deep gash and flowing blood made his legs give way.'

'You think that's what made him faint?'

Sarah looked at her 'Of course … don't you?'

'You saw something when you were alone in here. And you fainted. So why not Chris?' she continued sweeping.

'Because he's not pregnant.' There, it was out.

Eleanor stopped working and looked at Sarah. There was an awkward silence. The expression on her face was unreadable for a few seconds, then she said 'Really? That's wonderful, … do the others know?'

Sarah shook her head and wondered if Eleanor was thinking that it was all a little close to home given the subject of the babies in the grave. She said that she had wanted to keep it a secret for the first twelve weeks and had just had the scan. Before Eleanor could congratulate her, she admitted that it had not been planned and she did not know what Adam would say when she told him.

'Why, because he might be losing an able and experienced assistant?'

'Because he's the father.'

Eleanor opened her mouth but before she could speak

Sarah said hurriedly 'Yes I know, don't look at me like that. He and his wife have a sort of open marriage. Mea culpa. But if it wasn't me it would be someone else.' She raised her hands. 'I know that's a feeble excuse, but we spend so much time in each other's company at remote digs all over the country.'

'But it is you.'

'Yes, I'm just saying. It's like pass the parcel. Only I'm going to have to deal with the parcel.'

'It's not a parcel Sarah. It's a baby. And it isn't safe for you here.' Eleanor sat down 'This is a place of death' she looked up 'it may be a place of sacrifice.'

There was a long pause as Eleanor deposited the shards of glass and waste into an empty carrier bag. 'Your presence may have a significant effect on the outcome tonight.'

'What do you mean? What outcome?'

'It's already started. Blood has been spilled and the spirits of the dead have been seen.' She stood up and approached Sarah with a look of concern. 'Please take my Land Rover and drive away.'

Sarah was touched and surprised. 'I know that you believe all this Eleanor, and maybe some part of it is true, but there are four of us here and we can fight this thing, whatever it is. Isn't that what you want to do really?'

'Yes, I do. I want a resolution to the vile mystery that resides here. But I'm afraid for you and for the baby.' She thought for a few seconds and then said 'Look, if you need it, the Land Rover is open, and the keys are behind the sun visor. Don't forget that I know this church is haunted. My father saw something, and it broke him. I want to know what it was. That's why I'm here. I'm not peddling the silly booklet, I want answers Sarah. I want to know what frightened my father half to death and changed him forever.'

'We want answers too Eleanor. Well, I know I do' said Sarah.

'What we really need is a cup of hot sweet tea, but we don't have any, so fruit juice will have to do. I have a feeling that coffee would only make things worse.'

Sarah grimaced 'Coffee. Yuk.' They both smiled and

Eleanor took the waste bag through to the vestry. She quickly returned.

'Is it ok if Chris comes out here? He doesn't want to stay with his uncle.'

Sarah nodded and soon Chris joined her. He looked pale and serious, so she checked the dressing on his hand; it had stopped bleeding and the wound looked clean. She wrapped a new dressing on it and asked how he felt now, had he ever fainted before? He looked completely different from the jaunty slightly resentful young man that had turned up at her flat that morning. His hair was flat and stuck to his head and he was white. He looked sick and afraid.

'Sarah, I saw something.'

She knew it must have been bad to have caused him to collapse and break the lantern. She said 'Go on. We're in this together Chris and we need to be open with each other.'

'I didn't really believe before, when the man appeared, and Adam knew straight away that it was not a living person.'

'Adam saw a ghost?' Typical, she thought, he kept that to himself.

'It was after he hurt his hands on the panelling, something started reciting the prayer for the dead, in Latin. I spoke to it and it spoke to us in Latin. But we weren't near it. It was over here' Chris went to the pew nearest the panel 'It was dark but I thought it was an old priest who was kneeling and praying but it felt … unclean somehow. It said that it was a father, that it had a son, something about blood. Oh, and that we should save ourselves.'

'Why didn't Adam tell us? This is really important. Did you get any idea of how he was dressed? What period of time?'

'I'm sorry Sarah, but we never really saw it. It was more of a felt presence and it was …' he hesitated 'dreadful somehow.'

'But you must have had a strong impression Chris. Didn't you get a sense of who it was? Could it have been Little William's father? The combination of words – father and son suggest it might have been.'

'I thought it was a priest but I suppose so, yes. It was praying in Latin. Look Sarah, this will seem fanciful but it didn't feel human. You spoke of the man in your dream as though he was real. This creature ... well it felt as though it had lost its humanity and the words it said were more of a curse than a prayer.'

He looked around the church and moving closer to her said, in a voice not much more than a whisper: 'When Adam had fled to the safety of you ladies ... I saw something else.'

Sarah waited for him to continue.

'Sarah, it shocked more than frightened me. It was awful in the true sense of the word and I really only glimpsed it in different parts of the church. The air felt cold, not like it was with the creature, harsh and bone chilling, but the damp cold of despair, and yet - hope still hanging on like a sad little thread. And I felt weakness in my arms and legs ...'

Sarah's sense of dread increased, and she could not resist looking round the church at the plain expressionless walls. It was a pitiless place, but she had to know and urged him to tell her what he had seen.

'I saw a child.' A sob escaped from Sarah and he said 'Did you see it too?'

'No I didn't. Please describe it Chris. What exactly did it look like?'

Chris reached for one the piles of newspaper copies. He showed her a drawing of the skeleton of a child that had accompanied the article in 1847. There was just one little body in a shroud, no babies.

'They must have removed the other skeletons when they made this drawing' Sarah said, holding back tears. It was a pencil drawing, skilfully done and delicately shaded. The shroud was intact, but the head exposed. The skull was large compared to the narrow body and it lolled to one side. In the way that skeletons do he seemed to be grinning malevolently, but the overall impression was pathos. The artist had written *Length of the coffin 3 feet 4 inches.*

'You definitely saw Little William?'

'I think so. And it seemed to be a boy's voice. He said 'Papa'. Then something about his legs, and then 'Papa please'. And lastly 'Papa no'. Then he seemed to be really close. Sarah I was terrified, and I don't remember anything until I came round and you were all there.'

'Why didn't you say anything then?'

'Adam was making such a fuss about the cut and the blood. I just wanted some time to recover.' He paused and then whispered 'So this place must be haunted…right?'

'Of course it's haunted' said Eleanor entering carrying rolls and cartons of fruit juice. Chris told her what he had seen and then remembered that he had been holding his phone and if they could find it there might be a photograph.

The presence of Eleanor broke the spell that had held Sarah and Chris. She seemed so matter of fact and accepting of theories that the others would have laughed at the day before. She explained

'To the Stansham villagers the supernatural was, and had always been, part of normal life. Using it to attract visitors, be they mystics or devil worshippers, is a way to make a living. The devil is just the Green Man and he was simply the pre-Christian pagan god representing nature.

'There have always been 'wise' women in the village.' She said 'My family have lived here for generations. My grandmother was a land girl; she married a local farrier despite his reputation as being a warlock, a male witch. His mother was a midwife and I have inherited some old books with 'recipes' for natural remedies.'

Chris stood suddenly 'Oh God, you've spiked our drinks with magic mushrooms. No wonder we saw things - we've been hallucinating.'

Sarah looked accusingly at Eleanor. 'Tell me you haven't.' Her hand instinctively went to her belly.

'Of course I haven't. We all drank the coffee and those fruit cartons are completely untouched - from the village shop. You pierced them with the straws yourselves. I haven't put any spells on you.' Chris looked at Sarah for reassurance and she nodded so he sat again.

He felt sufficiently recovered to eat a roll, but Sarah had no appetite. She suspected that her father's experience and its background of medieval murder and the Victorian hauntings were not the only reasons Eleanor had invited them to St Jude's. If she practiced the old religion or Wicca, then the feast of Samhain was significant. She had spoken several times about an ancient evil and that the Christian church was just a relatively recent layer in the story of this hill and its history. For at least five thousand years there had been Neolithic settlements, beaker people, bronze age religious structures, iron age hill forts, Romans, Saxons, Christians and now, a godless vacuum.

'What's the real reason you invited us here Eleanor?'

For a moment the older woman's face was a stony mask. Then Sarah said 'You believe in the presence of older gods at St Jude's, don't you?'

Eleanor nodded.

'And you believe that hauntings by Little William and his father are happening again because the church has been deconsecrated.'

She nodded again.

Sarah continued 'And the ground has been opened with the coffins of the dead exposed by the subsidence? Are you saying that William's murder in 1275 was a sacrifice by a local person to the pagan gods, and as usual the Jews of Winchester were just the scapegoat?'

Eleanor stood and began pacing. 'You must have wondered why there is stone under the church? On land like this the builders would usually just scrape off the topsoil and build straight onto the chalk. But here, surprisingly, they appear to have laid stone foundations. They only became visible after this recent storm washed away part of the mound on which the church was built. Adam noticed them when I showed him round. He became excited.'

'How does that fit into the story about a crypt and the anchorite's cell?' Sarah asked.

'People have looked for the crypt before. I believe the architects noticed the stones when they were poking around at the time of the proposed sale. It's unusual in an area of chalk like this, most of the houses here are flint because it's freely available. Stone was not a common building material for a rural church so far from a river.'

'I thought the Normans always built in stone though' said Chris 'like the cathedral in Winchester.'

'That was usually French stone brought in barges on the river. All the great Norman cathedrals were constructed at the highest navigable point of the river.' She stopped as she realised the implications.

'Where did the stone underlying St Jude's come from? Are you saying that the stone is pre-Norman?'

'I'm saying it's pre-Saxon, pre-Christian; I'm saying it's ancient. You know that there is a prehistoric stone called the Devil's Finger on a hill on the opposite side of the village, well, I think there was a prehistoric circle made of stone on the site of St Jude's.'

'And you think that stone circle is now underneath this church?'

Eleanor said 'I found some additional information I would like to share with you, perhaps I should have done it earlier but I thought Dr Glover might disapprove. I'll just fetch it from the vestry.' She left them.

'Sarah, I have a sketchy idea of this but what sort of timescale are we talking about? Are we talking Stonehenge, built about four and a half thousand years ago?'

'The British Isles have been occupied by humans for thousands of years and hills like this were common areas of occupation because as the country was heavily forested it was probably safer. The later iron age hill forts were defensive, but we don't know enough about the people who built the oldest henges. They may have had some sort of ritual aspect and there is a theory that they marked a decline in the neolithic people who were using them to seek help from their gods. At about that time 3000 BCE there was the migration into Britain of the beaker people who came from Europe and seem to have displaced them about five thousand years ago. We only know about these peoples because of rituals of the dead.'

'What do you mean?' said Chris 'Human sacrifice?'

'Well, I meant that the neolithic dead were exposed or cremated and the bones buried in a barrow. The beaker people favoured a cist grave and were buried intact with grave goods often consisting of a beaker.'

Chris persisted 'I've heard of bodies found in peat bogs and they were sacrificed.'

Eleanor came back into the church with her briefcase and sat with them. 'When the deconsecration of the church took place and the land was put up for sale the surveyors sunk shafts near the foundations to establish the geomorphology of the site. They found the stones and the rumour soon spread amongst some of the villagers that there was truth in the legend of the church being built on a stone circle.'

Sarah said 'Why doesn't the village advertise the stone circle as well?'

'It's our secret. We don't have to share it. The other ancient monuments are enough for most visitors and the village doesn't want to wash all its dirty linen in public. Some things need to stay hidden. After all we have kept our pagan beliefs hidden for a long time. Along with their money, outsiders have brought bad things, like plague, and the interference of government. There was a witch trial in the seventeenth century and a woman was crushed to death at the crossroads where she is said to have been buried. We have had to close ranks at times.'

'But this is the twenty-first century. There'll be no witch hunts' said Sarah.

'Perhaps not, but there are other types of persecution. You should have seen the animal packs of journalists when the little girls were killed by their father, even though it happened in Scotland. There were some ordinary people who brought flowers to the house where the children had lived. You could see they were genuinely grieving, but they never knew those girls or their dad. One couldn't help feeling that they revelled in it and it fed a febrile atmosphere. Emotions like that can only stimulate the primitive hunger of St Jude's hill.'

Before Sarah could respond Eleanor continued.

'I told you what happened with my husband and his friend's wife. They were surveying the ring of yews looking for Saxon or later artifacts. As you know the trees probably date from the time of Alfred's Wessex and may have been planted to commemorate a battle against the Vikings at about the time the original Anglo-Saxon church was constructed.

'One day my husband came home very late and accused his friend of finding something that he wouldn't share or discuss.

After that a coldness grew between them and a few weeks later all hell broke loose when he ran off with his friend's wife.'

'You think he may have found something important?'

'I think he found the crypt, and I think we have a good chance of finding it now that this storm has exposed the stones. You must agree they're worth investigating.'

Sarah was quiet for a few moments she was thinking: what about the ghosts? It seemed such a ridiculous question. The silence became uneasy as though something was listening. It was Adam standing at the vestry door.

He was changed and seems relaxed, Sarah thought, and was obviously not in pain from the migraine or his fingers, and his face was flushed. He said, 'Tell us more about the stones Eleanor.'

'How are you Adam? Has the pain gone?' asked Sarah.

He said 'I feel wonderful. The meds have kicked in and the coffee has helped. Thank you, Eleanor.'

Chris said, 'I've told them about the man that we heard.' Adam did not respond but Sarah thought she noticed a flicker of fear about his eyes. He shot her an angry glance, and she dropped her gaze.

'And I saw something too, Adam' there was no response and he seemed irritated, so Chris said, 'I'll tell you about it later.'

Eleanor continued 'The local legend is that twelve stones originally stood as an upright circle on the site of the church. I've got some Victorian notes on it here.'

She leafed through her papers and started to read '*A Charter granted in the year 972 AD, in the reign of King Edgar, refers to an 'Egsanmor' (slaughter stone) at Stansham.* If the Saxon church was built over it, it would have concealed it.'

Chris said 'But a slaughter stone. It means blood sacrifices?'

'It must still be here. This place has long been a place of sacrifice, of blood.' Eleanor stopped when there was a scraping noise, and they felt the floor vibrate again.

'It's the tree' Adam said quickly.

'I don't like the way that happens when we speak about

blood sacrifice' said Chris.

Adam scoffed 'It's been doing it all evening Chris. It's the effect of the wind on the tree that is so close to the church'.

'But there is no wind' Chris replied. Adam ignored him.

Sarah thought if the wind has dropped should the tree still be moving. Was it wise to be so complacent about potential danger; perhaps they should leave now and take up Eleanor's offer of spending the night at her cottage?

Chris resumed his questioning. 'Isn't it a bit sinister that they would build a Christian church on a pagan site? Especially one that had sacrifices carried out.'

Adam laughed 'But Chris, blood sacrifice is still a part of Christian beliefs.' At Chris's incredulity he added 'To take Holy Communion is to eat the body and drink the blood of Christ. Especially if you are Catholic.'

He took a fruit juice carton and whilst sipping it he paced the floor of the nave as though lecturing at university 'There is clear evidence of bronze age and iron age settlements in the area and there may have been a druid temple in pre-Roman times, and the druids did practice human sacrifice. There was a strong Roman presence in Winchester so it was likely that local settlements would have been sustained for agricultural value and as part of the road system.'

Eleanor said, 'There's no evidence of a Roman temple hereabouts, that was something we hoped to find if we located the crypt and the anchorite's cell, assuming that any Roman evidence would be below ground.'

Adam showed them the photographs he had taken earlier with his phone. 'From the tops of the stones visible under the Norman tower it would appear that they are standing. These means that someone took the trouble of filling the gaps between them and constructing a church on top. It would account for why the church sits on a hillock inside the churchyard.'

'I can't find my phone' muttered Chris.

Sarah cautiously said 'Although the Romans were fond of incorporating other countries' religions into their own, Christianity was a lot less tolerant, and it would have been suspicious of pagan stones. It possible that you were right

Eleanor and that the Saxon Christians were seeking to control the power of the old religion.'

She replied 'The old beliefs remain as do some of the old Celtic races. Their faith in God was strong but their belief in the power of the old religion didn't disappear overnight.'

Adam was expansive now as he enthusiastically said 'Ancient history is big business and we all know there are many people who would pay a considerable sum to visit the standing stones of Stansham as well as the Norman church on top of it. I mean, it's an important site encompassing a span of five thousand years.'

Chris and Sarah looked at each other. Adam seemed different, somehow, and Eleanor was encouraging him. What about keeping the mysteries of St Jude's hidden? Was she prepared to open everything to the public gaze or just to Adam's? And he was behaving as though nothing unusual had happened. What about the damage to his fingertips and the thing that had appeared to him in the church? Sarah had to challenge him.

'What about the supernatural things we've seen and heard. I know about the man's voice and I've seen what that wood did to your fingertips Adam' She stopped. She had moved to the front of the church and pointed her lantern at the panel that had caused so much damage. Adam joined her to look at the stain that had caused his fingers to stick and the skin to peel. His jaw dropped. There were no marks and no bloody smudges on the wood.

'It's gone. How could that happen?' She looked at Chris who shook his head.

Adam examined at his fingers. They were almost healed. He turned to Eleanor.

'That ointment you gave me has performed a miracle. I've hardly any pain and the skin looks less raw. What was in it?'

'Oh, it was just a recipe from my grandmother, a few herbs with cooling properties. But you should keep them covered' she retrieved a rough odd-looking pair of gloves from her bag and gave them to him. 'Here, why don't you put them on?'

He looked at them and laughed. 'Come on, these are very unfashionable. What will my public think?' He pulled on the strange green gloves and seemed quite comfortable. Sarah had never seen him so biddable.

'What are those gloves made of?' she asked.

'Nettles, of course.' Eleanor laughed 'They'll stop him turning into a swan.'

Magic, thought Sarah, she has worked some sort of magic and healed his hands. That must be good, surely? They clustered around him and the wooden panel. What had happened to the bloody stains? It had been real, Sarah had seen the red weeping wounds. Looking at the unblemished panelling Adam pretended to be unconcerned; putting the injury down to a chemical reaction as a result of damp conditions and poorly mixed varnish from a time when health and safety rules were less rigorous.

Leaving the men together the women walked to the back of the church and Sarah asked Eleanor if she had some special recipe for Chris's wound which was still leaking blood slightly.

'Oh dear me no. Only magic can be healed by magic.' She beckoned to Sarah and at the vestry door she whispered:

'I'm worried about Adam; I can only protect him for so long from the compromising of his soul that began when the corruption entered his blood.'

Sarah looked back at him with concern. He stood under the filthy boarded up window, the newer stains spreading behind him like dark wings as he looked across at Chris who was bending over William's grave. Their body language was eloquent. Adam was resurgent as though strengthened by his experiences and Chris was humbled. Adam sensed her gaze; he turned and looked at her and she was shocked by the look on his face. She whispered 'What do you think has happened to him? Is he possessed?'

Eleanor took her arm 'The evil enters men's souls and reveals their true nature. Men who love to kill become insatiable; greed is unrestrained. It's not safe, especially with your pregnancy and with the child sacrifice connected to this place. Remember Sarah if you want to leave, you can take the Land Rover.'

She stopped speaking because Adam, trailed by Chris, was

moving towards them.

'Whispering in corners? I think you should share your thoughts with everyone.'

'Chris has seen the ghost of a child, that's what caused him to faint' she said to distract Adam. 'We're all upset by this. I'm afraid to stay in the church overnight, especially with the vibration and noise created by the tree and the weather. Perhaps we could go and stay with Eleanor at her cottage?'

Adam ignored her request but pressed Chris to tell them what he had seen. Chris was embarrassed to be telling his uncle a ghost story. But as he talked, he brought to life the terror and pathos of his encounter. He described the darkness, the cold and the child's voice. Then he described the skeletal creature and again started looking for his phone to see if there was a picture. He had it when he fainted, so it should be in the church unless someone picked it up.

Chris was convinced that he had seen the ghost of Little William and that it wanted to speak to its father; he believed this to be the dark man that had terrified them both earlier. 'It's the reason I fainted and smashed the lamp and cut my hand. Honestly, Adam, I'm not making it up. You heard that man earlier.' He took the illustration from the newspaper 'I saw a skeletal child like this illustration' He showed Adam the Victorian drawing of Little William.

Adam looked at it dispassionately. 'Are you sure you didn't see the drawing then imagine the ghost?'

'I hadn't seen the drawing at that time, and you had only just left when I saw him. Why would I make up something like this? You heard the thing earlier.'

Adam looked at their pale faces, but he just shrugged 'I don't know what I heard earlier, it may have been my imagination. Look at my fingertips, there is no trace of any injury, maybe it was mass hysteria – or the result of my migraine.'

Sarah tried to avoid looking at Eleanor in case it provoked Adam. He was increasingly a man she did not recognise.

Chris was becoming frustrated. 'We saw the raw flesh on your fingers and how do you explain the blood disappearing from that panelling, we all saw it earlier. I think something has consumed the blood and the skin.' He stopped as they heard sound of stones and roots again creating a vibration that shivered through the church. 'I can't stay in here. I'm going outside to see what's happening to the tree. Anyone going to join me?'

Adam made to go but Sarah said 'Wait a minute Adam, I need to speak to you.' Then to Eleanor 'You go with Chris, we'll be out soon.' Eleanor was reluctant to leave them but, in the end, she did agree to show the younger man around the dark graveyard to the tree.

After the door was shut Adam and Sarah looked at each other. He seemed darker, as though he needed a shave; and somehow unclean. He had changed physically in a few hours. She thought: I don't recognise him anymore; he seemed tainted. How long has this been coming on? Had she been withdrawing from him because of the pregnancy? He looked back at her, daring her to, what? Challenge him?

Sarah said, 'I've something important to tell you.'

'Of course you have.'

'I'm pregnant.' She did not know whether to expect him to be surprised, shocked or even angry. She looked away from him waiting for a reaction. When he said nothing, she turned towards him with a reassuring smile but was fascinated by the expressions changing on his face. He was unable to control the spasms as it changed between anger, despair, delight, terror until it grew dark and unreadable, and he turned away and walked into the vestry.

Eleanor had mentioned possession and there seemed to be more than one person fighting for control of Adam now. Was he dangerous? She had to try to reach him. She followed, determined to talk about it and found him searching the bag he had taken in there. Perhaps he has some cigarettes? He has a hidden packet when he was supposed to have given up, but he brought out a hip flask and helped himself to a hefty slug.

Although Sarah had not expected warm words or a hug, she suddenly felt completely alone and vulnerable. He still did not face her and the shape of his back suggested a suppressed violence so that when he spun around, she flinched.

'I suppose it's mine.'

'Of course.'

Sarah had rehearsed this many times in her mind, she knew that she had expected the old Adam to make a great dramatic scene which they would talk through. When he realised that his career and marriage were not in jeopardy, he would have accepted the situation, even been proud of himself. Jane had never wanted children; she managed every aspect of her life, even rationing the number of friends she maintained.

Sarah put on her coat. 'We have to go now Adam. It isn't safe here.'

'But we can't leave!' He paused. 'I mean, the road is flooded. You won't be able to get to the village. Eleanor said so, and the Volvo doesn't have four-wheel drive.'

'The church and the tree may not be safe when so much soil has been washed away. I thought perhaps I would spend the night in the Land Rover as it's furthest away from the church.'

'Nonsense, spend the night in the Volvo if you must. I'll help you.'

He took her by the arm, picked up her backpack and almost marched her through the church to the porch door, his fingers pinching the flesh of her arm so that she almost cried out. The others were not in sight and Sarah wondered what they would think when they found she had left. Adam pushed her in front of him as they followed the path to the car park.

He carried her backpack to the car and opened the back door for her. 'You can lie down in here and sleep.' She was about to argue but something about him stopped her. He thrust the bag in and she obediently climbed into the back of the car and lay down. He was about to lock the car when he remembered the alarm sensors and didn't, but he took the keys with him. She looked in her bag and found that he had taken her phone.

'Adam, I need my phone' she shouted.

'You have a torch. Lock the doors and get some sleep.' Then he walked away and was gone.

She lay in the darkness and let her emotions take hold. Sarah wept, partly from loneliness but also because she realised that she was terrified of him.

Through blurred eyes Sarah watched Adam join the others at the side of the church. She went through her backpack again and concluded that he must have taken her phone as he carried it. She felt like a trapped animal, and the worst of it was that she could not guess her fate. She could see Adam gesturing back at the car. So he had told them she was sleeping here. They went into the porch and Sarah thought she saw Eleanor turn back and look in her direction before disappearing into the church.

As soon as they had entered the church Adam insisted that they look for hidden doors. He wanted to be sure that no one could get in or out of the church without them knowing. Sarah had locked herself in the Volvo and he said she was safe there, he was certain.

They shone their lanterns and torches into every corner and tried to find any hidden doors or access points. They could see nothing that suggested a way into the crypt or any other exits. Adam drew their attention to the panelling that had burned his fingers. It was still smooth and unmarked and there was no pattern or grain on the wood. He asked Eleanor if anyone would object to the panel being removed. She took a little time to clean her glasses and appear to consider his request, then she said that it seemed the only sensible thing to do, given the circumstances. It would be interesting to see if the anchorite brass was concealed by it and if it had been left behind when the other brasses were taken.

Adam picked up the crowbar and, being careful not to touch the panel with his bare skin, he inserted the bar behind it and wrenched. It squealed and groaned at first, so he applied more power and part of the wood splintered.

'Give me a hand Chris, can't you' Adam asked and Chris added his strength to the pressure on the bar. The sounds changed to a cracking like small gunshots, but still the wood resisted the steel. When both men had put their full weight behind it the panel sprang away from the brass plate and they flinched away from its poison. But Chris's damaged hand was caught by the split panel and his wound reopened. Adam grabbed it quickly as though to examine it and in so doing he splashed a small amount of blood onto the blackened brass plate.

'Oh God. That hurt. Damn it! Why did you do that?' Chris clasped his injured hand and staggered back from the wall. Eleanor led him further away and examined it under torchlight. Adam muttered that it was an accident. She curtly replied that they were going into the vestry to clean and close the cut again. He barely heard them, he was sitting on his haunches in front of the brass. His torch illuminated an image crusted in soft grey-white mould.

By moving the torch about to highlight the features they could make out that it was a stylised bas relief of the anchorite, a thin man, bearded, Christ-like, naked but for a loin cloth, his hands joined in prayer. He was kneeling side on, but his face looking to his left and out at the viewer. Adam followed his gaze. He was looking in the direction of Little William's grave. There was something odd about his face and because the brass was mouldy he would need to wipe it.

Adam raised his gloved hands and made as if to polish the brass but the strange gloves would not let him touch it. The nettle gloves seemed to have a will of their own and a small panic gripped him so that he tried to pull them off. They tightened as he did so but when he stopped they relaxed again. He accepted them and part of his soul slept, comfortable and pain-free. The gloves knew what was best for him and he slipped into a fugue state; waiting, compliant.

'You've been sitting here for almost half an hour' Chris was behind him, looking over his shoulder. 'He doesn't have any eyes. They've been gouged out. He's blind.' He looked up at the boarded windows in the church. 'A bit like this church with its Christian protection removed and its windows gone.'

'He's not blind. He's looking at William's grave. It just needs cleaning.'

'What is that white stuff? It looks sticky and it stinks' said Chris.

'It looks like adipocere, grave wax, but it really shouldn't be here. It's a whited sepulchre' Adam muttered.

'Eleanor wants to know if you need any medical treatment' Chris's hand was wrapped in what looked like kitchen roll. Run out of bandages he explained. Adam did not reply. He stood up, awkwardly, and suggested they go into the vestry and do some research using the photocopy documents that Eleanor had brought with her.

'But it's almost midnight' said Chris 'Shouldn't we try to get a few hours' sleep? And are you sure that Sarah will be ok alone out there in the car?'

Adam brushed off his enquiry saying that Sarah would be safer if not inside the church and the Volvo was very comfortable. She was probably sound asleep by now.

Chris muttered something about no one wanting to sleep alone in a haunted graveyard but Adam said:

'It's the church that's haunted, not the churchyard.'

They joined Eleanor in the vestry and she agreed to continue their research into the archives. A few dregs of cold coffee were shared out to kickstart their scrutiny of Victorian newspapers and court cases.

An hour or so passed then Eleanor said 'Dr Glover I've found something on Hugh Critchley.'

'Does it say why he gave up his lands and property and became a hermit?'

'The caption says: *It was an unlucky and ill-omened house that Sir Hugh Critchley built with the wealth he acquired from the Jews of Winchester...*'

'Well,' said Adam 'That just means he was influential enough and wealthy enough to take advantage of the cheap property offered by the king. It doesn't mean that he had anything to do with the accusations against the Jews.'

'I didn't suggest that he did,' Eleanor continued reading '*...and a sequence of misfortunes befell it from its building to its destruction. Evil begot evil and the house could not escape from the dark cloud of influence that hung over it. The house that seemed built for ever has been sponged out, and Time has drawn other and meaner pictures on his transparent slate.*'

Chris said 'I like that expression – the transparent slate of time. Rubbed out and replaced. How transient we are. And why did it say e*vil begot evil*? That suggests the Victorian writer had some information about the circumstances in which the great house fell. Perhaps something relating to the family.'

'I daresay it's just typical Victorian prose,' replied Adam 'Eleanor do you know what house they're talking about? I wouldn't expect there to be anything of that age in the village now, but it sounds as though it was a substantial property and might have been in a prominent position. Perhaps a more recent house has been built over an earlier building from this period?'

'I have something that may be relevant in here.' Eleanor produced her booklet on the village and showed Adam the description of the shape of a building that had become visible from the air during the previous year's drought. 'It's a little off the beaten track, just beyond my own cottage, and no one has built on it.'

'What did the geo physics turn up? Adam asked her.

'We were all very excited, but it didn't get much further. The surveyors had been convinced that the foundations of some structure lay under the soil. But look at this.' She brought out a newspaper article that had been written six months after the one that Chris had found on William's disinterment. She pointed out a section of the text.

'On the following page there is a picture of William's body, from when his grave was opened, sketched in 1847. The article describes it as *The tomb of William Critchley believed martyred by the Jews of Winchester aged 9 years. May his soul rest in peace.* That report was May 1848.

Chris looked at it. 'It's the same picture I showed you from 1847. That means the ghost I saw was talking to Hugh Critchley when he said 'Papa', and he seemed afraid. Adam, the man we heard was Hugh Critchley and he must have been praying for his son's soul. Their brass memorials were on either side of the altar, does that mean that Hugh is buried on the opposite side of the church from William?' He looked at the door to the main body of the church, unwilling to enter it alone.

He stopped, waiting for their opinions. Nobody spoke so he continued 'He is kneeling facing the altar, but his head is turned in the direction of his murdered son. He must have become an anchorite in grief when his little boy was killed. That's tragic. But why did the villagers decide to cover over the panel of the anchorite? Apart from the eyes it didn't look too bad.'

'The timing is wrong,' Adam spoke slowly. 'William died 1275 and Hugh became an anchorite in about 1290, according to the reports we have seen. Little William probably was Hugh Critchley's son, but his murder is not what led him to the cell. Let's look. There must be a reason his brass was installed on the other side of the altar to William.' They left the vestry and took their lights into the church.

They stood in the space of the altar and contemplated the pale brass on one side and the site of William's shrine on the other.

'We are assuming that the body is still under the site of William's brass, so let's open the grave.' Adam said as he grabbed the crowbar.

Chris appealed to Eleanor. 'Surely we can't just dig him up, can we? Aren't there rules?'

Eleanor shrugged.

Adam was kneeling next to the slabs that had held the old brass plate, screw holes visible at each corner. It was pitiably small. He was loosening the mortar around it. 'Come on Chris, this is what we do. It's what you're here for, find another levering tool and help me.'

Chris cautiously went to the toolbox and found a long chisel.

'Adam, what do we do if there are babies in here?' He and Eleanor exchanged a glance, but Adam just laughed coldly.

Between them they prised the stone slabs out of their places and leaned them against the wall. With a trowel Adam gently removed the granular spoil that had supported them until he came to a wooden lid, obviously replaced by the Victorian archaeologists; the original one must have rotted.

With a brief glance at the sickly white brass of Hugh Critchley, Adam prised open the lid.

'Papa look upon your son' he said with unhealthy relish.

There were no babies this time. No little sacrifices to keep

William company. Just the shrouded body of a small under-developed child. Adam unwrapped the corpse revealing the skeletonised remains of a boy.

'That's what I saw. That's it.' Chris said. He drew back in horror, but Eleanor drew closer and held her lantern over the grave.

'There's something wrong with this body' said Adam.

'He had been mutilated' Eleanor reminded him 'his arms and legs had been broken.'

'Then it must be William, look, the long bones have been broken. We could expect that, but this child was a cripple before he was attacked. His limbs are deformed, as though they were bowed.'

'Ricketts?' asked Eleanor

'That would have been common in under-nourished children of that time, but this was a knight's son, he should have been well fed.'

'Perhaps a poor child was passed off as Critchley's son' said Eleanor.

'Possible, but unlikely, because what had become of the real William? No, it would mean Hugh was complicit, because he would have had to identify him. It would have been a massive fraud, and then why would he become an anchorite for life? I think this is a congenital deformity and would have been obvious to anyone who saw him.'

Eleanor looked through the newspaper article. 'They don't mention it in 1847, probably too shocked at finding the babies. But I don't think we ever saw a contemporary account that mentions William being disabled.'

'If his bones had been deliberately broken when his body was found, you might not notice the deformity but as he is now a skeleton, the distortions are obvious.'

Chris said 'He was telling his father about his legs. You don't think the killer did that when he was alive?'

'After all this time there's no way of knowing, but it would have been at about the time of death.' Adam started taking photographs with his phone and Chris continued searching for his.

'Eleanor, have you seen my phone?'

She said no and then to Adam 'I think you should rebury him now.'

Adam seemed reluctant but Chris said 'Requiescat in pacc' and made the sign of the cross.

Adam stood up and left Chris and Eleanor to replace the lid and re-cover the grave. He went into the vestry and they heard him rifling through the documents. He shouted back to them 'It might be possible to trace the timeline of the Critchley family.'

Eleanor walked into the vestry. She said, 'I'm going to check on Sarah and see if she's ok'.

'No' Adam said forcefully. Then took her hands in his gloved ones and said more gently 'You'll only disturb her, and I think you know about the pregnancy, she needs her sleep at the moment.'

They stood in the vestry holding hands and Eleanor looked into his eyes searching for signs of something within him. Eventually she seemed satisfied, smiled up at him, let go of his hands and said, 'Very well Adam. Perhaps if you tell me what you are looking for in the photocopy archive I may be able to help.'

'We now know that the anchorite was William's father, and we need to build a timeline of events to understand what happened. To do that we have to pin down the dates of these occurrences. Assuming the body was that of William and not some unfortunate pauper obtained for the purpose, why did Hugh become an anchorite some seventeen years after his son's murder? How did the newly built house fit into the timeline and did he have any other children?'

Chris came quickly into the vestry and shut the door. 'I hate being out there on my own. The skeleton was bad enough but that brass makes me feel ill.'

'Take these papers and look through them for anything relating to the Critchley family.' He gave a bundle to Chris. 'According to the newspapers Hugh had built the 'ill-omened' house with money effectively acquired from the Jews accused of William's murder. He obviously didn't have himself walled up in 1275, especially if he had other sons and William was disabled in some way. In fact, the murder resulted in good fortune and wealth for Hugh Critchley and his remaining family. We need to trawl through the research of the Victorian archivists and historians. It is likely that some of those original medieval papers don't exist now and it was a good idea of yours Eleanor to bring copies.'

Chris reluctantly began reading, his eyes wanting close, but then he found a writer who had obviously immersed himself in the period. 'I think I've got something relevant' he said 'One of the essays, published in the Archaeological Journal in 1848 has a genealogical table of the Critchleys, drawn up to illustrate who had made gifts of land to the Church. The writer has quoted substantial chunks from the medieval manuscripts but also has plates illustrating some of the names on the table with images made from brass rubbings of their memorials in this church.'

He expanded a paper and smoothed it out. It showed the Critchley family from the beginning of the thirteenth century and ending with Sir Hugh and his four sons. There were also two daughters, but they were not shown as marrying or producing any issue. The prints showed Hugh as an anchorite, kneeling half naked and turned to one side. Little William was a stylised child-saint holding a lamb, but without a halo. Two of his brothers were represented, one as a child and the other in armour. The fourth son was not shown.

'What are their names?' Adam brought a piece of green chalk out of his bag and began to draw the family tree on one of the orange vestry walls. 'William was the eldest, let us assume that we know what happened to him. 1275 for the murder of William.'

Chris said 'I think I've got something in the essay. From the table we can see that Hugh Critchley had four sons that survived infancy – William – we think we know about him – there was a John, then Geoffrey, and lastly Simon. It appears that the whole estate was gifted to the church in 1290 when Hugh became the anchorite. By that time all of his sons had died.'

'All of them?' asked Eleanor 'Does it say how they died?'

'It says John died in *the 6th year of Edward*. He was crushed when part of the house fell on him as it was being built.'

They looked at Adam who said, 'That would be 1280' and wrote it on the wall.

Chris continued reading; 'Ah, Geoffrey died in the 16th year of Edward.'

Adam wrote 1290 on the wall and said, 'When Hugh became an anchorite.'

'It says *a terrible calamity befell the family and its servants when they all died*' Chris read.

'Obviously not the head of the household - Hugh' said Eleanor drily.

'What about Simon?' asked Chris.

'It says that a terrible disaster killed the entire household and the house caught fire.' Adam took the documents from Chris and said that he would study these himself.

'I assume that is what drove him to the cell. So, the Victorian take of 'evil begot evil' was really just an unfortunate series of events. Nothing more.' Adam studied the papers.

He chalked up the two heads of household shown on the genealogical table before Hugh, they were his grandfather Stephen and his father Richard, and then he settled down to immerse himself in the papers. Eleanor and Chris, unwilling to return to the church, sat silently. Chris looked at the wall with the lineage of William's family.

The Critchley family tree as chalked up by Dr Adam Glover glowed faintly green on the dark orange wall of the vestry. Grandfather Stephen Critchley had died in 1248 and was not buried at St Jude's. His son Richard had died in 1265, the time of final battle of the second Barons' War when Simon de Montfort had been defeated by Henry III's son Prince Edward, who became Edward I. Richard Critchley was not buried at St Jude's either and there was no indication of which side he had supported, assuming he had been involved in the rebellion. Chris knew enough about the middle ages to know that under feudal law a knight owed his military support to the service of his liege lord and ultimately the king. Taking part in a rebellion against the king on the losing side would have been a disaster for the family.

There had been other children of Richard, including an older brother to Hugh, called Guy and his death was recorded as 1266. He was not shown to have had issue, so the title passed to Hugh. The illustration plates showed earlier members of the family, none of whom were buried in St Jude's parish. The only brasses that had hung here until deconsecration were of William, his brothers John and Geoffrey and his father, the anchorite. The genealogical table ended with them.

Chapter Five - 1251

Licoricia of Winchester

Asher and his mother Licoricia walked around the medieval city of Winchester hand in hand. She was twice widowed, well known and respected, especially among the Jews who relied on her network of contacts throughout the country. She was liked by her neighbours and had a Christian maid, although this was strictly forbidden. The Church preferred Christians to have as few dealings as possible with other religions.

Her two husbands had been wealthy and successful moneylenders and she had learned much from their experience, but she was a sensible woman, clever in business and personable to the extent that she was sometimes consulted by the king and his queen. It was 1251 and King Henry III had been on the throne for 35 years. He had been nine, the same age as Asher was now, when his father King John had died whilst fighting a war against his own barons.

Henry had been born in Winchester and maintained close ties with the city. He was a king in a feudal society which meant that his power was derived from those who owed their duty to him. He relied upon the goodwill of the most powerful men in the country. Men who were usually at loggerheads over land, wealth and divided loyalties.

In order to carry on the same business as his mother and his father before him, Asher would need to be able to speak Norman French, the language of government, English, the language of the common man and Hebrew, the language of his own people. He would also need to be able to read and write in Latin, the language of the law.

These were the last of prosperous times for the Jews of Winchester. Their little community was soon to be persecuted and scapegoated from all sides. Many towns had already expelled their Jewish enclave so that they were able to live and work in only a few cities. The protection of the king was needed more than ever as the Church became increasingly vociferous against anyone not Christian. The constant wars of the Plantagenet kings to try and recover their ancestral lands in Normandy, Anjou and Aquitaine were expensive and led to increasing demands for tax. Any wealth accumulated by the Jewish population was fuel for an atmosphere of distrust against non-Christians.

Asher knew that he would be expected to run a similar business to his parents when he was old enough. They had extensive networks that enabled financial transactions to take place in a world with no banking systems. The loans he would make to the gentry and to the business community would create wealth, part of which would go to the king. It would also make him hated and a target for unscrupulous individuals.

Licoricia had spent time imprisoned in the Tower of London, then furnished as royal apartments, as surety for the tax that fell due on her second husband's estate when he died. Her confidence and efficiency had impressed the king, and the huge sum of tax she yielded was spent by Henry on creating a shrine to Edward the Confessor. Thereafter she was granted an exemption from the annual tax that all Jews bore, the tallage, and which provided essential funds for the royal exchequer.

His mother's house in Winchester was substantial and was close to the synagogue; it had its own mikveh, ritual baths, and covered almost an acre of land. Licoricia had three sons and one daughter from her previous marriage, as well as many friends in what was a close-knit community. Asher's father David of Oxford had loved books and fine horses and he inherited these passions along with such a pleasant nature that he was given the nickname 'Sweetman' by those who knew him. Ironic given that his mother had been named after liquorice, a sweetmeat.

Asher's older brother Benedict was an influential businessman in Winchester, with a number of Christian friends and also powerful enemies. He would become a guildsman, the only Jew known to have achieved this level of acceptance by a Christian community. His fate was to be hanged for 'coin-clipping', probably a trumped-up charge by his detractors.

As they walked through the medieval city, mother and son

could not know what fate awaited them.

During the turbulent mid 1260s Asher, then an adult, left Winchester and based himself in Marlborough in the county of Wiltshire. By 1272 Henry III was dead and his son Edward had become king, returning from crusade to take the throne. Asher inherited his mother's property in Winchester when she was murdered in 1277. He had by then been expelled from Marlborough with other Jews. The net was tightening, and in 1290 all Jews were expelled from England.

During the seventeenth century, a historian called Patrick Junius examined the castle ruins of Winchester where he found an inscription carved on a wall in a vault in the South Tower. The inscription was in Hebrew and read: 'On Friday, eve of the Sabbath in which the pericope Emor is read, all the Jews of the land of the isle were imprisoned. I, Asher, inscribed this…'. Junius reported his finding to John Seldon, the historian and map maker, who published it in his Treatise on the Jews in England 1617.[1]

---

[1] Suzanne Bartlet, *Licoricia of Winchester Marriage, Motherhood and Murder in the Medieval Anglo-Jewish Community* p.143

Chapter Six

In the Volvo Sarah had closed her eyes for a moment and had fallen into a fitful sleep. She woke with a sense of having received more information into the haunting of George Macey. Although she was not sure how she could know that Macey was haunted by a medieval Jewess, she could remember it with surprising clarity.

He had been a presence in her dreams for years while in a liminal state between waking and sleeping and he always brought comfort and a sense of reassurance. She was sure that he had been to St Jude's and that he had made brass-rubbings. His story must be interwoven with the circumstances in which she now found herself. Either that or she was going mad, and her sleeping brain had packaged everything into a neat parcel to deceive her into thinking it was manageable, a déjà vu paradox.

How much could she remember? It was important to recall as much as possible before it vanished into waking life. She found a paper and pencil in the glove box and began to make notes. Sarah knew that a Dr Macey had opened the grave of Little William in 1847. Now it seemed as though the reason he did that was prompted by the veiled woman's ghost. She had continued to haunt him until he acted and prevented more babies being buried in William's tomb, her urgency perhaps prompted by the possibility that live sacrifices were being made to some nameless ancient deity.

The latest dream revealed that the woman was the ghost of a Jewess who had been called Licoricia. Sarah remembered reading about her a few years ago when a statue was proposed for Winchester city centre to commemorate this notable of medieval women. She had not come to a good end; she recalled that too. She was murdered in her own home. What was her connection with Little William? That was a mystery and that was what she would now investigate if she got the opportunity.

It appeared that George Macey had been convinced by

Licoricia and if he had found answers then they might be in the archives. It made sense to look at the past through the recorded work of Victorian historians, and even earlier ones if they could be found. He may have had access to more original material. She felt sure that he had returned to St Jude's in the following year.

Sarah closed her eyes and reached into the dream for other less obvious findings. The intervention of Licoricia was deliberate and persistent because babies were not just buried in the tomb, some of them had been deliberate sacrifices by people of the village who sought some benefit from older gods with grosser appetites. This haunting had continued until Macey acted.

Sarah knew that as a pregnant woman she was particularly sensitive to the suffering of babies and children. Licoricia was a mother too and she had lived in the middle ages, at a time when injustice and cruelty were commonplace. But in this place, there was an overwhelming miasma of bereavement and loss. Sarah wondered if Licoricia's strong sense of maternal responsibility had summoned her soul from its rest to stop the cruelty and she had done this by haunting George Macey.

As the memory of the dream became less vibrant, she was tempted to lie down and try to re-enter the intoxication of sleep to wash away the coldness of reality. It's a drug, she thought, endorphins that my brain have created. She sat upright and accepted that she had to do something. The account that Chris had described of the haunting he experienced from the child-ghost of William meant that there was a disturbance at St Jude's church, and she was in some way, through Macey, connected to it. Sarah was not afraid of the dead. They were to be pitied. The danger would be from the living and Adam in particular.

Why were these things happening now? Eleanor appeared never to have seen the ghosts, but she had invited the archaeologists here. Sarah now suspected that she was not the simple middle-aged lady with an interest in history that she had at first seemed. She and her family had been involved in pagan practices. She was, to some extent a follower of the old religion and it was unclear to what extent she had power. She had apparently healed Adam's damaged fingers with a potion and a pair of nettle gloves. What had Eleanor said about Adam not turning into a swan? She racked her brains for the folk tale that she was referencing. An enchantress has turned a girl's brothers into swans and the only way to defeat the curse was for her to pick nettles at night in a graveyard. She then must weave a coat of nettles overnight and cast it onto the boys before the dawn without speaking, and despite the blisters and pain she suffered.

Sarah discounted the obvious moral lesson of the silent sister suffering for her male siblings. Perhaps the magic nettle cloaks curbed the wilder instincts of the boys and made them biddable and human. Perhaps Eleanor had used the gloves to exert control over Adam and surely that would be a good thing if he had been possessed by something at St Jude's?

Eleanor genuinely believed in the pervading evil of the church and its history and she believed it was capable of influencing the actions of people. She had even cited the desertion of her husband and the deaths of a man and his two little girls as somehow the result of supernatural interference. Sarah struggled to accept this but what she and Chris had seen and heard tonight was not rational.

She decided to go into the church and tell the others what she had seen and that they should research the writings of Dr Macey. Then she remembered that she did not know exactly where his work was published, and what had happened to him. She would check her phone to see if the signal had been restored, then she remembered that Adam had taken it from her when leaving the church and given her an ordinary torch.

The fear returned. He was behaving strangely, as though everyone was suddenly his enemy, and it had started before she had told him she was pregnant. The word 'possession' was fixed in her mind and where, if not in this haunted place, is possession more likely to occur?

If she could not join them in the church, then she should try to leave. Adam seemed to be obsessed with the unwholesome image of the anchorite and the murdered boy, Chris was out of his depth and Eleanor was, what, playing devil's advocate in some way? The church may not be safe structurally so it made sense to alert the authorities and to let them know that they were at St Jude's and cut off.

She climbed out of the Volvo and went across to Eleanor's Land Rover. As she had promised the key was inside the sun visor and Sarah sat in the driver's seat and put it into the ignition, depressed the heavy clutch and turned over the engine. It did not start, but the noise was so loud that she was afraid it would alert Adam. The vehicle was old and it might still have a choke. She looked for it while listening for sounds in the churchyard that might indicate he had heard it but there was no sign of him or the others. She tried again and it almost fired but she dared not risk it a third time.

Remembering boyfriends with old bangers she decided to try and bump start it by rolling it down the hill away from the church. She located the headlights, switched on the ignition and put the vehicle into second gear, depressed the clutch and let down the hand brake. It slowly rolled forward until there was a reasonable motion, then she released the clutch and it fired into life.

Without a thought for the noise, she turned on the lights and drove it forward. She steered it down the track quickly turning out of sight through the yew trees and began the winding progress to the main road. She would go to the village now the storm had abated and tell them that there were people in the church. There would be no need to explain about the hauntings, Eleanor was well known, and they could arrange assistance as soon as possible.

Eleanor had said something about a culvert being blocked but she could not remember the details. She drove slowly because the wet trees hung low over the road and the car was heavy to steer. About a quarter of a mile from the church the grotesque trunk and lower branches of a yew appeared in the dim yellow headlights. She skidded to a halt. The road was blocked.

After a second when tears of frustration welled, Sarah shook herself and climbed out, and with the aid of the torch and the headlights was able to establish that it was too heavy to be pushed out of the way by the Land Rover and to try might damage the lights. She set about finding a way past it on foot.

With an effort she was able to clamber around the massive root plate that had lifted from the shallow soil. By this time her boots were caked with mud and as she slid down the other side onto the roadway, she heard running water. She was near the fork in the road and might have been able to walk to Stansham except that the ditches were full and water flowed along the road. It was very dark.

The culvert being blocked must have diverted the stream from its usual course onto the roads, adding to the flood. Even with her torch she could not distinguish where the road ended and the ditches began. There might be drains and potholes, and she was not familiar with the road to Stansham. It would be dangerous, should she risk it or go back to the Land Rover?

She decided to return to the vehicle and wait it out. She was tired and cold and if she locked the doors, she was sure that she would feel safe, even if Adam had heard her leaving and decided to come after her. She listened for the engine of the Volvo but heard nothing. The sky was dark with no reflected light from the settlement. Perhaps there had been a power cut. She would hide in the Land Rover and find a way in the morning. Her watch said it was 12.42 am, so she would have a long wait.

Sarah systematically locked all the doors and the tail gate, and finding a blanket on the back seat she covered herself completely and closed her eyes. The silence was oppressive, the smell in the Land Rover was of petrol and possibly dog, but her ears and her eyes were entirely devoid of sensation. She wasn't sure if her eyes were shut as she strained to hear the approach of someone or something towards the car. She jumped at the clicking sound of the cooling engine, and later when a few drops of water hit the roof. She lay still for as long as she could, but there was no relaxation in her limbs, all hope of sleep had gone.

Sarah sat up, relieved to be out of the stifling closeness of the blanket. After earlier tears, haunted sleep and the panic of her failed flight, she realised that her body was tense and she had been running like a hunted animal. She ran her fingers through her hair and tried to straighten her shoulders.

Was she really afraid of Adam? She had known him for so many years. Eleanor's stories had planted the seed of some nameless horror lurking on St Jude's hill, and this might have prompted a fear that she now acknowledged, but fear is the mind killer and it was time to take her destiny into her own hands again and return to the church.

She felt around the back of the Land Rover for something that she might use and found a tin of travel sweets, a box of tissues, a pair of sunglasses, an umbrella, gloves and a black beanie. She put the hat on to cover her blonde hair. Further rooting provided her with what she could use: a pair of Nordic walking poles. She would use them to navigate the path back to the churchyard and need not rely on the torch. Her eyes would become accustomed to the dark.

The door creaked a little as she opened it and listened carefully to the sound of dripping branches and water running beyond the fallen tree. The crescent moon was just visible above the overhead canopy, she tried not to look at it as she needed her night vision. Sarah quietly closed the door and then remembered the key was in the ignition; well, the Land Rover wasn't going anywhere tonight. She kept to the dark shadows where she could, using the poles to check that the path was clear, as she walked back up the hill. It seemed to take a long time and every so often she paused to listen and catch her breath.

She grew accustomed to dripping trees and an occasional rustle of small claws in the deep litter under them. The lychgate loomed out of the darkness and the smell changed from the warm tang of the great yews to the earth and mould smell of the graveyard.

Sarah now felt quite comfortable to be walking without light, she had the poles and was able to make out obstacles reasonably well. She was about to start anti-clockwise when she remembered the old superstition about walking widdershins around a church. It was ridiculous but she was unwilling to tempt fate. There was a path going off to the left and she decided to walk outside the boundary wall of the churchyard to see where it would take her, reminding herself that at some point there would be a collapse of earth where the new farm road had caused a landslide.

The path had been gravelled and remained quite stable under her feet, but she put both sticks in her left hand and used her right to keep in contact with the wall. About six metres from the lychgate she could make out the other building. It was square and built of brick with a tiled roof; she determined to examine it more closely when she had circled the church.

The wall passed continued passable for about fifty metres and then the path became overgrown but Sarah found a gap and climbed through into the churchyard. Again, she carefully followed the inside of the wall keeping it close to her and continued the circumnavigation. There were no sounds from the church and only a faint glow from the vestry windows on the north side. She had walked further than the square tower, which had the large yew growing close to it. It seemed to embrace the building. Sarah was fascinated by the tree, it was the only one close to the church, the others had been planted in a circle around the top of the hill. She forced herself to stop looking at it and concentrate on where she was treading.

The vestry windows were lit so she assumed the others were talking or reading in there. Sarah found another break in the wall under her left hand and saw that there was a path leading from the vestry though the churchyard and into the yews. It might be the route to Eleanor's cottage.

She continued walking carefully through overgrown vegetation and gravestones until she had progressed further towards the east than the end of the church and turned the corner to bring her parallel with the large east windows. Suddenly the wall disappeared from under her hand and she slid a few feet towards a chasm. She clambered back, dislodging loose flints and soil.

This must be the collapsed area, she thought, instinctively crouching down behind a large modern gravestone. She could see the shapes of yews against the sky but there was a gap, and the land between the trees and the church had sunk. She searched her pockets for the torch and shone it along the remains of the wall. The ground here was not chalk, it looked like a combination of flint and other spoil.

Why would the builders of the church make such an effort

to disguise the henge? It did not make sense to build here so far from the village. Sarah could see why someone might believe the hill itself was significant and that there were older superstitions at work in that Christian community of Alfred's Wessex.

Her archaeologist's senses were tingling. If there were earthworks, whether they were neolithic or iron age, the ditches may have been filled in. She thought of the western approach by road, passing through the steep banks and yews. It was possible that this was the original gateway into the henge from the east so that when the farm road was cut, there was only the spoil remaining in that gap and no chalk. It could easily have been washed away by the heavy and continuous rainfall of the last two months.

Apart from the exposure of the more recent graves distressing as it was, there could be a lot of archaeology in the ditch. Was it filled in when the Anglo-Saxon church was built, or by the Normans when they demolished the wooden structure and built the current church? She could not wait to tell Adam. Then she remembered that he might not react with the same enthusiasm that she felt and was used to seeing in him. She controlled her excitement and reminded herself that there were more urgent matters that needed to be dealt with tonight.

She was not sure how far a person would fall if they slipped over that edge or if there were hazards unseen on the slope, but the unstable ground was treacherous. She was careful to stay well back. Even if she were not seriously injured it would take an effort to clamber back up to the churchyard and there could be stone monuments and other obstacles lying in wait for someone who fell headfirst down the muddy bank.

Sarah carefully made her way towards the church, seeking the firm ground of the older graves until she stood beneath the high boarded up windows. She turned to the right and made her way past the vestry towards the tree and walked close to its massive circumference. How old was it? Could it be more than one thousand years since these were planted? According to Eleanor they were planted after the Viking battle at around

900 AD.

From the other side she could just make out the tower with its small, rounded arch Norman windows high up, and realised that inside it there must be a staircase leading to the bells, although the bells may have been removed years ago. It was odd that they had not noticed any doors inside the church when they were looking for the access to the crypt. Like the boarded-up windows on the east side of the church they presented a blank face to the world. The church appeared sealed, whether deliberately or by accident she did not know.

She shuddered at the thought and turned back towards the vestry where she knew the others were working or sleeping. At the eastern end of the church, she set out towards the boundary again. Moving methodically along the sound edge of the collapsed bank Sarah found herself back at the boundary wall and made her way along the southern side of the churchyard. It took a long time to reach the lychgate again, but by then she was confident that she had the measure of the area.

She decided to investigate the structure she had noticed earlier and she passed inside the lychgate to a building that appeared to be a Victorian brick construction. She carefully shone the torch, shielded by her body from the church, and she saw a weathered painted sign that read 'Danger – deep well. Access only by arrangement' and which gave details of now long-gone parish contacts. The door had been padlocked but the wood had rotted, and it would be easy to prise the screws out.

For a few moments Sarah listened, and the silence convinced her that she should take a look inside. Pulling open the door was not easy because the long grass impeded its outward movement. She knelt and cleared the area to enable it to open a small way. She slid into the darkness and stayed close to the wall. Luckily, she was not afraid of spiders and small animals, but she need not have feared. The inside of the well house was clear and uncluttered, the ceiling was high, up to the apex of the tiled roof and supported by sturdy timbers.

The floor was concrete; she supposed that must have been a twentieth century addition and in the centre of the building was the well. A brick wall had been built around it and a hand operated pump installed to enable easier drawing of water to fill the flower vases on the graves. It seemed safe so she looked inside the well. There was a metal grill over the drop and when she found a stone to drop into it the water was close, understandably, given the recent exceptionally heavy rainfall.

For a few moments she allowed herself to reflect that this was the same well that Little William had been found in so many centuries ago. A movement caught her eye and she saw a small newt on the side of the wall. She smiled, and for a moment felt delight in the natural world and a flush of joy filled her at the thought of teaching her child about these things.

It occurred to Sarah that there were contradictions at this site, good and evil, nature and religion. Whether they were result of history or magic only time would tell, but somehow Sarah knew that tonight the shrouds that had hidden St Jude's would be opened and its dark heart exposed.

She decided to walk closer to the church and see the exposed stones under the tower for herself. She left the well-house with the door slightly open and made her way in darkness along the path to the west side of the church.

The tree loomed on the other side of the tower but at the southwest corner she could clearly see the stones that they thought might be Neolithic. The soil had been washed away more thoroughly here and, in her torchlight, Sarah noticed what might be a window arch, half buried to the south of the tower.

She wanted to investigate it further but was wary of using her torch too much, so she passed along the western edge of the tower, returning to the yew tree and examined it more closely. At its base a grey stone sat out of the ground and exposed roots ran around it like veins. She was not convinced that the tree was safe, but the wind had dropped so there was not much likelihood of it blowing down tonight.

Circumventing the tree was a challenge in itself as the ground was uneven but she remembered some information about ageing yews and their hollow centres. She shone her torch into the centre of the tree and she saw that there was space for a slim person to climb into it. She spent some time looking at the tree and the way it appeared to lean into the church. Indeed, it was impossible to see the corner of the tower and the church's main body; it was completely obscured by the tree.

As she made her way carefully along the north wall to the vestry, Sarah remembered the dragging sound and the whimpering child that she had heard earlier. She looked around and could see nothing that should frighten her yet an irrational wave of panic began to push adrenaline into her body and she didn't want to stay out in the darkness any longer.

There were lights in the vestry, and she moved close to the window to hear what was being said, wanting to feel part of the world of the living. Adam was reading aloud something he had discovered in one of the Victorian documents. Sarah remembered that she wanted to follow up on her connection with George Macey and she did not think she could bear to be denied access to the documents any longer. There was an external door to the vestry, so she hid the Nordic poles on the other side of the yew tree. She tried the door but it was still locked, so she knocked.

Adam stopped speaking and Sarah heard Chris exclaim that there was someone knocking at the door and Eleanor saying that she knew where the key was. When the door was opened Sarah pretended to be disoriented and they welcomed her in.

'How did you get here Sarah?' asked Adam.

'Are you alright?' said Chris.

'Come and sit down.' Eleanor beckoned her in and soon she was sitting on a bench with Chris on one side of her and Eleanor on the other in the light and warmth of the room again. Adam stood apart from them.

'You're looking so much better' said Adam 'you must have had a good sleep.' Then, slightly sarcastically 'Did you dream anything useful to our investigation?'

'Well, yes I did' Sarah decided to conceal her exploration of the churchyard. 'I dreamt that this church was built on an iron age hill fort' she lied, 'and that the east gate – the gap in the earthworks – was filled in with flint and soil and that is what the heavy rain and farm service road have now dislodged. If it was filled in Anglo Saxon times when the wooden church was built, Adam, it's likely to be full of archaeology. What's more there may be Viking artifacts too if the rumour is correct and there was a battle against the Vikings on this hill.'

There was a glint in Adam's eye but he said nothing. Chris and Eleanor were delighted to have her back and they wanted to show her something that they had discovered.

Chris said 'Hugh Critchley, the anchorite was Little William's father. So, there is a connection between the ghosts that we saw.'

Adam said 'Come and see the brass plaque to Hugh of Stansham. We've been trying to piece together the timeline between the murder and the fall of the house of Critchley. There seems to have been a series of accidents beginning with the murder of William.'

'It sounds more like a curse to me' said Chris as he followed Adam through the door into the church.

As they left Sarah turned to Eleanor and whispered 'I took the Land Rover, but it wasn't possible to get down off the hill because a tree has fallen across the road. I decided not to walk as I could hear water running. I left it there I'm afraid.'

'Don't worry about that' replied Eleanor, 'as long as you're alright. Adam seems quite reasonable now, but you had better stick with me or Chris while we are in the church.'

They went through into the nave and joined Chris and Adam who were looking at the grey-white brass.

Chris beckoned her over 'Look Sarah. What do you think of this?'

'What is that disgusting stuff? It looks like grave wax,' she said.

He continued 'Don't touch it. Don't you think it's odd that his body is turned sideways and yet his face is staring out at the viewer, or at William's grave.'

'They say it's the fate of the damned,' said Sarah.

'What do you mean?' said Chris.

'Being obliged to relive their sins for eternity.'

'What if you enjoyed your sins?'

Sarah smiled. 'Sorry, I put it badly. The damned are defined by their sins. If you are greedy, you become a perpetually hungry mouth … like, erm, a ….'

'A zombie.'

'I suppose so, in modern horror film terms.'

'What sin makes you blind?'

They looked again at the brass of Hugh, until Adam said 'The inability to appreciate what you have so that you lose the possibility of seeing it. Perhaps he's not blind, he just has perpetually weeping eyes.'

He took them again to the vestry where he showed Sarah the chalked timeline on the orange wall. 'He seems to have lived the life of a normal knight of the period and built a house in Stansham. Although the family appears to have been in reduced circumstances after his father's and brother's deaths.'

Eleanor said, 'Dr Glover thinks they were on the wrong side in the Barons' War with Henry III, and as a result they were punished by losing most of their manors.'

'I think they lost more than their property,' said Adam. 'From the timing on the genealogical table at least one lost his life. Sir Richard died in 1265 and has no commemorative brass and his eldest son Guy in 1266. Yes, I rather think they were on the rebels' side, and when Hugh inherited, he tried to regain the family's wealth and position.'

'And had given it all up by 1290,' said Chris.

Sarah said, 'The blood libel against the Jews resulted in the deaths of men who were probably innocent and a profit to Sir Hugh of Stansham. Do you think that might have weighed on his conscience?'

Adam said, '1290 was the year the Jews were expelled from England.'

'Perhaps his eyes perpetually weep because he felt guilty in some way over William's death and didn't want to look at his grave,' said Chris.

'Then he waited a long time between the murder and

becoming an anchorite,' Adam said. 'It's more likely that he gave up the secular life when his entire family died, in some catastrophe, and his house was consumed by fire.'

'That's definitely more like a curse than bad luck' Chris insisted. 'So he must have done something to deserve it.'

'I haven't found any mention in any of the contemporary or Victorian documents that Hugh was blind either as an anchorite or as a living man,' Eleanor said. 'Perhaps the damage to the brass was carried out by someone else as punishment for his crimes.' They thought about that and wondered who would hate him so much for eternity, and why was the image covered in a waxy substance?

'What if you were a murderer?' Chris asked Sarah. 'What is your eternal punishment then?'

'The worst fate of all. Perpetual unrest. Living death. No chance of peace.'

'Hence the prayer Requiescat in pace. Perhaps he was praying for his own soul.'

'I suppose that's possible,' said Sarah. 'He would be doomed to wander the earth, seeking some sort of redemption.'

'The only way to recover his soul would be by atonement. As in Yom Kippur, Sarah.' Adam said.

Sarah wanted to discuss the dream she had not disclosed to them and the role of medieval Jewess Licoricia of Winchester and her involvement with Macey.

'If you like. Yom Kippur occurs in autumn. As we prepare for the hardship of winter, we should also be preparing our souls in case we don't survive it.'

Chris considered this and said, 'I'm not sure we should have done it on Halloween but, while you were sleeping, we dug up William's bones.'

Sarah was astonished 'He was still there?' she asked Adam 'After all this time?'

Chris continued 'And there was something odd about his bones. Wasn't there Adam? He was a disabled before he was murdered. And the mutilation must have concealed it.'

'Was it Hugh's son?' said Sarah. 'Or a peasant's child, but I suppose either way that puts Hugh in the frame for the murder, since he benefitted more than most.'

'We thought about that, but if so, what happened to the real William? No,' said Adam. 'That's the real William Critchley, in that grave.'

Chris said, 'I saw the boy's ghost. He said Papa. Whoever he was, he must surely be blameless; why should an innocent be cursed to haunt this church and possibly the graveyard, after his bones were disturbed by that chap in the nineteenth century. He was a victim.'

'Any child in distress would call for his father, to help him,' Eleanor said, looking at Adam.

Sarah asked Eleanor 'Do you know what type of apparitions have been encountered before, and what sort of people have seen them? Apart from the man that your father saw. I assume he saw the anchorite who we now believe to have been Hugh Critchley.'

'I suppose the most recent ones were the men who investigated the church for potential sale and the various surveyors....' She paused 'To be honest nobody actually said, 'I've seen a ghost and I'm not going back'. The most I could get out of them was that they were just not going back. That was enough to have it taken off the market by the Church authorities. I got the impression it was connected to the place rather than being associated with a person. Some people have experienced nothing. I'm one of those.'

Adam turned to Sarah 'Well it's been quiet since you went to sleep in the car Sarah. Perhaps you are the catalyst. A previous life of yours has disturbed the spirits. Or possibly the fact that you're pregnant has woken the souls of dead babies left here for years.'

Chris exclaimed, 'Pregnant! Really! Bloody hell!' He shuffled about and tried to control his feelings at this revelation.

Before he could say any more Eleanor suggested that perhaps it was simply that so many graves had been disturbed that had woken the spirits. She added 'We all now accept that there are hauntings, don't we?'

'I suppose so,' said Adam 'I can agree that something is being replayed or repeated here and that there has been great bloodshed and trauma in the place itself. But I don't accept that we are in danger.'

Sarah said, 'How can you say that? You and Chris have been injured and Eleanor thinks it hasn't finished with us yet.'

They all looked at Eleanor and she said, 'I'm sorry but it wants a willing blood sacrifice.' She smiled apologetically.

After a few seconds Adam laughed and was followed by Chris and Sarah. 'You almost had me there. Surely the obvious disturbance is the boy and his father the anchorite.'

'It's a pity that William can't tell us who killed him,' said Chris.

He was anxious to help the child's spirit rest, Sarah could see he had not shaken the image of the little ghost from his mind.

'Well he can't. There's nothing to be done until it gets light and then I will secure the site and ensure that no one else looks at the stones. I am going to take charge of this investigation and bring in a team from the university. Before you leave, I want non-disclosure agreements from all of you.' Adam said firmly.

There was an awkward silence; Eleanor raised her eyebrows but they were all tired and it was the middle of the night. Then Sarah thought she heard something. She glanced at Chris, and he looked alarmed.

She said 'What makes you think that it's going to let us ignore it?' It was the sound of something being dragged across the floor of the church and it was getting louder. 'Can you hear that?'

Chris moved closer to Sarah and she thought that even Adam and Eleanor must be able to hear it now.

'There's something coming – towards the vestry,' said Chris.

Adam went to the door to the church and looked through it.

'I can't see anything.'

'Shut the door for God's sake!' said Chris and Sarah tucked her arm through his, as much for her own comfort as his. When the door was shut it stopped and they giggled a little from relief. Even Adam had looked worried.

Eleanor put her ear to the door and listened. She said 'You

know, it's now 31ˢᵗ October and the barrier between life and death is said to be weakest at Hallowe'en. And St Jude's feast day was 28ᵗʰ October. Not that he'll be much help, being the patron saint of hopeless causes.'

A crash against the door broke the short period of relief. Eleanor screamed and backed across the room with a look of horror on her face. She looked as though she had been struck.

'Are you ok?' asked Sarah, aware that this might have been the first genuine reaction she had seen from the woman. She and Chris huddled on the pew and Adam moved as far from the door as possible.

They waited in silence listening for any sounds, but there was only the dripping of water from rotten guttering and a slight increase in the whistle of the wind. The wind's picking up again, thought Sarah and her mind ran through the topography of the churchyard and the exterior of the church.

After a few minutes with no unnatural noises Sarah stood and without allowing herself to think, because she knew if she did, she would hesitate. 'We must see what has happened' she said and pulled open the vestry door. Then she gasped 'Oh no. How could it do this?'

They shuffled into the church, staying near the door. In shock they saw that the pews they had arranged into a square earlier had been stacked in a pyramid facing the white brass of the anchorite.

'How could this happen? Who did it?' asked Chris

'What did it? And why? Are we expected to find something at the front of the church? Have they been arranged for our benefit? What the hell are we going to see in this unhallowed performance space?' Adam sounded as though he was on the brink of hysteria.

Eleanor was particularly quiet. She was white and her eyes seemed to have shrunk in terror and panic. She looked left and right as though seeking the perpetrator, her calm assurance gone. Sarah took her arm, but she twitched it away and said 'Excuse me, I need to ...' and she ran back into the vestry.

Chris said 'It's a poltergeist, isn't it? I've heard about these things. It's really creepy but it's trying to communicate with us.'

'What's it saying?' asked Adam.

'I don't know; maybe it's just playing a trick.'

Sarah left them to their debate and went after Eleanor. She was in time to see her drinking from a small flask.

'Nerve tonic' she said.

'Can I have some?' asked Sarah.

'Better not' said Eleanor pointing to Sarah's belly.

'Will you be all right?'

Eleanor turned to Sarah 'There's something watching us, isn't there? Whatever we do is being observed and things thrown at us to see how we react. Like the spirits being released to haunt us and the poltergeist to unsettle us.'

'Look Eleanor, you say you believe that evil forces reside here. Are you really surprised that it has manifested in physical form? I know you've never seen a ghost, but did you think we were making it up?'

Eleanor sat down and removed her glasses. She cleaned them and rubbed her eyes but seemed to be calming down.

'I thought it was an evil influence that made men do bad things. I thought it just waited for people to deliver a blood sacrifice then gave them good fortune.'

'You said a willing sacrifice earlier.'

'Yes, perhaps.'

'Is that why it didn't help Hugh Critchley for long,' said Sarah.

'Assuming he was the killer. And you have to offer up a worthy sacrifice,' said Eleanor with contempt. 'A cripple just won't do.'

It was like a slap in the face but before Sarah could react, Adam and Chris walked in from the church and joined them, closing the vestry door.

'Hallowe'en and death are intricately linked,' said Adam desperately. 'Winter was coming and darkness and harsh weather, they never knew if they'd survive until spring. Blood sacrifices were usually made in October or November. It was simply a matter of animal husbandry. They had to slaughter most of their livestock – they couldn't feed all the animals through the winter. They'd keep the best breeding animals and the rest were salted, smoked and stored. They feasted at

Christmas and when stocks ran out, coincidentally at Lent, they went hungry. No eggs after Shrove Tuesday, they were needed for the next batch of summer chickens. It's only common sense.'

Chris said 'That doesn't explain the blood libel against the Jews. Why would people accept the ridiculous story of child blood sacrifice? I know there may be a slaughter stone here, under this church, but there hadn't been human sacrifices in this country for hundreds of years.'

'Human sacrifice or not, people of those times believed in the magical power of blood sacrifice. It was quite common in rural Ireland into the twentieth century. A goose would be slaughtered some time in November and its blood sprinkled in the corners of the kitchen. Catholics are still meant to believe that they are eating the body and drinking the blood of Christ, and in medieval England it had been declared as fact by the Fourth Lateran Council'.

Chris was disgusted by this 'You think that's the reason people were quite willing to believe that some Jews sacrificed William for religious reasons?'

Sarah added 'It can be linked to Abraham and Isaac in the Old Testament, at a stretch. It wouldn't take much to scapegoat the Jews – another biblical expression. The chosen goat took all the sins of the tribe on its back and was driven into the desert to starve or be eaten by wild animals.'

'That's barbaric' said Chris 'I can't get my head around the idea of clearing out sins by whatever method, scapegoats, sin eaters, confession and atonement etcetera and blood sacrifice.'

'Jesus was the ultimate willing blood sacrifice' said Sarah 'and the idea is that through him your soul can be saved.' She decided it was time to relate her dream 'Adam, have you ever heard of Licoricia of Winchester?'

He looked surprised. 'Yes, I have. I believe she was an influential businesswoman in the thirteenth century and a Jewess. Why do you ask?'

'I think she may have been the veiled woman who haunted George Macey and convinced him to investigate St Jude's in 1847.'

Eleanor and Chris asked how Sarah could possibly know

her identity, so she had no choice but to tell them. She had slept in the Volvo and again dreamt about Macey and his encounters with the ghost of a woman.

'She told him that blood sacrifice was again being carried out at St Jude's hill and that these sacrifices were of babies and infants. He didn't want to believe it but it was borne out by the remains found when Macey excavated the grave of William later in 1847.'

Adam continued 'Licoricia was murdered in her own home, wasn't she?'

'I believe so, in Winchester, and no one was brought to justice for it. There must be a connection between William and Licoricia; he was murdered in 1275, she in 1277 after five Jews of Winchester were hanged. Perhaps she tried to clear their names. Possibly she got too close to the truth.'

Chris looked between them. 'How is this connected to blood sacrifice and the babies?'

'William may have been a blood sacrifice, but not by Jews, by someone purportedly Christian who had more faith in the darkness of pagan myth.' Sarah was now inclined to believe that his father had done it.

'Yes,' said Eleanor eagerly 'as a blood sacrifice to the gods of old.'

'Oh, for goodness sake Eleanor, nobody believes that apart from you.' Adam sounded irritated.

Eleanor was ready for an argument 'The Vikings sacrificed valuable animals to their gods before a battle, usually their best stallion or a hunting hound. Those religions were not that far in the past in 1275 and the Normans were Vikings originally. And you're the one who was so keen to convince Chris about blood sacrifice a few minutes ago, Dr Glover.'

She's recovered well thought Sarah, she wondered what was in that nerve tonic. There was an uncomfortable silence, then Chris said 'William Critchley was a cripple.'

Adam looked annoyed with Chris for having disclosed what he was thinking. But for the benefit of Sarah, he described in more detail what they had found.

'It was the skeletonised body of a small boy in a shroud and I unwrapped it, the fabric was disintegrating anyway. As expected from the written accounts the long bones had been broken at about the time of death, but it was obvious that the child had been a cripple in several ways. His legs were not straight, and his back was also crooked; it might account for his small stature.'

'But who would kill such a child?'

'The obvious answer is Hugh Critchley himself,' said Adam

'Why would he do that?' Chris was aghast.

Adam was matter of fact about it 'To increase the size of his estates.'

Sarah was grim when she said, 'And because he was ashamed of him.'

'Of course as he had three other healthy sons by this time, he did not need his eldest son who would be unable to fight and hunt but would still inherit the estate,' said Adam.

'Two birds with one stone.'

Chris said 'If he did kill William then presumably, if she found out about it, he might have been responsible for the murder of Licoricia too. Do you know much about her?'

Sarah replied 'Licoricia was by that time an elderly Jewess who had, for a while, enjoyed the protection of King Henry III. She'd had two husbands, and both died before her, and four sons who all outlived her. But she had also run a profitable business although by this time the greed and prejudice of the barons and the Church had ruined the livelihoods of the remaining Jews in England. By the time she died Henry's son Edward I was on the throne and not inclined to protect the king's Jews for much longer.'

'What is her relevance to this Sarah?' Eleanor asked, 'Did the blood libel affect her family?'

'Not in this case, but a similar accusation had been levied against her first husband in London when she was quite a young woman. He was not convicted but died shortly afterwards. By the time of Little William's murder Licoricia must have been in her sixties and maybe she decided to make a stand.'

Chris said 'It's a murder mystery. Multiple murders in fact, and a brutal miscarriage of justice. Do you really think that there is a chance that we could uncover the guilty party after all these centuries? We would need supernatural help.'

Nobody responded so he prompted again 'How about a séance?' As soon as the words left his mouth, he regretted it. 'Oh, I forgot about the thing that was dragged across the floor. I'd be prepared to see William again but not whatever that was.'

Eleanor said 'Well, speaking as someone who has had no supernatural interaction, I heard the dragging noise, the crash and I am not anxious to meet whatever rearranged the furniture.'

Adam sat frowning in his corner of the vestry and said 'Well we'll never know. Will we?'

Sarah could tell he was planning how he would regain control of the situation and burnish his academic credentials. They lapsed into thoughtful silence again.

Sarah broke the reverie by saying 'Eleanor did you find anything in the court cases?'

Eleanor brightened, and brought out a sheaf of papers. 'Well, there is an article mentioning that at the time the five Jews were accused of murdering Little William, there was uproar amongst the people of Winchester. The archa, that's the chest that the bonds were stored in, was broken into and some went missing. As these were the official records showing who owed money to the moneylenders, the debtors stood to profit because the debt could not be proved. One was a substantial bond taken out by Sir Hugh's father secured on the family's remaining land in Stansham. Sir Hugh benefitted doubly out of the trouble arising from William's death.'

They were sober and silent for a few minutes. Then Chris said: 'You don't think that Hugh Critchley really murdered his own son, do you?'

Adam shook his head 'If he wanted to discredit Jews, any Christian child would have served the purpose and I'm sure that there were others he could have chosen.'

'But he disposed of a cripple in the process and gained a martyr in the family.' Sarah's voice was hard. 'Not to mention making a blood sacrifice, albeit a poor one. Sorry Chris.'

'There was a direct connection to Licoricia,' continued

Eleanor 'Because it says here that when Sir Hugh disputed the existence of the bond, a case was brought by 'Benedict fil Licoricia' and that suggests that the debt was not the property of one of the accused men but owing to Benedict or possibly his mother.'

'What happened in that case?' asked Sarah.

'It doesn't say. Quite possibly it was quietly dropped, or a deal was done.'

'So Licoricia had a double motive for going after the killer. It was an attack on people of her race and she or Benedict lost money as a result.'

'And she was murdered within a few years of the crisis,' said Chris. 'Didn't it say that when Licoricia was murdered, three men were accused.'

Eleanor had found the coverage 'They were released, due to lack of evidence, according to the article in the Gentleman's Magazine.'

'Lack of will more likely,' said Sarah.

'There were further burglaries of her property after her death. This was as usual attributed to heirs wishing to avoid tax on the value of the deceased's estate.' Eleanor turned to Sarah. 'I doubt we have any chance of discovering who killed William or Licoricia.'

'But she had a personal reason to want to get to the truth of the matter,' Sarah said. 'And she haunted George Macey until he agreed to investigate William's grave. If we can find the writings of Dr George Macey there may be some answers. I believe that he returned to St Jude's in 1848 and attempted to solve the puzzle.'

'And found the bodies of the babies. Surely that was her motive - to stop the sacrifice of more innocent children,' suggested Eleanor.

'In this place of ancient ritual,' said Adam. There was a sound like a sigh from the church.

They were huddled in the vestry, too afraid to go back into the church and it was cold. She shuddered. Perhaps Adam had seen that shudder, but she was startled when, before she could say anything, he came over to her and spoke.

'Sarah, it isn't safe in the church, don't you think that you should be in the Volvo? You slept earlier and I would be happier if you and the baby were out of harm's way.'

She was alarmed and saw a similar emotion cross Eleanor's face.

'I think Adam's right,' said Chris. 'You've got to think of the baby, it's just not safe in the church. I'll go with you to the car.'

He fetched a bag and put some drinks and chocolate in it; his solicitude was enough to convince her that she should go with them. While they were preparing Sarah's supplies Adam drank more of the potion Eleanor had given him for his damaged hand. He opened the vestry door and when Sarah was outside, he turned back and said firmly to Chris.

'Don't worry, I'll see Sarah safely to the car. You stay with Eleanor. We don't want anyone on their own for long.' He removed the key from the door.

Chris disagreed and made to push past him, causing Adam to lose his balance. The two men struggled in the doorway to Eleanor's shock and dismay. She tried to help Chris but Adam viciously jammed Chris's injured hand against the door frame. He cried out in pain and Adam pushed him back into Eleanor, so they fell back together.

'Sorry Chris. This is between me and Sarah. And before you say anything Eleanor it's none of your business, you look after the boy's hand.'

He shut the door and locked it and looked around for Sarah with his torch, but she was nowhere to be seen. He turned to his left towards the tower and walked up to the yew tree where he thought he caught a whiff of her scent, but it was soon gone in the earthy smells of trees and the graveyard. He carried on around the building searching with his torchlight and then followed the path down to the lychgate and, near it, the well-house. She must have gone to the car, he thought, and he went through the gate to look in the Volvo, it was empty. It was dark and quiet. He called her name.

Then he noticed that the Land Rover had gone. He felt viscerally overwhelmed by rage, he swore and started down the drive, away from the church but then listened and could hear no engine. She may have coasted down the track and he ran after her until he came to the vehicle and the fallen tree. She was not in the vehicle and from its state it had obviously been there for some time. The bitch must have taken it earlier, he thought. She had tried to get away. Again, the rage overwhelmed him.

She must still be here he thought, and turned back to the churchyard, after the uphill walk he entered through the lychgate stopping every few paces to listen. He could hear nothing except for the dripping yews. He was furious.

He retraced his steps to the vestry door and listened. He could hear Chris and Eleanor talking quietly as she re-dressed his cuts. He unlocked and opened it swiftly so that Sarah would not be able to hide, and they looked at him startled; he saw fear on their faces and it pleased him.

'Where is she?'

Eleanor stood and faced him, she seemed calm. 'She's not here Dr Glover.' He looked in the kitchen and the toilet and then charged through into the church. He scoured the place ensuring that there was nowhere she could have hidden from him. So, she must be hiding in the churchyard, unless she had been taken down to hell. The thought gave him pause as it was uncharacteristic; where had it come from?

He strode through the church door into the porch and began searching the churchyard again, he was becoming increasingly frustrated that she should be able to evade him. He was again at the lychgate when he noticed the well-house and that its door had been opened. So, he thought, that's where you're hiding. She didn't trust him was that it? He called out softly 'Sarah, I know you're in there.' She did not respond 'Don't be stupid, I'm not going to hurt you.' Still, she did not respond, and he felt a wave of fury. 'Come on you silly bitch, I warned you, I'm coming in.'

☦   ☦   ☦

In the hollow yew tree Sarah held her breath as Adam prowled around outside. She could see flickers from his torch light as he shone it all over the graveyard searching for her. There was one moment when he stopped by the tree and she thought he had realised where she was. She dared not move a muscle and was so relieved when she heard his feet on the gravel as he walked away. She decided to stay where she was. She had only just managed to wriggle through the split in the tree, but the interior was reasonably roomy, although it was wet and probably full of insects. She did not mind if Adam could not find her; she was afraid of him.

She listened with every fibre of her body for a long time and heard him return and burst into the vestry and then nothing. Her best bet was to get back to Eleanor and Chris while he was away and ask Eleanor to take them to her cottage. She had offered earlier, and Adam could take his chances over here.

She began to ease out of the space and as she did so a large piece of rotten yew broke and fell away from her, exposing part of the tower wall that had not been visible before. Sarah froze, and listened for signs that Adam had heard, but it was quiet, so she continued easing out of the space. She dared not risk using a torch, so she used her hands to feel down the wall and steady herself. She stopped. She could feel something round and metallic under her hand? Like a ring or possibly a handle, and she could also detect a groove that dropped down as low as she could reach. Above the handle the groove carried on but was full of lichen and then vanished behind the tree as it pressed against the wall.

Sarah forgot about Adam as she realised she had found a door in the tower. It was made of wood but still sound. She slipped out of the tree and ran to the vestry door and burst in. Chris stood with a mallet in his hand.

'Damn it, I thought you were Adam. Thank God you're ok. Where is he?'

'Looking for me, but listen, I've found something fantastic, a door to the tower. It's hidden behind the old yew tree. If we can make more space between the tree and the door, we may be able to open it.'

This was such a breakthrough they agreed that they would deal with Adam when and if he reappeared. They brought lights and one of the kit bags with tools that would enable them to hack away at the rotten tree. The confined space meant that only one person could work at a time and the other two stood guard with torches.

The deep red smooth wood was soaked with so much rain that it was soft and the person in the cavity was able to lever chunks out with a crowbar. Millipedes and woodlice ran about in panic to escape. Sarah regretted destroying this old tree and wished it could be used to make something beautiful.

After about ten minutes Adam appeared from the other side of the vestry; he saw their torches and came towards them, stopping when Chris told him not to approach or he would knock him down. Adam was trembling and almost incoherent, but not with rage. He squatted down and rubbed his head, then in a shaking voice he said:

'There's a man in the well, we have to try and help him. You must come with me. Please. I could hear crying and splashing but I can't see him. Please, it's awful but we can't leave him there.'

Chris said 'I didn't see a well. It's a trick. You're making it up.'

'It's in a building, it was open, and I thought... I heard something splashing and shouting. I thought it might be Sarah. I wanted to help her.' He was pleading now.

'That's where they found William,' Chris said. 'Are you sure it wasn't a child's voice?'

'No, it sounded like a man. You must come with me, we must try and help him.'

Eleanor stood next to Chris 'Nothing large could fall into the well Dr Glover, there's a grill over the top. You're lying to us' she paused. 'Or it's a haunting.'

Adam caught his breath and collapsed onto a grave.

Eleanor continued 'I expect a number of things have drowned in that well over the years. No one is going to fall for your tricks again. Sit there and don't interfere. We've found a door to the tower.'

Adam did not argue or approach but sat on the grave and watched them work. Eleanor offered to take a quick look at the well if the others felt safe enough and if Dr Glover would stay where he was. She soon returned to say that there was nothing unusual about the well, and this caused Adam to rush off again and check it for himself.

'The grill is strong, it's really thick and if he did hear something it must have been a small animal, the water is high and the walls would probably make it seem louder.'

Eventually Adam reappeared. 'There's nothing now, but I did hear a voice calling for help; I swear it.'

'Then you heard a ghost. Now let's get this door open.' Sarah and Chris had widened the gap that had allowed Sarah to enter; now they began to gouge away the upper part of the tree that abutted the door. Eleanor moved the debris away whilst keeping an eye on Adam, but he seemed quite compliant for the moment.

The lichen came away cleanly, having been softened by the rain and it did not take too long before the upper part of the door became completely visible. The bottom of the door was buried in the ground. By using trowels to remove earth and a mattock to cut away tree roots they were able to expose the threshold and soon the entire door was visible. It was small and Eleanor said she could not remember it ever being visible, or used, although it must have been, because a bell had sounded occasionally when she was a child.

By combining the use of the crowbar and turning the ring handle, they were able to push open the door. Eleanor stood back and said to Sarah 'You found it, so you should go first.' She raised the torch and shone it inside. There were stairs to the left spiralling upwards, she guessed to the place where the bells had been.

'Shall we go up?' she said and Chris offered to wait at the bottom in case they encountered a problem. He also wanted to ensure that Adam did not shut them in, so he armed himself with the mattock and guarded the door.

The spiral staircase wound clockwise up to a small room and a pair of Norman mullioned windows that looked to the west. The floor was covered with droppings and nesting materials from birds, but otherwise the room was empty. They were disappointed, and reluctantly returned down the stairs. During her slow and careful torch-lit progress, Sarah noticed that the stone steps were worn, and she was studying the tread pattern when they again reached the ground. Chris asked if he could go up and Eleanor offered to watch Adam. Sarah was still fascinated by the worn flagstones. She asked if she could close the door and then she shone her torch on the blank wall behind it. Yes, she was sure, the stairs continued downwards, the tread was clear, but the access had been blocked up.

When Chris returned, she explained quietly to both of them that this was probably the crypt entrance. They suppressed their excitement but agreed that Adam should be told and they would try and break through without his assistance. Despite his injured hand Chris offered to do most of the work and he began prising out the mortar and smaller stones. Eleanor helped by removing them and this enabled Sarah to sit down and talk to Adam.

'Did you really hear someone in the well?'

He nodded. 'Sarah, why are you doing this to me? It should be you and me making these discoveries. We're the professionals here. Goodness knows what mess Chris is making of the excavation of that door. Is he recording everything?'

'Stop it Adam. This has gone far beyond being a dig. We … I … need to know what happened in 1277 and why I am haunted by the ghost of a man who lived in 1848. You have seen the ghost of Hugh Critchley and now it appears heard the ghost of somebody who drowned in the well.'

'I heard something horrible in the church too, earlier, it sounded like the same man. He was terrified.'

'Why didn't you say something?'

'I don't know. Sarah, you need to be on my side in this. They are trying to take over.'

'They? You're being paranoid Adam. This is not a normal situation. Forget your ambition for a moment. You have heard a ghost and we've all experienced poltergeist activity. Your own nephew has seen the ghost of a murdered child. Isn't that enough to convince you that this is no longer about archaeology, but about something supernatural, about good and evil.' She stood and moved away from him. She noticed that he was rubbing and scratching his hands. 'Are your hands hurting? You're still wearing those nettle gloves.'

He reached inside his jacket and took a swig from his flask. 'You're jealous because I have contacts in the media, and you want me to fail. You'd like to take all the credit for this site.'

He was winding himself up into a rage, 'And I've seen the way you look at Chris.'

She was astonished at how quickly his mood had changed.

'Don't be ridiculous. This is nothing to do with you and me. You're becoming paranoid.'

'Don't talk to me like that' he stood up and walked towards her. She shone her torch into his face and could see that his pupils were dilated. Sarah caught her breath, unsure whether to run but Eleanor had heard the exchange. She moved from the tower doorway and stood between them, a large stone in each hand. Her presence seemed to calm him, the aggression subsided, and he shrugged and walked away cursing women as witches.

'I don't know what's got into him.' Sarah looked at his hunched retreating figure.

'Let him go. He's been infected by whatever resides here. I've seen it before, but he hasn't been here long, imagine what several months would do to him. He's already obsessed with ensuring that he benefits from the investigation no matter what the cost in terms of relationships and lives. This is what happened to my husband and his friends. This place makes you paranoid.'

'It has seen its share of tragedy. Do you know of the drowning of a man in the well?'

'You believe he heard it?' asked Eleanor.

'Yes, when I dreamed about George Macey he was going to return to St Jude's with his artist friend McKinley to make further investigations. Perhaps one of them drowned in the well. I don't even know what became of George, whether he survived and went on to live a long and happy life. I don't suppose you know of a gravestone in his name, do you?'

Eleanor shook her head. 'There is a section of Victorian graves but if he wasn't local, he wouldn't be buried here.'

Just then Chris called out. 'I've broken through and there's space on the other side of the wall. I can see steps going downwards.'

'You go' said Eleanor 'I'll stay here in case Adam comes back.'

Sarah helped Chris to remove a few more stones and she was able to squeeze into the dark space. The stairs descended in the same way as the others and had obviously not been used for a long time. She carefully stepped down until the way opened into a large underground room that her torch did little to illuminate. Chris brought a larger lantern and they shone it on the floor.

'Bones' he said, 'This confirms that it was a charnel house.' Most of the skulls had been laid in stacks against the walls supported by rough shelving, but some had fallen and littered the floor. The shelves were situated between large upright stones.

'Look, standing stones, said Sarah, awestruck. She reached out and touched the nearest, it was cool and damp. She counted them. There were seven, but there were supposed to be twelve, according to the archive material. The room was under the tower on the west side of the church and where she imagined the narthex to be, there was also a heap of rubble and tree roots.

'It looks as though they didn't excavate the whole site when they built the charnel house. Just the part under the tower. Watch where you tread Chris.' He was looking upwards at the vaulted ceiling and the supporting stones.

Chris stumbled and fell to his knees. 'Ouch, what's this?' he was kneeling in front of a rectangular grey stone with a dipped centre and a channel off one end. 'Oh no, no, no, not again.' The paper bandage on his hand was bloody from exertion and a smear of blood had been left on the stone. He stayed on his knees as though waiting 'It's the slaughter stone isn't it, Sarah? It's tasted my blood and now it wants me.' There was panic in his voice and they were both shaken by the accident.

Sarah tried to keep a tremor from her voice as she said 'Stand up and come over to me. You just stumbled. That's all.' He moved away from the stone and they looked at it, but nothing happened. 'See, it was just a coincidence. Now use the camera on your phone to record what we've found here.'

'I can't find my phone Sarah. It's been missing for ages. Don't you have yours?'

'No, that's gone too.'

She was amazed to have found the slaughter stone exactly as predicted but it troubled her that Chris should have spilt blood on it. She tried to look analytically at the room, from the stairs clockwise she could see a stone, then the rubble and roots where the main body of the church must be. Then another stone, half visible, and a shelf containing intact sets of bones and skulls, shallow but orderly. There was another stone and more bones, a stone and a disturbed area of bones, another stone and more disturbed bones behind the slaughter stone, then two more stones with the most disturbed area of bones between them.

On the beaten earth floor lay bones and fragments of skull as though there had been a struggle around the slaughter stone and near the stairs. Perhaps someone trying to get out, she shuddered to imagine what it would like to be trapped down here alone in the dark. The ceiling was vaulted, obviously Norman and in poor shape; some water had made its way in and dripped onto the slaughter stone diluting poor Chris's blood and making it look more than it was.

'Can I have a look?' Eleanor appeared at the foot of the stairs 'I couldn't wait much longer; I was dying to see it.' Chris gladly took this opportunity to leave.

As Eleanor walked carefully around the room, using her phone flashlight, Sarah moved to the shelves containing the most disturbed bones. She asked Eleanor to film as much as she could on her phone which the other woman was happy to do.

She wanted to pick up the scattered bones and return them to the shelves, and she picked up one skull that looked charred and then noticed others the same. Hadn't the Critchley house been burned? Could these be the remnants of that family? She reached into the shelf and felt something other than bone under her fingers. A cloth-wrapped object. With an almost unbearable thrill of excitement Sarah lifted it from among the bones and brought it into the light of the lantern.

She held her breath as she unwrapped a leather-bound book, opened it and read the inscription 'Journal of Dr George Macey'. This was his book, and she knew that she had been meant to find it. She showed it to Eleanor.

'Do you think you're descended from him Sarah?' she said, 'Is that why you have a strong paranormal bond?'

Sarah admitted that the name did appear in her family's history, but she had no recollection of the details of that side of the family.

'I must go and read this Eleanor. I hope it will help us to understand some of the Critchleys' history and the Licoricia connection. Do you mind if I go back into the vestry? You could come with me or stay here.'

Eleanor said that she would prefer to accompany Sarah and hear what the journal contained, so they mounted the stairs and joined Chris outside. The night was clear now, and quiet, and he agreed to remain at the doorway to guard the entrance. In the vestry there was no sign of Adam, so Sarah started to read aloud from George Macey's journal.

Chapter Seven - January 24th, 1848

The haunting of George Macey

I write this account of the supernatural manifestations that have haunted me for almost a year, so that if something should happen to me or to my companions and friends, then our fate may be explained even if it cannot be understood. It will not be published, at least not in my lifetime, but it may be made known after my death and I fear that this will not be long in coming.

But first something of my background. I am the second son in a family of three sons and two daughters; both my parents are well, and they live a blameless, if conventional life on the family estate near Worcester. The estate will pass to my elder brother and my younger brother has made a career in the army, as is the convention with families such as ours. I was destined for the church and to that end I was taught classical languages and encouraged in the study of theology. It was at Oxford that my life changed when I met and fell in love with a young woman, the sister of a college friend. I courted her and we became engaged and married soon after my graduation when I became a curate at a parish near my family home.

If there was such a thing as paradise, it was the time I spent with Sophie. She was an English rose, slender and pink, with fine brown hair and such gentle manners that every man became civilised in her company. That year I woke each morning with the thrill of knowing that we would spend our leisure time together. Our joy was multiplied when she told me that she was carrying our child.

When the time came for her confinement I was banished to the stables as her labour continued for longer than I could endure. Her cries filled the house and I can write no more of that terrible time. She did not survive and the child, a girl, also perished.

I remember the hours after her death very clearly. The

bloody sheets that the housemaids tried to hide when I went to the room to see her. A waxen complexion replaced skin that had once been luminous and had flushed with delight at simple pleasures. The dark shadows under her eyes told of the long struggle to birth my child. I hated myself, and I hated God, for we both allowed this to happen. The baby was hurriedly baptised by the rector so that she could be buried alongside her mother. I did not see her.

After the funeral I resigned from my clerical position and went home where my family tried to comfort me. When various attempts to interest me in the farms did not succeed, they suggested I should go to Europe where I might be distracted from grief. I went as far as London where I found escape in laudanum and alcohol. I became too ashamed to visit Sophie's grave.

I spent much of my time in the stews with the lowest forms of humanity and I revelled in their beastly company as they could never remind me of Sophie and my previous life. It was in a tavern near the hospital of St Bartholomew that I met fellows who were students at that teaching hospital and I drunkenly engaged them in debate that was fuelled by my hubris and their lack of skill and knowledge. They invited me to attend one their lectures and I found myself watching the dissection of a pregnant woman who had been found drowned in the Fleet.

I am sure they expected me to faint or vomit but her waxen features bore such a close resemblance to my dead Sophie that I watched with fascination as she was dismembered by the surgeon. It gave me a perverse pleasure to see another human being as an empty husk and I was able to absorb all that was being taught with curious dispassion. As a result, they convinced me to take up the study of medicine and I did so out of intellectual curiosity. It curbed my drinking, but I still occasionally indulged in the taking of laudanum to dull the pain of my empty heart.

My family were pleased to find that I had taken an interest in medicine and funded my studies. Although I am a qualified doctor I do not practice and am fortunate in having a private income so that my specialism is now the study of long dead individuals and the times in which they lived. In that way I do not need to engage with the living, and I can do no harm to the dead. My atheism convinced me that I had nothing to fear from the dead. I believed that until I visited St Jude's church in the Hampshire village of Stansham in April 1847.

When I present my paper to the History Society in a fortnight's time it will be scientific and factual. But there is more to tell that I cannot make public for fear of losing my reputation and my career, such as it is. I have changed address twice to avoid intrusion into my private life from people who have no shame and who would allow me no privacy. But a year ago I resided in an old house in Jewry Street Winchester in the topmost set of apartments. It is a hilly town, and I had an impressive view over the rooftops of the city, with the stately tower of the cathedral beyond.

I had become fascinated by monuments to the dead, and although I have never visited Sophie's grave, I am comforted by memorials to others. As a pastime I began a collection of brass rubbings made on paper with a heel of wax. This includes the brass plaques installed in many churches and I have been accustomed to spend my weekends travelling the countryside visiting small churches and always keen to find old medieval brasses to record.

On one particular weekend in April 1847, almost a year ago, I was in Hampshire, exploring the downs to its north east of Winchester. I had ridden my horse to the church of St Jude on a hill some distance from the village of Stansham and surrounded by old yew trees.

The church was a dismal sight, despite the spring sunshine and the flowers that were in abundance along the country lanes. I was intending to explore the church and its grounds and collect brass rubbings before riding down to the village inn for luncheon. Inside the church the atmosphere was still and quiet and I felt unwelcome. However, I was determined to collect my specimens and then perhaps research the place in greater detail when I was far away from its malign influence.

I finished five brass rubbings as quickly as I could. Two of them struck me as odd and were both near the altar. A grim looking man in a loincloth on a pale brass purported to be an anchorite was fixed to the wall, and an angelic looking child called 'Little William' lay on the floor on the other side of the altar. The rubbing I made of the child was difficult as the screws holding it in place were loose and the paper was occasionally displaced. I may have cursed once or twice, and I apologised, for I felt as though someone, or something, was watching me. I left immediately.

That night I slept badly and resorted to laudanum to quiet my mind. As I stood in my room looking at the disturbing images I had made, I was approached by a veiled woman in quaint attire; it was apparent that she was a creature walking between the two worlds of life and death.

She wore tabards and an embroidered girdle so I should have been aware that she was not a woman of my time. She had gold rings on her fingers but only her eyes were visible as the veil covered most of her face. They were brown, compassionate eyes and the lines surrounding them were that of a careworn woman in her sixties.

She did not speak directly to me, but she touched my face. From that moment I fell into an airless void that deprived me of sense and my connection to the earth. I knew that in the grave of Little William directly beneath the brass where I had dispassionately made a copy of his image, were the bodies of babies. It was with horror that she conveyed to me the certainty that they were sacrifices and that the ritual of blood sacrifice was being practiced in this village. I had fallen upon the floor but had the sensation that I was falling further and when my senses returned the woman was gone, but the two brass rubbings were fixed to the wall before me. That of Little William, a child holding a lamb, the symbol of sacrifice; and …. The other.

I rose and peeled the papers from the wall; they seemed to be held by nothing. I vowed to put it behind me as a disturbance of the psyche. I splashed my face with water and determined to destroy both images in the morning. I hid them from view and went back to bed for a fitful night with little rest.

The next day I ripped up the paper containing the brass rubbings of the child and the anchorite and gave them to my landlady to light the fires. I woke early the following morning, and the same papers were again fastened to the wall so that they were the first thing I saw when I opened my eyes. That day I burned the papers in my own fire to ensure their destruction. The next morning, they were again on the wall before me.

This was repeated for seven nights in all, during which time I tried to dispose of them by taking them out of the city, by leaving them in a church and by burying them. Each morning they had reappeared. Then one night, at midnight, I awoke in a cold sweat and was aware that she was standing, veiled, at the foot of my bed.

She wanted me to converse with her, but I was able to refuse, and I convinced myself that I could block any discourse from my dreams. I was mistaken. She returned the next night and was again at the foot of my bed and importuned me, her clothing now entirely a grey shroud, the colour of cobweb. The next night she returned and every night thereafter, so that I was afraid to go to sleep and kept a candle burning by my bed. Each night she returned and implored me to listen to her, but I would not. And each morning the hideous and the piteous brass rubbing images were replaced on the wall.

Lack of sleep and fear that I was losing my mind prevented me from working efficiently. I ate little, and an old school friend, Robert McKinley, commented on my lethargy and drawn face and eventually he was so concerned for my health that he prised my secret from me. I feared that he would attribute the ghostly visits to insanity, but he was convinced that my addiction to laudanum lay at the root of my condition. He was anxious to help me reduce my use of the drug and I confessed that it had increased in my attempts to find sleep. He suggested that the drug allowed the creature to present herself and I agreed to give up my use of the opiate under his supervision and with the assistance of my servant, Rudd.

What followed was physical and mental torture. For five days my body felt as though it was tearing itself apart to find any remnant of the drug in a forgotten piece of my flesh. I saw terrible things, dead babies and broken skeletal children crawling over the ceiling, evil eyeless demons that crawled after them. Grey clad ghosts that lay next to me in my bed with skeleton hands and filthy nails on the point of touching me.

Eventually I woke in a state of sanity and nausea to a room that stank of faeces and vomit, and to my poor exhausted friend. I wept in my weakness and thankfulness; and I pledged never to take laudanum again. I shall be forever grateful to Robert for his loyalty and practical help in recovering my life, but I am sorry that I have dragged him into this nightmare.

Then one night in June I lay in a heatwave unable to sleep, tossing and turning in a luckless attempt to find some cool part of the bed. The window was open, and the moon was passing across it, its movement almost perceptible to the naked eye. I must have closed my eyes for I opened them to see the lady in front of the window. She appeared to be looking out, and not at me, but she spoke to me.

This was where her son's house had been, and he had lived here until they killed him. It was a fine building. She knew that I could not deny her existence tonight, perhaps the absence of laudanum in my body allowed her to enter my mind. She turned and I could see that she was still veiled.

Was I asleep? I sat up and she remained in front of me before the window. A welcome breeze lifted the curtains and made her veil flutter slightly. Who are you? I asked. Why do you haunt me?

She told me that the brass plate of Little William's shrine was loose because it had been moved regularly and his grave disturbed, and what began as the disposal of another unwanted infant has woken something terrible that has lain dormant for centuries. There is an old blood lust in that place that is now being temporarily sated by the sacrifice of young and innocent lives. It must be stopped before the beast is freed from its bonds. I had to do something to stop the killing and burial of babies at the church in Stansham; it was an abomination that I instinctively knew to be true.

I was fascinated and frightened by what she said and again asked who she was and when she had lived. To this she replied that she was Licoricia of Winchester and had lived at the time of Henry, son of John and father of Edward known as Longshanks. She was a Jewess and carried on the business of money lending.

She said that she had several sons who prospered for a while in the city of Winchester and other towns open to their business, but it was increasingly a time of trouble for the children of Israel. The cruel murder of William Critchley at St Jude's church led to five notable Jews of the town being blamed for his death. They were hanged and their property confiscated.

The child and his killer haunt that church. The child's body was found in a well in the churchyard. Somebody close must have killed him. It was well known that his limbs had been smashed. They say he was like a rag doll when they brought him out of the well, poor child.

She knew that his death was not some Jewish blood sacrifice. She had sons of her own and was certain that the Jews who had been hanged for his death had not been responsible. Children are not sacrificed in Jewish rituals. It was a lie. It was the blood libel.

She was a soul out of time disturbed by the abominations of the hill they call St Jude's. My own damaged soul was half in the world of the dead and my body polluted with laudanum that she saw me. She told me that her spirit was now like a seed in my heart that could blossom at any time.

I could persuade the Church to allow a scientific enquiry into William's grave because I was an investigator of history. Now the blood sacrifice is restarted, it must be stopped by intervention.

I had so many questions of her and my mind raced to find the words, but when I looked up, she had gone, evaporated into a mist that seemed to come from the window and clouded the moonlight. My candle guttered out and I became fully awake. The room was filled with mist, and outside the air in Winchester was so thick with it that I shut the window. Such miasmas arising from the river were common in that great and historic city.

I shivered and retreated to my bed where I lay in a fever for more than a week, to the consternation of my friends and the great inconvenience of the household, the members of which were afraid that they would catch the sweating sickness from me. I had fully recovered by the end of the month and I determined to find out as much as possible about this Licoricia of Winchester. Did she exist? Could there be any possible truth in her story?

To settle this turmoil once and for all I told myself that if I could establish her life to have been real, then I would make enquiries about investigating the tomb of Little William of Stansham. That he was never canonised as a saint should make it easier to gain permission. It was an historical fact-finding mission after all and would put the old church of St Jude's into the spotlight for a short time only. I had no idea what I would find, nor the cost to me, and to my servant.

The account of the fate of my manservant Rudd is now common knowledge having been the subject of much journalistic speculation and surmise, following the public enquiry. Accounts of ghostly apparitions in the churchyard have fed popular imagination and Stansham has found itself the object of sensation seekers.

I began my research into the archives of medieval Winchester and became completely engrossed in the life and troubles of a medieval Jewess called Licoricia, a name based on the sweetmeat and a conceit popular with women of the time. She was a Jewess born sometime in the early part of the 13th century. She had three sons and daughter with her first husband, Abraham of Kent.

When Abraham died Licoricia wed a second time, to David of Oxford. They had one son, named Asher, but David's death a few years later gave King Henry III the opportunity to impose a tallage or tax comprising 30% of David's estate and this large sum funded a shrine to Edward the Confessor at Westminster Abbey.

Licoricia lived in Winchester and carried on her money-lending business and one of her sons, named Benedict, was a guildsman of the city and was well regarded, but he was hanged for coin clipping in 1279. Her youngest son, Asher was expelled from England in 1290 along with all his race.

Licoricia was brutally murdered in 1277, a few years after

Little William died. Her body was found by her daughter, she had been stabbed to death along with her maid Alice of Bickton. Three men were accused but never brought to trial. A sum of money had been taken and that was accepted as being the reason for her murder.

I had sworn to pursue her wish if I could prove that she had been a living person. That she had, so I approached the Church with the request to conduct an enquiry into the life and times of Little William Critchley of Stansham. I expected some resistance from the local parson, so my approach was made using the good offices of the Gentleman's Magazine and the upper echelons of the See were agreeable to my pursuit of historical information.

I confess that I was initially afraid of the church and the local people and that was one reason I took my man Rudd with me in addition to the representatives of the diocese. Overall the work was carried out inside the church and the villagers were kept outside. It did not take long to remove the brass on William's grave and to lever up the stone slabs and reveal the loosened gravel and soil. I had not warned Rudd what we might find and indeed, I was the only man in that church who was not surprised by the sight of the small bones laid upon and around the old shroud, which itself had not been disturbed.

The vicar was terribly upset, he dropped to his knees praying for the souls of the children. I did not mention that they may have been unbaptised and illegitimate. Rudd wept openly and refused to touch the remains; he could not understand my coldness. After the discovery, when recriminations were being held in the vestry, I carefully excavated the bones and cadavers. I felt sympathy for the vicar who was a bookish and kindly old gentleman, and almost certainly ignorant of the abominations that had occurred.

Further winding cloths were sought from the villagers, at which a wailing arose that chilled my blood. The light had faded early as it does in October and when I looked out of the church door, I could only see a few candle lights, but I heard their owners' cries.

As Rudd would not participate in the disinterment, I took him to one side and asked him, in all innocence, to make enquiry of the villagers and try to find why these babies were buried in this manner. He was a man of the people, and as I said, not usually given to over-imaginings but he was reluctant to interfere in their grief, so I gave him some money for himself and to reward them if they talked. He told me later that the men had melted away, seeing that nothing was to be done to prevent the opening of the grave and left the women to mourn.

He returned after about three quarters of an hour and took me aside to a privy place where we would not be overheard. The women had been largely ignorant of the origin of the burials, but a very old woman seated in a chair brought for her was persuaded to recall her younger days and tell them what she remembered.

She said that the babies were 'gifts' and had been left since the year after the great battle of Waterloo, when the anti-Christ Bonaparte had been finally defeated. I knew that year to be 1816, the year of no Summer, when frosts in June and snow in July destroyed the crops growing in England. A baby had been born to an unmarried girl and was weak and sickly and not expected to live long. Its presence had to be kept secret and the old woman believed it had been the result of family relations and such abominations would not be tolerated. I took this to mean incest or incestuous rape and could imagine the horror of all right-thinking people.

It was just before Christmas, and a poor one it was expected to be with little food saved and with new laws restricting the taking of wild game, so that many were expected to starve in the lean months to come. The head of the family had taken the child from its mother and rumour had it, was going to kill and butcher it to make meat for the pot. He walked as far away from the village as he could and found himself in the churchyard. She supposed he must have had a morsel of Christian compassion in him for he entered the church lit by advent candles and housing a simple nativity scene.

This much I could believe, but then she told a story that makes my blood run cold. I cannot help but think of what occurred just a short while after Rudd recounted it. The man remembered the door to the crypt in the Norman tower. Thinking that he might find something valuable, for he was not above robbing the dead, the man ventured down the stone steps carrying the defenceless infant. In the crypt his one candle revealed great standing stones on every side of him, and in front of him, surrounding by bones was the sacrificial stone. When she said this, Rudd said, the other women cried out and crossed themselves. Standing behind that stone was the devil himself demanding that the babe be sacrificed to him and promising riches.

What happened then, they could only surmise, but the child was never seen again, and the man returned home that night with a cock pheasant and a bag of money. It was thought he had found the bird half frozen to death and the money was almost certainly robbed from the church. But the following year the harvest was good and a measure of prosperity returned to the village. The local landowner permitted limited taking of game from his lands and there was generally considered to have been a change of fortune. Of course, the man could not resist boasting about his activities on that night before Christmas, although it was met with a good deal of scepticism. Then in 1818 the story began to be repeated, when a failing crop and starvation was once again visited upon the country.

The old woman was reluctant to say much more, but that the village men met in secret and thereafter any stillborn or miscarried children found their way into William's grave. Having heard the story, Rudd told me that the other women berated her for making up such wickedness about a crypt and a sacrificial stone. It was the good grace of the little saint on receiving the souls of the innocent that had saved the village. Everyone knew that there was no crypt. When Rudd asked what had happened to the man, did he find his way back to the crypt for more money, they said that he drank himself to death. But he heard the old woman mutter under her breath, in the well, they found him in the well. At that they all clammed up and hustled the old dame away with much scolding and reproval.

I have often considered since that time that if I had

immediately removed us both from the church at Stansham then he might still be alive. Whilst Rudd was making his enquiries of the women, I had carefully removed the small bones, documented them and laid them to one side. When the Dean's men reappeared with the worried vicar, I said that in my opinion they were quite ancient and had probably been placed there in medieval times when William was commonly believed to be a saint.

There was universal relief at this and one of the men suggested their lodgement in a museum in London where such curios were eagerly attended by persons hungry for either knowledge or sensation. I agreed but said I thought a contribution should be made to the local parish in recompense. Arrangements were made to transfer the relics that very night and as they were moved from the church the wailing of the women started up again.

It is a matter of public record what happened later that evening. I left Rudd on his own and he was later found dead. Whatever he encountered must have been a truly terrifying and hideous thing to make such a reliable and unimaginative man take leave of his wits and die in those circumstances.

I kept telling myself that a crypt in so small a church would have been unusual, but I was somewhat startled by the old woman's tale of giant stones and a slaughter stone beneath the church. It is true that many ancient monuments surround Stansham. There are the grave mounds and ditches and a single standing stone on a hill some way off. These things would be visible from the church but for the massive yew trees that surround it and hide it from view.

Often at night I am transported in my dreams to that awful hill, unable to look away as clouds race against the dark sky, the church of St Jude seems blind to all the cruelty that lies within it. It is strange and out of place, squatting on its mound in the cold churchyard and, in my dream, its windows are blank boards. After many sleepless nights lying in fear of the nightmare, I discovered that if I can conjure the presence of Licoricia her appearance helps to clear the image from my closed eyes and I can sleep.

Although she has not again manifested as a ghostly form in

my presence, I feel that she is in some way a benign spirit and I derive comfort in knowing that we have stopped a bloody practice that has no place in a modern society. From the guidance she gave me and with my own research I have discovered something of what happened to William Critchley in 1275 and subsequently to the people who were affected by his murder.

January 29th, 1848

My account of the end of the Critchley family is complete and I have arranged with my good friend, the artist Robert McKinley, to travel back to St Jude's at Stansham as soon as the weather will allow. The hubbub that arose after the grave of Little William was disturbed has not entirely died down. There seems to be an ever-increasing appetite among the people of this country from all classes to read as much as possible about ghostly events. The publication of Mr Dickens's book 'A Christmas Carol' has created an expectation of thrills and fortune-telling from ghostly emanations.

Last year the church was subject to the scrutiny of day visitors and some who remained until nightfall in the hope of seeing the spectre that the newspapers had reported. The snow will have reduced their numbers, but I have no doubt that it will restart once the weather improves. We must therefore act as soon as circumstances permit, for I am determined that we shall find the crypt where the slaughter stone lies and I believe we may find the cell of Sir Hugh Critchley, the anchorite of Stansham.

Chapter Eight

In the vestry Sarah had read about half the journal and it confirmed her knowledge of Licoricia's haunting of Macey. Before she could continue Eleanor reminded her that they should check with Chris and ensure that Adam had not made more trouble. They decided to fetch him and then go to Eleanor's cottage and wait for dawn.

Sarah ached to be able to sit around a kitchen table and have a cup of tea and fall asleep in a proper house. They stood and gathered up their rucksacks and the most important papers. Sarah was keen to know what had happened to Macey, and Eleanor promised that they would finish reading the journal when they were safe at Hare Cottage. They left through the vestry door and turned towards the hollow yew and the tower door.

There was no sign of Chris, nor of Adam. Sarah called him but there was no reply. Eleanor immediately went into the tower and down into the crypt. She screamed and Sarah rushed after her. Chris was lying on the floor next to the slaughter stone. Sarah clasped a hand to her mouth to prevent herself from crying out. Eleanor kneeled next to him and felt for a pulse.

'He's alive and his pulse is strong. He's been knocked out.'

She checked his body for signs of injury. There was a cut on his head and grazes on his knuckles and he would have a black eye in the morning.

'I think he's been in a fight with Adam.' Eleanor put him in the recovery position in case he vomited before regaining consciousness. 'We need to bring him round, have you got anything that might act as smelling salts?'

They both checked their bags and settled on burning something and extinguishing it holding the acrid smoke next to Chris's nostrils. With a match and some of Eleanor's hair a pungent odour managed to bring Chris round. He panicked on reaching consciousness but was quickly reassured when he heard and saw Sarah and Eleanor bending over him. He recovered quickly and they reckoned he had not been unconscious for long, the blow had stunned him. They agreed that a trip to the hospital for a check-up was going to be necessary, as well careful monitoring.

Eleanor cleaned up his head wound and reapplied cut closures to his hand while he explained what had happened.

'I would have got the better of him if my hand hadn't been so bloody painful. He caught me off-guard, but I dodged his second swing and we wrestled a bit. I managed to hit him a couple of times, but when I really clouted him my hand seemed to explode in pain. He hit me on the eye, and I don't remember much more.'

'You caught your head on the slaughter stone. Fortunately, just a glancing blow or it would have been a lot worse.' Eleanor said to Sarah 'We really need to leave in case Adam comes back and finds us here.'

'Why did you fight each other, Chris? What was the cause?'

'I told him to stay out of the crypt.'

'That would do it. His professional pride and vanity are piqued that we discovered it without him.'

'He started shouting that this was his dig and we were ganging up on him and stealing artifacts and documents. He accused me of disloyalty to my family and of disappointing my parents. He seems to think he's the victim here.' He turned to Eleanor 'Then he accused you of being a witch and putting a curse on the people who betrayed you. He said the trouble with curses is that you can never tell how they'll come to pass, hurting innocent people along the way.'

'He's a fool,' said Eleanor 'Come on, we have to get out of here.' They stood, Chris shakily, but as they reached the foot of the spiral stone staircase, they heard a door shut above them. Sarah ran up the last few steps. The outer door was closed against the downward spiral staircase as it had hidden the blocked-up entrance when they had first broken through.

'Adam! Don't be stupid, let us out! Chris needs medical attention, said Sarah. She looked at Eleanor 'I'm sorry Eleanor. He is obviously crazy and now he's trapped us in here.'

Chris cautiously mounted the stairs and put his weight against the door. It was impossible to move the door more than a few centimetres.

'He's jammed something against it,' said Chris.

He came down into the crypt where Sarah said 'He doesn't know about Macey's journal, and I don't think we should tell him. Let's ask him what he wants.'

'I'll do it,' said Eleanor, 'he has less of an axe to grind with me.' She went alone up the stairs and called for Adam. There was no reply at first, but she continued and began saying how much she had enjoyed his TV show, and he didn't really think she was a witch did he? She was amazed that she had been lucky enough to have healed his fingers so easily. The flattery and cajoling seemed to work and after a few minutes he responded from just outside the door.

'Is Chris all right?' he asked, and she reassured him that he would be fine. He sounded pathetic. 'I thought I'd killed him. I didn't know what to do.'

'He just needs to get checked out by a doctor to make sure there's no concussion, but he's up and talking.'

'He provoked me. You've all ganged up on me. I'm not a violent man, you've made me do this.'

'I know it was an accident, Dr Glover, and you didn't intend to hurt him. Now will you let us out?'

'I want to speak to Sarah, alone.' There was a pause, then he said, 'I promise I won't hurt her.'

'I'll ask her' Eleanor went back down, and they quietly discussed whether he could be trusted. They really had no choice if they wanted to leave the crypt, and Sarah did not relish spending the night in the damp charnel house so they had to get out. She also was worried about the tree. Had they really needed to do so much damage to the yew? They may have destabilised it, and the roots must have suffered during the storm. If the tower collapsed, they would have no chance. As if to prove the point there was a small fall of soil from the blocked area to the right of the door.

Sarah thought she could persuade him to let them out so she agreed to talk to him. She gave Macey's journal to Eleanor for safe keeping and mounted the spiral staircase to the top step. There was only room for one person there so she was alone when the door opened violently, and he grabbed her. He hauled her through and flung her down on the rising stone stairs.

Sarah cried out from the pain in her hands and legs on the steps, but she kept her wits and as he fumbled to replace the branch he had been using as a wedge to keep the door closed, she jumped over his kneeling form and dodged around the tree into the night. She could hear Chris and Eleanor calling out from the crypt, but she was not going back.

She ran around the yew and grabbed the Nordic poles she had hidden behind it. She could hear the others as they pushed against Adam for mastery of the door, but he had a stout piece of wood and they were struggling uphill in a tiny space.

She could not hide easily as the sky was now clear, but the moon had set so she decided to make for the well-house in the hope that his earlier experience might deter him from following her. He shouted her name as he turned the corner of the church onto the gravel path. Instead of going inside she threw herself over the low flint wall behind it, he might confuse the sounds she made with those of someone inside the well-house.

She waited, panting and shivering slightly, tears stinging her eyes from the grazes on her hands and the discomfort of her knees. She heard his feet on the gravel path.

'I know you're in there Sarah. Don't be stupid. I just want to talk to you without the others interfering.' He waited 'I know you think I won't come in because …. But I'm not that afraid. If you can stomach it, so can I.'

A soft gurgling came from the well.

He still made no move to enter the well-house and was obviously reluctant. He tried a different tack. 'Can you hear him Sarah, struggling to stay afloat, struggling to breathe. Can you hear his cries for help?'

She did not respond, so eventually he said, 'I'm coming in to get you anyway' and took a deep breath, it was clear that this was not something he wanted to do, and he cursed her stubbornness. He wrenched open the rotten door and cautiously entered the darkness stopping just inside to illuminate the whole of the small space with his torch. He couldn't see her so she must be behind the well and he would have to go all the way in.

When she was certain that he was fully inside Sarah crept along the churchyard wall hoping that the sound of her movement would be muted inside the building. Her intention was to follow the same path northwards that she had discovered earlier around the outside of the graveyard. She would then dodge back inside where the wall had crumbled so that she could make her way back to the church and free the others. They could then escape to Eleanor's cottage.

She had covered about twenty metres when Adam burst out of the well-house and shouted.

'You bitch. I'm going to find you.'

His flashlight caught her before she could duck down so she ran along the path, climbing over the wall when she reached the gap. He had her in his torchlight now and was shouting curses as he ran among the gravestones. She suspected that more than once he fell, because he was not lighting his way but trying to keep his torch on her.

Sarah realised that she was near the landslide and she would have to turn right towards the eastern face of the church or risk going over the top. At that point Adam fell and his torch light dipped away from her. She crouched behind a large gravestone and then took one of the poles and, with the distant memory of field athletics from school, threw it like a javelin high over the collapsed end of the churchyard. Then she hunkered down and prayed.

As Adam stood up his torch caught the movement of the shiny red Nordic pole and he began running towards it. Then he heard it crash into some shrubbery and he had no hesitation in following the sound. His flashlight was trained straight ahead as his feet trod thin air and he fell, headfirst, down the exposed slopes of the ancient hill fort.

She heard a cry but Sarah didn't wait, she sprinted over to the church and around the tower to the yew tree door. There she released Chris and Eleanor and together they followed the narrow path away from St Jude's to Eleanor's dark cottage on the other side of the valley.

Chapter Nine

At 4.30 am on 24th January 1848, in a room in his Winchester lodgings, Dr George Macey considered his task before putting pen to paper. The house was quieter than usual. A heavy fall of snow the previous day meant that the tradesmen who moved about the city in the early hours were still abed or their usual sounds were muffled by the snow.

Macey had banked the fire to keep it going all night and now he broke its crust and heaped on more coal to bring it to life. The room was still cold but by staying in bed and keeping the curtains closed he would be able to write what he had determined during a night of troubled sleep.

He had initiated the investigation into the peculiar burials at St Jude's church Stansham following the disclosures by the veiled woman last April and had now completed the essay that would be published in the Archaeological Journal. There was a great deal of interest in the disinterment of Little William, a putative saint from the twelfth and thirteenth centuries. The History Society would applaud its economy and scientific approach, and the newspaper coverage with sketch illustrations by his friend Robert McKinley had already assured him a large audience when he presented his paper in London next week.

It was what he had left out that disturbed him and he purposed to write it in his private journal.

The vicar, a Reverend Gibson was a scholarly man with more than a passing interest in history, and he could see no problem with examining the remains of someone who had lived and died so long ago. There were no family members to object and Little William's status as a religious martyr made him of particular interest.

When he had found the bones of babies Macey was not surprised for reasons that he would record and keep secret. The fate of his servant had been ruled an accident but there were inconsistencies that would not let him rest. Rudd had a solid, down-to-earth fellow who was literate but generally unimaginative and would do as he was bidden. As part of his archaeological research, they had excavated round barrows, and uncovered the intact or cremated remains of people from the distant past, removing them to private collections. They had never had a disagreement until they were given permission to open the grave at St Jude's.

He had not discussed with Rudd the possibility of finding recent remains in a medieval grave and was surprised at his reaction. This taciturn man was unmarried, but Macey knew that he had a reputation with the local women on his family's estate and he suspected that there might have been a few 'by-blows' in the areas where they had worked. He was careful to stick with married women so there was never a scandal over parentage.

He cast his mind back to the day of the disinterment and the incident he needed to record. The plan was kept secret for as long as possible. He did not need to divulge the suspicion of other bones in the grave, and the accepted notion that working people were superstitious meant that the Church itself was not keen to inform them until the day of the opening of the grave. It was afternoon and must have appeared to be a burial when the wagon and carriages arrived containing the Dean's proxy and his servants, together with Macey and Rudd.

They had arrived in the afternoon to a find few local people at the churchyard, some women had come to gawp at the spectacle of so many gentlemen from Winchester. Soon the rumour that a grave was to be opened caused a ripple of excitement among the small gathering and a child was despatched to inform others. Word spread and men appeared from the fields with the implements of their trades. Macey was afraid there would be violence, but the churchmen used the argument that none of their family graves would be disturbed and this was a matter of history and archaeology. When they did not disperse, a man was sent to bring back the sheriff and some bailiffs to read the riot act and by the evening, they had been persuaded to leave the site. The onset of darkness and a bitterly cold wind probably assisted with this, and in the darkness, they appeared to melt away.

When the babies were discovered, the coroner needed to be

informed. Rudd was stunned and his hands were the first to touch them. He was genuinely upset, and Macey regretted not warning him; but how could he explain that he had been given this knowledge in a vision granted to him by the ghost of a woman from another time?

The coroner's officer and the minister had officiated in their temporal and spiritual capacities with as much sensitivity as possible, and they took away the small remains with care and dignity. Local women were hidden in the darkness of the surrounding yew trees, unable to be seen. But their distressed wailing sounded like the cries of banshees. The sheriff was restrained from chasing them out, for they did not interfere with the proceedings. Macey accompanied the bones down to the waiting cart and horses. He did not know for sure, but assumed that they were now going to be part of some scientific exhibit.

Rudd had complained about being left alone in the church when Macey had instructed him to continue removing soil from around the shroud, still marked where the babies' remains had lain. He was going to accompany the cortege down to the main road. He now saw that had been a mistake.

He had only been gone for forty-five minutes or so, he thought, as he hurried back up the path through the yews. In truth he had been reluctant to leave the company of the coroner and the sheriff and their people. The women seemed to have melted away. The church was silent and the lychgate loomed ahead with the churchyard's well to the left of it. The yews were a cathedral, towering and majestic against the milky moonlit sky and he had the notion that the church was somehow an unnecessary imposition.

He paused to catch his breath before entering, then pushed open the oak door in the porch and took up the lantern he had left on the font. He called Rudd's name to let him know he was back. It would not do to startle him at such a task. There was no reply. Faint moonlight came through the windows and he could see a lantern at the front of the church to the left of the altar but heard no sound and saw no movement. Macey went along the centre aisle to the grave; there was the William brass, removed and placed out of harm's way against the wall.

The slabs of stone also were neatly stacked to one side, the tools placed on the floor around the grave and some spoil had been carefully placed on a cloth laid down for the purpose. The shroud was exposed, still intact although dirty grey and soiled by later interments. Of his man, there was no sign.

Damn him thought Macey; he has given up and gone into the village for refreshments. He thought he might continue with the work, but then he glanced at the other prominent brass near the altar. It was the anchorite brass and with a shudder he remembered what the veiled woman had told him.

He forced himself to approach it with the lantern. It was fixed to the wall and low down, unlike William who was in the floor. He noticed once again that it hadn't been cleaned. It was whitish grey and worse than when he had made the brass rubbing earlier in the year. The resulting image had startled him.

The expression was one of terrible despair. Rivulets ran from the eyes, like tears. Macey could see none of that now as the metal was almost white. He shuddered and gave a cursory glance around the church then, leaving the lantern burning, he retraced his steps through the churchyard and back to the village where he had a room at the inn.

The Star was a moderately clean establishment that made its money from travellers on the old pilgrim's road. The landlord was expecting him to be late, but he was surprised to find a group of men clustered around the bar drinking. They fell silent as he entered and, as one, turned their accusatory stares at him. He removed his hat but decided not to take any refreshment and beat a retreat to his bedroom.

He was too tired to wash so lay upon the bed in his outer clothes, but not before wedging a chair against the door. Macey closed his eyes and hoped desperately that oblivion would reward him with some escape from the things he had seen tonight.

It was to be the first of a long series of nights that he came to think of as being like a disturbed narrative. As though there was something he should be able to recall and describe but could not. He would have words with Rudd tomorrow; leaving without permission was unacceptable.

He must have fallen into a fitful sleep just before dawn because he was woken by the sounds of horses in the yard and of domestic geese being driven up the main street. He could smell bacon and his stomach grumbled, so he emptied the pitcher into the basin and ran a washcloth over his head, neck and hands. He would not be returning, so he packed his bag. He was a reasonably competent whip and would take his trap up to the church and leave from there to go home. His man should reappear sometime today, and he had an appointment with McKinley, to record the image of Little William.

Macey ordered the readying of his horse and trap and went into breakfast. Rudd had not appeared, but his friend was in the breakfast room enjoying a hearty repast and Macey was pleased to join him. McKinley was an old friend from school, scratching a living as a jobbing artist and illustrator of novels. He was excited at the prospect of recording a scene that promised to be as Gothic as the ghostly stories he had often been paid to illustrate. Macey had difficulty dampening his friend's noisy enthusiasm in the face of residual local hostility but was glad to have a companion in the absence of Rudd.

The two men left with provisions for themselves and the horse and drove up the road through the arch of dark yew trees to an area near the lychgate where carriages were left on service days.

Macey tried to reflect on the difference between night and day as a way of shaking the emotions left with him from the night before, but he had to acknowledge that the church was squat and ugly, and perched on a mound so that the graveyard sloped away from it. He assumed that it would not have been much smaller in its original wooden Anglo-Saxon form. A square west tower provided its most architecturally interesting feature with a couple of round-arched windows high up, presumably Norman. There was now a plan to replace the simple stained-glass windows, funded partly by a contribution from the museum taking the remains and also from the See of Winchester.

He led McKinley through the churchyard to the chancel with some inexplicable feelings of dread, but everything was just as he had left it the night before. Between them they uncovered the small coffin and then unwrapped part of the shroud. At first glance it was exactly as Macey had expected the body of a child of about nine years, skeletonised but otherwise undisturbed by the frequent intrusions visited upon him during the years. Then he noticed breakages in the long bones of the arms. He decided not to open the entire shroud as the sight was distressing and because the shroud was holding the body intact. If it were removed the body would fall apart. He could not bring himself to look more closely at the child and left his friend to produce something acceptable to the newspaper.

Macey left him to his work and began a perambulation around the church. Damn Rudd he thought, he should have been here by now. He needed some fresh air, so he went outside and began to walk in the graveyard, stopping to read the names of the dead. No doubt some new place would be found for unbaptised infants in the future. He thought to provide fresh water for his horse and went to the well. It occurred to him that this was where they had found Little William all those years ago. He didn't think his old pony would mind drinking from the well and he would pull up the bucket and fill the horse trough so that he could take a drink after eating the hard feed in the nosebag they had brought from the village. He grumbled to himself that Rudd should be doing all this.

The bucket was down so he just had to haul it up, and he gripped the rope and pulled. It would not come. Damn it, he thought, will nothing go right in this cursed place? He tried harder and it shifted a little. He walked around the well to try another angle; again, it moved but did not rise. He heard voices and saw that village folk were coming to the churchyard to tend graves before tomorrow's Sunday service. He would not let them see him struggling with the well rope, so he walked to his horse and began preparing the feed.

Two young women and a scrawny lad hailed into view and stopped their chatter when they saw him; the girls bobbed curtsies and the lad doffed his cap. They took their flowers to the chosen graves and began to remove the old ones, placing them tidily on a compost heap. One of the girls asked the lad to fetch some water and Macey watched with interest as the youth approached the well. He was satisfied to see that the bucket did not move for him either, and soon both the girls and the boy were hauling on it with all their might.

He politely offered to assist and all four of them managed to move the rope a short way; it seemed to have a dead weight on it. After about fifteen minutes they were exhausted and tied off the rope. One of the girls said it was like the time a sheep had fallen in and got stuck on the bucket. It had taken three men to pull it out. She thought this was like to weigh heavier.

Macey felt a chill of fear pass through him. No, it couldn't be Rudd. He was a countryman and perfectly able to take care of himself; what would he have been doing at the well anyway? As he was debating whether to tell the young people about Rudd's disappearance, McKinley joined them and on hearing of the difficulty he blurted out that he thought it might be Rudd in the well. One of the girls ran back to the village and soon a group of silent men were heaving on that rope until a foot and a leg appeared and then the rest of Rudd.

He had been alive at some time in the well, for he had tied the rope around his waist. But it was clear that he had died soon after from loss of blood, for there was a huge gash in his inner thigh, severing the femoral artery. Macey thought to his horror that he had probably injured himself in the church and then passed out when leaning on the well on his way to the lychgate and come round when he hit the water. He could have done nothing to save him, he knew, but he still felt guilty.

The men took the body down to the village, for there would need to be a coroner's inquest, and he joined McKinley inside the church to repair the grave site, replace the brass and clear away the tools. They were sweeping up when McKinley asked: where was the blood? Surely there should be a lot if he had injured himself while working on the grave? They searched every inch of the church but found nothing.

A chisel was missing so they deduced he must have heard something that alarmed him, and he went outside to investigate, and may have received the injury in the churchyard. They set off in different directions, prying apart the grasses to try and find a trace of his flight towards the well.

Macey started at the well but could find nothing.

No further light was shed on the case of Rudd's untimely death, and the Coroner ruled that it was accidental, perhaps he had been drinking and stumbled onto the chisel which was still missing and thought to be at the bottom of the well.

His body was taken home, and after the funeral Macey returned to Winchester where he continued his researches into the story of Little William and wrote up the findings for his paper. He was not haunted by Rudd, or even by William, but his fragmented sleep was haunted by another figure, the grey, increasingly unnatural image of the veiled woman he had met in St Jude's church the previous April. Her physical presence was waning, but the strength of her spirit was as strong as ever.

Chapter Ten

Sarah breathed the fragrant scent of the bedroom that Eleanor had shown her into. After the fraught chase in the graveyard and the hurried and silent escape along the narrow path to Hare Cottage in the near dark it was heaven to be inside a cosy well-furnished room with a soft bed and hot water on tap. She would have loved to take a bath and to sleep under that plump duvet with the pattern of roses and matching curtains. Even the walls were decorated with flowers.

They had left their boots and coats in the porch and were so relieved to find that the lights were working, it felt like a return to civilisation. Chris was given first use of the bathroom as he needed to clean up his wounds and Sarah could hear him washing ostentatiously in that way that men do, as if their mothers were listening through the walls. She turned as the door opened and Eleanor came in with towels.

'Do you want a cup of tea? I've got herbal as well as builders. Then you can have a sleep. I expect you're exhausted. It's been a hellish day and the kitchen is nice and warm as the aga is alight. The kettle will be boiled soon.'

'I'm sorry Eleanor but I really must finish reading George Macey's journal.'

'Are you sure you want to do it now? Both you and Chris could use some rest.'

Sarah was grateful for her consideration but said she did not feel tired. On the contrary she was fired up to find out what had happened. Eleanor had told Chris about the first part of the journal when they were trapped in the crypt.

'Well, if you're sure' said Eleanor 'Come with me to the kitchen.'

Sarah followed her down the narrow staircase to the front door where they turned right through a sitting room with a large inglenook fireplace, and into the kitchen at the back of the cottage. The woody smell brought back memories of country pubs and leisurely dinners in autumn and winter. Usually with Adam, she thought, and then remembered that

Adam might be lying injured or worse at the bottom of the slope.

'What shall we do about Adam? He might be seriously injured; we should call for help.'

To her relief Eleanor replied 'I've already phoned the emergency services while you were upstairs. It may be some time before they arrive, but I will go back to the church when we've had tea and you're settled, so that I can show them where he might be. You mustn't feel guilty Sarah, he gave you no choice. He was out of control.'

'You'd better meet them at the fallen tree' Sarah remembered that she had abandoned the Land Rover on the track.

'No need. I've told them to come along the new farm road, the one that's caused the subsidence. That way they can locate him more easily. I can find my way around the hill and intercept them. It's only on the other side of the valley.'

They heard Chris lumbering down the stairs. He followed the lights through to the kitchen and smiled broadly when he saw Eleanor preparing to make tea and bringing out a cake tin. He was pink and clean and spotted with plasters and bandages and carried a distinct whiff of antiseptic. His left eye was bloodshot and almost closed from the swelling, knuckle marks visible on his brow.

They all relaxed at the prospect of sitting together and discussing the evening's events. There was the palpable relief at being safe and a flood of endorphins from the extraordinary events they had experienced. Chris was grateful to have escaped the nightmare of the church and the graveyard and the hauntings.

'How long have you lived here?' asked Chris.

'I moved in after my husband had left and my aunt died. It was old-fashioned because she lived here with my parents originally and she liked it that way. I haven't been inclined to make many changes.'

'I thought you grew up here,' said Sarah.

'I lived here until I was 11 when my mother inherited the blacksmith's house and we moved there. Auntie lived with us because she never married.'

Sarah looked around the kitchen. It was old-fashioned, with free standing units and dressers made of wood, and there was an old brown aga giving off a cheering warmth. The walls were painted red, and a long pine table and chairs took up most of the space. Horse brasses hung on the exposed beams above the aga but there were no family photos anywhere. The only image, a big oil painting of a hare, took pride of place on the free wall space. The floor was tiled and the curtains at the three windows were decorated by red cherries and outside it was very dark.

Sarah wanted to know more about the cottage, but the kettle came to the boil and Eleanor changed the subject as she closed the curtains. 'Let's have tea. Would you like chamomile Sarah? It'll help you to sleep.'

Sarah accepted and they sat around the table with the mugs of tea that Eleanor had placed in front of them.

'Eleanor's called the emergency services. They'll sort out Adam when they arrive.'

'That's a relief' said Chris through a mouthful of fruit cake 'I wasn't looking forward to daybreak and what we might find when we go over there. So, you tricked him into rushing past you and he must have fallen down the collapsed slope?'

'I threw one of Eleanor's Nordic poles over and he followed it. Sorry Eleanor.'

'Don't worry I'll find it tomorrow anyway. Or today I should say.'

'The title deeds to this cottage must have made interesting reading' Sarah said.

'The current house was built sometime around 1820 and had its own well; it's still in the back garden but has a grill over it for safety. We know the vicar occupied this cottage for a while until the living was shared with another parish for economic reasons. In more modern times it has been extended to include a bathroom and a few home comforts.'

Sarah could wait no longer and with apologies to Chris she set her tea aside to cool and started to speed read Macey's journal, pointing up facts relevant to their circumstances as she was able to find them.

Chapter Eleven – George Macey's Journal

March 23ʳᵈ, 1848

Robert Mckinley and I had met at school but he had not found the academic life to his liking, nor did he wish to pursue a career in the army as his family were hoping, despite being a fit and courageous fellow. He is stocky of frame but quick and observant of everything, his hair curly and a great wit when in the mood. His overwhelming talent was for art and he managed to find the funds to study at the Royal Academy, but like so many others, making a living was a constant struggle and he was reduced to illustrating books and journals to support his vocation. Had he been prepared to turn his hand to portrait commissions he might have flourished, but he was of a romantic disposition and would only paint people he liked, or beautiful women in fanciful compositions.

I had carried out research on the Critchley family from the court documents in Winchester and those of the diocese held in the church archives. I felt that I was getting closer to discovering the mystery of Hugh Critchley and his murdered son and their connection with Licoricia of Winchester.

McKinley's presence was a great comfort to me on that frosty March morning when we hacked over to Stansham to look in depth at the parish registers. We decided to leave our horses at the inn and walk the three quarters of a mile or so to the church. If the landlord recognised us, he said nothing, and I preferred it that way. We were investigating something from long before the memories of any living person and did not want to be reminded of last year's tragedy.

On the journey we had conversed about the unfortunate events of the previous visit and I explained to McKinley what I had found out about the anchorite. His name was Sir Hugh Critchley, and he was the father of the murdered child known as Little William. The event that appeared to have driven him to become an anchorite was the death of his entire family in

1290 in a fire that destroyed his house. At that time, his whole estate was given to the Church and he became resident in a cell under the church of St Jude's.

He remained there until 1305 when he was accused of the crime of murder and was ordered to appear in front of a clerical court. The outcome was not clear from the records and the exact details of the case had been removed.

I had discovered some of the history of the Critchley family. They had prospered during the twelfth century under the reign of Henry II. How they had fared under his sons Richard Lionheart and John was not clear, but the reconciliation of the barons and the crown on the accession of John's young son Henry III meant that they had probably not suffered much loss of land and wealth.

However, it was clear that in the middle of the following century Hugh's father, Sir Richard, had joined the forces of Simon de Montfort and rebelled against Henry III, now elderly and increasingly frail. They had taken the king captive in 1263 and for fifteen months Henry had been a puppet whilst de Montfort and his followers were de facto rulers of the kingdom. This ended in 1265 at the battle of Evesham when the rebels were soundly defeated by Prince Edward and his loyalist army.

I was sure that Hugh's father had been killed at Evesham, a terrible battle in which the usual practice of sparing the wealthy knights and ransoming them, was set aside and Edward's forces killed with unprecedented brutality. Hugh's older brother, called Guy, had managed to escape. Hugh was aged about twenty years at this time and had remained at home with his mother and sisters, otherwise he might have lost more than the greater part of his family's lands. As the second son Hugh Critchley had not expected to inherit his father's demesnes but as the son and brother of a traitor, with no influence at court, he was personally vulnerable.

For a short time, the residue of de Montfort's army continued to resist in pockets around the country and the older brother Guy did not flee to France as many others did but became an outlaw in Alton Wood. He and his men waylaid travellers on the road from Winchester to London. As long as he remained at large the fortune of the Critchley family could not hope to be restored.

Legend had it that Hugh and his mother tricked him into a meeting with the promise of coin to pay for a passage abroad. They were to meet at the church in Stansham, the only property remaining to the family. The small house and poor land at Stansham had remained available to the Critchley family whilst their more valuable properties had been forfeited as punishment for treason. When Guy arrived with two of his men it was to find that he had been betrayed by his own brother. The sheriff and his armed men were hidden amongst the yew trees, and Guy and his men tried to fight their way out. His men were cut down and one of the sheriff's men was killed and another injured. Guy surrendered and was said to have called down a curse upon his brother when he realised that he had been betrayed by his own family.

Guy Critchley was to be tried in Winchester, and because of his rank he would have to be tried by his peers. Fortunately for the family he died in prison, either from injuries sustained or from some other sickness, and there was a suggestion that he might have been poisoned. Since food was often provided by the prisoner's family it is possible that they had a hand in removing him, to avoid the embarrassment of a trial and to limit the exposure of his father's treason against the king.

Perhaps because of their actions in bringing Guy to book, no further punishment was meted out to the Critchley family and Hugh inherited the single remaining homestead and was dubbed Sir Hugh of Stansham. He pledged loyalty to Henry and was thereby compelled to provide fighting men or pay scutage, a tax in lieu of military support. Either way he would have needed money. Stansham was a poor manor and would not be sufficient to enable him to fulfil his feudal duties as a knight, so he needed to rebuild his finances quickly.

From this I was able to deduce that Sir Hugh had been very keen to recover his position and prestige at the time of William's murder in 1275. This information had been available from the court records of 1265 and 1266, but a later case, the accusation in 1305 of murder against Sir Hugh himself, was heard in a clerical court. He had bequeathed his property to the Church when he became an anchorite in 1290 and so he fell within ecclesiastical jurisdiction.

It must have been a matter of severe embarrassment for the Church who had supported a man and treated him as a living saint to find that he was accused of murder. The accuser's name was in the records and he was listed as hailing from Stansham so I needed to know more about him and his background. During my researches in the archives of Winchester I had befriended some of the clerks who worked for the municipality and they were helpful in finding alternate sources of information. There were reputed to be documents of interest that related back to the middle ages kept by the vicar of Stansham. His name was Frederick Gibson and I hoped to persuade him to allow me to examine them. He was the same elderly cleric who had presided over William's disinterment.

McKinley and I arrived at Stansham in the early afternoon, and we partook of a ploughman's lunch with ale at the Star Inn before walking to the vicarage. I was unsure of the welcome I might receive. He had been fortunate in retaining his living after that and my insistence in presenting the bones as the result of ancient ossuary activities rather than a modern-day pagan sacrificial ritual might have been instrumental in preserving his position.

Fortified by our ale, McKinley and I knocked at the door of the vicarage on the hill opposite St Jude's and the old gentleman himself opened it. I need not have worried. The Reverend Gibson was greatly relieved that the unholy practice had been stopped. His parish was now recognised as being of historical interest and the number of visitors from districts outside the village had increased, improving the quality of his congregation.

He was a fussy gentleman, tall and thin and bald as an egg, but effusive in his welcome and I had the impression that he would be extremely conscientious as a priest. He bade us enter the cottage and called his housekeeper to bring refreshments in the form of tea, which we gladly accepted. The house was built of brick and flint under a thatched roof and the living quarters of the vicar comprised a comfortable study at the front and a large sitting room at the rear. His housekeeper was a grey haired but energetic woman who resided on the other side of the house where there was small front room that she used as a bedroom and from where she had easy access to a cosy kitchen and scullery. I imagine that there were several bedrooms upstairs as this would have been a house that could support a small family.

There was a fire blazing in the study, and he had obviously been working on a sermon, so in view of the cold outside we sat in that room to take our tea. The walls were lined with books and I had great difficulty in focusing on the vicar's words because my eyes kept wandering to the titles on display. McKinley was better at engaging in social conversation, and they discussed at some length the newspaper accounts of a ghost being seen in the churchyard. The tea came and was poured by the housekeeper and the Reverend Gibson was silent until she had left. He then stoked the fire and lit two lamps as though to cheer the room, before telling us of his recent experiences.

He gravely admitted that he had seen the reported apparition, and this brought my attention onto him entirely. He said that he would be glad of our scientific observation because he could not find an explanation except to rely upon his faith, and the event had consumed him since he first experienced it.

In October of 1847, shortly after the distressing occurrences at the church, he had taken a break from composing his sermon and had glanced out of the study window towards the yews surrounding the church. It was his habit to gaze at those majestic but melancholy trees and to contemplate the passing of time. On that day he had seen a mist arise from the floor of the valley, creep up the steep slope, and disappear into the trees. I pointed out that such a thing was surely a natural phenomenon in a valley like this. He agreed, he had observed mists before, but they would be general, in patches, drifting here and there and that this was a definable shape and seemed to move as though it had its own will. He described it as being, oddly, like a loaf of bread, moving up the grassy slope and into the trees.

Being of a curious disposition and unafraid, he had left the house and followed the small path that led directly from the vicarage to the church, passing close to where the mist had disappeared. The yews were silent on that evening with no rustling or birdsong but before reaching the vestry on the north side of the building he saw the shape to his left. He stopped walking, stood still, and held his breath as the cold mist moved across the graveyard and along the side of the church in front of him. It gathered around the large yew that stood next to the Norman tower and then it melted through the door and disappeared.

He had no explanation how the thing had manifested and why it went into the oldest part of the church. He had no sight of a creature in a shroud. That was all he saw but he had seen it several times since. McKinley asked him if he had been afraid and he said no, it was exciting to see the thing, but he had felt no malevolence from it.

I tried to imagine the exterior of the church from my memory but as we had entered from the other side where the lychgate, path and main door were, I had not noticed an external door in the tower. I asked the vicar where it led and he said that it was just the staircase to the bell tower and there was no access inside the church. McKinley was keen to explore the door and the tower, but I was doubtful that we would see more than we had on the previous visit.

The Reverend Gibson said that flowers were regularly laid on the grave of Little William and it had become a place of pilgrimage for mothers who had lost their own children whether they were from the local area or further afield. The newspaper coverage had stirred a great deal of interest in St Jude's church, and the new stained-glass windows would be installed later in the year. Services were well attended, and overall his congregations were of a quite superior quality. In general, the villagers seemed to accept the fame of St Jude's and the Star Inn had profited from increased numbers of visitors as the area was becoming popular amongst travellers seeking both interest and sensation.

We agreed to look at the church again today and to return the following day to examine the extensive library inherited by the Reverend Gibson from his predecessors and added to by his own efforts as a bibliophile. He confessed that he had not yet catalogued the collection and did not know the whole history of Stansham.

I asked if he had a curate or any younger member of the clergy assisting in running the parish and he said that sadly he was likely to be the last vicar living in the village as there was a proposal to merge it with the neighbouring village of East Wellsley. Although he still hoped that the recent flurry of interest might persuade the Church to look again at the arrangement, he knew in his heart that St Jude's would soon be little more than a chapel of ease.

We donned our outer clothes and once again went out into the bitter weather this time guided by Gibson along the single path down a valley and up into the yews. We came out near the ramshackle lean-to vestry and could see the large yew tree near the tower that shadowed the door. The church seemed peaceful, even benign although the surrounding trees gave it a secretive air and I never found it to be a welcoming church.

We entered through the tower door and climbed the stairs to the bell tower, where there hung a single bell rung on occasion by the verger. The tower contained a fine pair of Norman windows but lacked any view except over the graveyard because the yews entirely encompassed the site. Throughout the walk and the visit to St Jude's the vicar talked incessantly and I had the impression he enjoyed holding forth about his parish to those who were interested.

I asked if we might take a closer look at the church inside and out to try to discover the entrance to the anchorite's cell and he became even more animated, describing a book he had been translating from Latin that was a detailed account of the man, Sir Hugh Critchley, and his fall from grace. I could not have been more pleased, and we made arrangements to spend the whole of the next day examining his collections. McKinley offered to make sketches of all aspects of the church, provided he was furnished with plenty of hot tea and somewhere to warm his hands.

So, with an air of anticipation, we entered the church. I breathed at once the smell of hopelessness that brought back the memory of Rudd's mysterious death. A quiet fell over our little party and even McKinley became sober and serious. We allowed Gibson to guide us, as he no doubt did frequently with visitors and he drew our attention to the medieval oak door and surround.

The church was quite dark, the small windows did little to brighten it and I saw again the brasses on the walls that had attracted me the previous year. I held my breath and looked around for some sign of Licoricia. I realised that I would never find her there, her appearance in my rooms had been an extraordinary visitation, perhaps prompted by some desperation either on her part or that of William's spirit.

The altar was below the stained-glass window to the east; it was quite a simple window and not especially colourful. At the western end of the building there was the Norman tower which was dark and uninviting. There was a wooden pulpit and a very small choir stall, a tiny organ at the front and a stone font near the porch door, upon which I had rested my lantern the previous year.

Gibson then picked up a portfolio and showed us a design for the new triple window with its beneficent Jesus in the centre window and St Jude, otherwise called Thaddeus, patron saint of hopeless causes, in the window on his right. This, he explained was to distinguish him from Judas Iscariot who had born the same name. I thought to myself that alone was a hopeless cause: to bear the same name as the man cursed for all time as being our Lord's betrayer.

Then I noticed the design in the third window and was shocked: it showed Judas hanging from a tree. I pointed it out to McKinley who was delighted with the drama of the design. The vicar noticed my horrified expression and said the artist had found it appropriate to place the good Judas on the right-hand side of God and the bad Judas on the left side of God. What could be a more sombre warning to the congregation as they contemplated their weaknesses and misdeeds. I could see that McKinley was quite taken with it and he studied it as Gibson and I continued searching.

The church is so small that we quickly examined the walls and the brasses and speculated whether access to another room might be possible through one of them. Nothing looked promising but when we examined Hugh Critchley's odd anchorite brass I was drawn to look closely and remembered the image from the rubbing that had shown a weeping kneeling man. His sense of hopelessness reminded me of the hanging man design for Judas in the window and I was struck that this would be directly above the anchorite brass. Was this a sign of damnation? Giving up hope means a lack of faith and loss of access to the redeemer, the key to the Christian religion. The suicide of Judas represented this despair. It was a feeling I had known only too well.

McKinley came up and signed that we should carry on, following Gibson as he continued his peregrination. He whispered to me that he would have a closer look at it tomorrow when he was making his sketches. He asked the vicar why the anchorite brass was allowed to become so dirty and whether he might clean it, as it appeared to be badly tarnished. Of course, said our host and explained that no matter how often it was cleaned that brass always discoloured more quickly than any of the others.

I stood above the altar and looked out over the tiny church with its rows of dark wooden pews and tried to imagine where the anchorite's cell could have been. I resolved to research the history of the church before engaging in further speculation, for I did not want to arouse suspicion.

The Reverend Gibson was loquacious as he showed us around the churchyard pointing out graves of note and only becoming quiet when we reached the well and he recalled the previous year's incident. Poor Rudd, I still could not understand his death and had failed to explain it to his grieving mother and sister. The lack of blood in the church and the possibility that he might have gone to the well carrying a chisel, if that is what he did, were incomprehensible. I could only speculate that he had taken it to defend himself or someone else. What had he seen?

We walked back to the house and gratefully settled again in the warm study where the fire had been fed by the old housekeeper. She had also made scones and brought these out proudly with butter and jam and more tea for our afternoon refreshment. Gibson showed me his system for finding his books. Sermons predominated in the library; at least fifty authors some of which were multi-volume editions. He proudly showed me a copy of Paley's A View of the Evidence of Christianity, published in 1807, with its exposition of Natural Theology and its reference to nature rather than scripture. He had found books that assisted in preaching sermons that could be understood and appreciated by all in his country congregation.

Gibson was an inveterate collector of anything written or printed. His tastes ranged from copies of Lloyds Weekly newspaper, a salacious choice for a country clergyman, to copies of handwritten journals and bibles that he had found at local fairs or discovered in the vicarage when he had taken it over. These were the books that I desperately wanted to examine. He had even acquired documents that had been found in a cottage demolished in 1839 and that were being used as kindling by the blacksmith. He could not bear to see this wanton destruction and had bought them all.

In view of my serious interest, he was happy for me to take them and begin a study tonight, many were damaged by years of damp but they were now dry and some were legible. McKinley and I carried the small chest between us and tramped back to the inn for an evening of mutton and indifferent wine followed by close study which we carried out in our room to avoid arousing unwanted local interest.

I was pleased to discover that the old documents were legal ones and related to the possession of the cottage that had been demolished. With careful handling and the aid of a magnifying glass I have been able to identify several separate transactions in which the tenancy had passed to various persons and the constant name that cropped up was Morton. I could find no references to the Critchley family in these papers.

My friend had lost interest in the few documents I had given him and was busy sketching me. A good likeness but for the frown lines which I should prefer not to be wearing at the age of six and twenty. We retired early with the intention of starting promptly in the morning and passed an uneventful night. I was not troubled by Licoricia of Winchester nor did I experience the night terrors of the yew trees at St Jude's church, although its physical presence was so close to me.

March 24^{th,} 1848

After an excellent breakfast we took the small chest back to the vicarage and were greeted with much enthusiasm by our host. He had spent the previous evening searching his Latin information on the Critchley family and had found an account of the court case translated in 1763 by one Broadbent, a previous holder of the position of vicar, who had been fascinated by the history of St Jude's. He carefully opened the journal and began reading a translated account of the trial of the anchorite.

The accuser was a crusader recently returned from Jerusalem and was described as a man of some 40 years, tanned, bearded and battle scarred. He gave his name as Simon Moortmain and he accused Hugh Critchley of the murder of his own son William Critchley, known as the martyr Little William. The accusation was sworn in the sheriff's court, there being no manor in existence for Stansham but it was immediately transferred to the ecclesiastical court because the property was church land having been gifted by Sir Hugh when he became anchorite.

The anchorite could not be brought to the court as he was outside the law having been consigned to God some fifteen years earlier, but the clerical representatives promised to take a statement from him and act as his attorneys. The case was heard in camera and the findings would not be available to the commoners. Fortunately, our intrepid vicar had pursued his quarry and uncovered more of the records from 1305 and Gibson was able to convey them to us.

Hugh Critchley, son of the rebel knight Sir Richard Critchley had murdered his own child and thrown him into a well. The timing coincided with a Jewish festival in Winchester and the common rumour was put about that the child's blood had been used to make Passover bread; it was sufficient excuse for a purge against Jewry in the middle ages. This had enabled Hugh to profit from the forfeiture of the accused's property and wealth had found its way into the hands of the father of the murdered child as compensation.

During the subsequent rioting, the chest holding details of bonds owing to the Jews was broken into and ransacked. There was at least one accusation that Hugh had escaped payment of a substantial debt that could have cost him his remaining land at Stansham. Gibson was keen to point out that this in itself was a serious matter, and if the crown's agents had found out that Hugh Critchley had anything to do with the theft of the bond, he would have been guilty of cheating the king. The bond was an asset and all the forfeited assets of a Jew belonged to the king.

I was intrigued by this information and asked the Reverend Gibson if Licoricia or one of her sons had been involved in this particular blood libel. He was surprised that I had heard of her and McKinley gave me a warning glance so I did not explain that she had been haunting me but passed it off as a general interest.

She had not been involved he said, but she had brought a case against Critchley relating to bonds that had been stolen during the riots. Broadbent had been fascinated by her and had revealed that, in his deposition, Simon Moortmain had alleged that he had knowledge about her murder. He had been informed by her son, Asher Sweetman, that his mother had uncovered information about the killing of William before she and her maid Alice of Bickton had been brutally murdered in 1277.

That stunned me. Was there a connection between the death of William and Licoricia? I asked if Hugh might have been responsible for the murder of Licoricia? Gibson said that Broadbent did not comment on that and, in any event, by 1305 all the Jews had been expelled by order of Edward I so there would have been no one to plead her case.

We sat contemplating the significance of this, and I felt strongly the connection of the veiled lady with the tragedy of Little William and her ghostly presence. What a place this was. What malevolent presence exerts its influence over the minds of men on St Jude's hill? There were stories of a battle between Saxons and Vikings; there had been child sacrifices; and what had claimed the life of my manservant?

McKinley interrupted my reverie and said he thought it was unnatural for a man to murder his own child. Surely any Christian child would have sufficed to initiate the blood libel? And who was this Moortmain to appear so long after the event with the accusation?

That was the interesting part said Gibson, becoming very excited: he was a Critchley. He was Simon Critchley the youngest son who had left home in 1290 at the age of 20 years. He had met Asher in Winchester, possibly just before his exile and, having nothing to lose, Asher had told him that Simon's own father, Hugh, had murdered William. The reason he knew this was his mother's enquiry into the murder.

She had paid two Christian men from London to investigate the death and find out who was responsible. Presumably, they had visited the shrine, ostensibly from Christian piety, and begun asking questions. She was careful to ensure that there was nothing to connect them to her family. They had not visited her in Winchester, but her youngest son Asher had met with them on the London road and brought their information to her.

It would have been difficult to find proof that Hugh had killed William and she did not act upon the information for some time. The court case that Licoricia brought against Sir Hugh in relation to the missing debt documentation from the archa was several months before her death. Licoricia was killed in her home in Winchester by intruders who stole money to make it look like a robbery.

It is possible that she was using the knowledge of Hugh's guilt as leverage in reinstating her claim to the missing debts. In any event it had led to two more bloody murders and Asher had the good sense to keep quiet about his suspicions, until he had the opportunity to tell Simon whilst they were drinking together in Winchester in 1290. At that time, he had little to lose with his business in ruins and his exile imminent.

We can only surmise what happened next. A drunken and furious Simon, who was then aged only 20, might have confronted his father with the hideous accusation, and then felt driven to leave the country. It appeared from his affidavit in the court records that Simon changed his surname and became a man at arms to a French nobleman setting out on crusade to Outremer as soon as he could on crossing the Channel. He must have seen terrible bloodshed in the Holy Land yet he could not forget or forgive what his father had done to his older brother.

The Reverend Gibson pointed out that he was only four or five years old when William was killed and may not have remembered him. However, as a pious Christian he would have heard much about the murder from his mother and brothers, and of course Little William was virtually a saint and every visit his family had paid to the church would have been a reminder of his martyrdom.

Gibson continued reading from the old text. It appeared that Simon had been destined to join the clergy but showed a greater inclination for military matters, together with wenching and carousing. Like many young men he did not get on with his father, who he alleged to be a brute in all things. He returned from the crusades expecting to find his older brother Geoffrey and his sisters possibly alive, even if his mother and father were not. What he then learned must have appalled him. It had all taken place soon after he left, and if he had stayed, he might have prevented it. And it was possible that his angry argument with his father might have precipitated the disaster.

Broadbent must have spent months researching this tale, of course it was all in a clerk's notes from the trial hearings and cannot be substantiated. It seems that Hugh acquired property cheaply in Winchester and mortgaged it for money with which to build a great house at Stansham. This was probably nothing more than a hall, but it was constructed of stone acquired from a local source. My mind began to think where that might be, and I deduced that some of the original local standing stones could have been used for this purpose. There was currently one on the other side of the village.

The house had been a disaster from the start. Critchley's second son John had been an adventurous boy and loved to climb so that one day he climbed the partly completed building and fell bring heavy timbers down on him. He lingered for a few weeks then died. Infant mortality was common, but his mother and father were devastated. He has a small brass memorial in the church.

When Simon left, he still had an older brother and two younger sisters. When he returned it was to find that nothing remained. The house had burned to the ground and all its occupants had been killed. The land was now part of a farmer's field rented from the Church. His mother and siblings were buried within St Jude's and his father lived with them as an anchorite.

This was his testimony: hearsay evidence about William's murder from a Jew who was no longer in the country and no proof. Just a story by a man who alleged that he had been Simon Critchley and had returned to find everything he called home had vanished.

The case against the anchorite was dismissed but the taint of the accusation and the fact that the family had met such ill fortune made people suspicious. The pilgrimages to William declined. Hugh Critchley, by then an old man of 60 years or so, died soon afterwards. Simon Moortmain left the area and was thought to have returned abroad. I asked if Sir Hugh's burial site were known but the Reverend Gibson had never come across it and supposed that his bones would be in the ossuary below the church.

The crypt. We had come here to find it and I glanced at McKinley who straightway requested a viewing of the ossuary, and this threw Gibson into a state of confusion. All he knew was that when he arrived at St Jude's in 1831 there was no entrance. There might be a trap door, but he did not know where it was. We pressed home the advantage and he agreed that we might move the pews until we found a likely area of floor. It would help if we knew roughly which area of the church, and he suggested the narthex as he believed it was likely to be under the Norman tower. It was mid-morning and we immediately made our way across the valley and through the trees to the church which looked quiet in the pale sunshine.

Fortunately, there were no visitors and McKinley and I proceeded to lift the heavy pews away from the back of the church. Disappointingly the flags all looked the same. We systematically tapped them to determine if a different echo might be heard, but there was no indication from that source. Sometimes a crypt might be provided with a small window, so we scoured the outside of the building for any sign of a blocked area of masonry.

We borrowed a hoe from the gardener's lean-to and scraped the ground away from the walls. It astonishes me how much higher the ground becomes with the passage of time. All archaeology is found by digging, and we laboured for several hours until hunger got the better of us. We agreed that one would stay and continue working while the other went to purchase victuals from the innkeeper. I remained and McKinley left.

After about twenty minutes I saw the top of a stone mullion appear just to the east of the tree and as part of the nave rather than the Norman tower. I needed a shovel to remove the compacted earth and it was close to an ancient grave with illegible inscriptions. I apologised to the occupant and set to with renewed vigour and by the time McKinley returned I had uncovered a dark patch which had probably been a metal grill but which was now rotted to a dark stain on the clay. I am ashamed to say that I did not preserve this layer but did lay it side and had McKinley make a drawing of it with a description.

We took a short break to eat our ploughman's lunch and drink the small ale provided for us; and we discussed what to do about the proximity of the headstone which was likely to fall into the hole that I had been digging. Should we tell the Reverend or carry on and then try and make good? I agreed to go back to the vicarage and inform the Reverend Gibson of our find, for I felt sure that he would be as excited as we were. McKinley would continue digging along the wall, but I impressed upon him not to take any risks, mindful of what had happened to Rudd on my previous visit.

When I arrived at the cottage the verger was talking to the vicar in the garden and as expected Gibson was very keen to proceed and accompanied me back to the church bringing the verger as added manpower. I was relieved to see my friend knee deep in a trench beside the wall, unharmed and smiling.

We agreed the window and the remains of the grill

indicated that this may have been the access to the cell of the anchorite. The plaintiffs would kneel in front of the grill and receive counselling or predictions from the holy man. It was the window to his prison, and he would never leave that place. I was determined to excavate the window and see what lay beyond.

Between the three of us we moved the gravestone to one side and leaned it against the wall. The vicar set about scraping off the lichen and algae with a penknife to try and decipher the inscription, but I feared that it was too weathered to be translatable. Our trench was three feet deep when we stopped work as the light began to fade. The window was about two and a half feet deep, and a man might squeeze through if we were able to remove the soil that lay inside it. The verger brought boards from the lean-to and covered the trench so that no one could fall in during the night and we retreated back to the vicarage to wash ourselves to avoid marching covered in dirt through the village and arousing more suspicion than we already had. The verger had his instructions to keep quiet and Gibson said that he was a loyal man and valued his generally easy job.

As dusk fell, in that warm study, I looked out of the window and hoped to see the loaf-like mist arising from the valley and moving up to the yews. I fancied that it was the souls of the Vikings that had been ambushed here a thousand years ago and slaughtered by the Saxons of Wessex. Were they searching for their lost honour? Had they been denied entry to the feasting halls of the dead for some reason? I almost thought I could hear the cries of battle. Then I saw a family of cats outside waiting for the housekeeper to feed them scraps from the kitchen.

I turned laughing and explained my imaginings and the plethora of cats and kittens. Gibson explained that they were feral but they did an excellent job of culling the mice and rats hereabout, and sometimes the big tom was to be found hunting in the churchyard. We drank our tea and talked at length about the life of a hermit and the importance of superstition to the people of the middle ages. Such was their reliance on the supernatural that a prediction of the death of a powerful person, even a king, by a fortune teller or astrologer could provoke an attempt upon that person's life. A tarnished anchorite was an embarrassment to the clergy and his death shortly after the trial must have been a relief.

Gibson was keen to find an old journal he had discovered and to that end McKinley and I spent an hour examining the books on his shelves. When we had found where it was not, he said, he would make light work of finding where it was. With that thought we parted company and we returned to the inn for a rest and a hearty meal. I am writing this journal in our room while McKinley records his experiences of the day by drawings. I hope to sleep as well tonight as I did last night.

March 25th, 1848

Sadly, I did not achieve a sound sleep but woke the whole inn with shouts of alarm, and I was very sick. I dreamed that Gibson and I were walking across the valley from the vicarage to the church and we were accompanied by ghostly Viking warriors with neither shields nor weapons. They were grey and misty in form and were muddy and blood spattered, whether it was their own blood or that of their enemies I could not tell. Some were injured, but they walked with fatalistic certainty towards the trees.

When we entered the trees there were mournful sounds like mewing and calling followed by the thud of a falling axe as though one of the great trees was being felled. As the axe blade cut into it the tree seemed to give a great sigh and shuddered; something fell onto the grass and the axe moved on. As we passed out of the yews there was nothing to see except the church sitting above a pool of mist and surrounded by gravestones. The circle of yews was intact and there was no axeman.

I walked to the place where the window had been found and I looked for McKinley. He was not there, and the window was concealed again. Gibson walked off around the church calling his name, but I knew that my friend had entered the cell and was entombed in it. I dug at the earth with my hands calling him and scrabbling down into the soil between the grave and the wall.

That is when he woke me sweating and tearing at the sheets on the bed trying to find him between the bed and the wall. I shook and vomited and within minutes the landlord was banging on the door. McKinley let him in and explained that it was the night terrors that I had experienced since my man Rudd had died the previous year. Luckily, he was sympathetic and gave me brandy and lovage and forbore from advising me to leave St Jude's and to go home. I would not have listened as I was hell-bent on finding the cell and the charnel house if I could.

In the morning everything seemed unreal and dreamlike, but we made a good breakfast and returned subdued to the vicarage to meet our host, the Reverend Gibson. We did not tell him about my dream, lest it should prove prophetic. Despite our modern grasp of science there is still much about our ways that are owed to the superstitions of our fathers. We found him most jovial, and he produced the result of his labours the previous evening.

He bade us sit as his ever-helpful housekeeper prepared coffee and rolls. Then he held up a long wavering finger and said that he had been bequeathed a treasure from the house in which we sat. Whilst searching for old texts he had questioned his housekeeper and she revealed something she had found many years before hidden behind a disused bread oven inside an old pot. Thinking to reuse the pot she emptied out the contents and his housekeeper had been surprised by a grubby little parcel which turned out to be a small book wrapped in leather. Knowing the Reverend's affection for all things written she had not thrown it away. She had simply put it with his family bible. He produced it carefully; it was a Book of Hours.

This small book, written in English on vellum had been kept by several soldiers on campaign in the holy land during the crusades and probably been preserved by being taken from the body of slain comrades. Several of the names were illegible but one stood out; that of Simon Moortmain of Hampshire. We had found something tangible that had belonged to the youngest son and accuser of Hugh Critchley.

It was apparent that he had brought the book back to England when he finished fighting and settled down to marry. His name was stated to be the owner of the Book of Hours and was followed by others of the same name and latterly the name was shown as Morton.

The Reverend Gibson surmised that after the reformation or perhaps during the English civil war it was considered dangerous to possess something that would tie the owner to the practice of Catholic rites, so it had been hidden; and miraculously had survived. It meant that a son of Hugh Critchley had returned to the area and a descendant of his had lived in that cottage in Stansham at a later date, perhaps as vicar.

Did the Book of Hours give any clues about what had happened all those years ago? Did Hugh kill his eldest son and what happened to his wife, daughters, and the remaining son Geoffrey? He allowed me to examine the Book of Hours. It appeared to have been drawn up for a lady in English and perhaps she had given it to a knight as a favour when he went on crusade. Each page's capital was illuminated but there were no pictures. I closed my eyes and tried to imagine all the events that had occurred since the book was created and before it was hidden in a cook's pot.

McKinley broke the spell by repeating my name several times, and Gibson remarked that I looked pale and perhaps should remain at the vicarage whilst they carried on with the digging. But I replied that fresh air was what I needed, and I insisted on going with them. The verger had agreed to assist so we expected to make good progress; and the sun was shining.

We made our way to the church. Although elderly, the Reverend Gibson was a sprightly gentleman and put us city laggards to shame. After about an hour's work I became faint, and they sent me back to the vicarage where I recommenced my journal as you find here. They will join me for luncheon and then we will all return to the church for the afternoon's session.

The same day

It is later and you will see that I write, not with a pen and ink, but with one of McKinley's pencils. I have only a few inches of candle left and I must write down what has happened before it is too late. God help me. I am trapped in the crypt of St Jude's church beneath the Norman tower and have been here for some time, enough to burn most of my one candle. I had heard the efforts of the men to reach me after the earthslide but now all is quiet. It seems that the more they dig, the more the soil fills the trench. I will set out what I discovered so that when they find me, be it alive or dead they shall have a record of the events.

I returned with McKinley, the vicar and the verger in the afternoon and we continued to dig until the shadows had lengthened and we decided to stop for the night. As we were leaving, I saw a pale streak out of the corner of my eye, and it made me stop and turn my head. The thing, whatever it was, vanished and I heard a sound as of dry sand falling onto a soft surface. I could not ignore it and walked back to the window that we had once more covered with planks. I kneeled and pulled them aside to look into a black hole where before there had been earth.

I called to the others and prepared myself to descend, tying the rope we had brought around my waist and readying the candle and flint. They objected and the vicar offered the verger as first to explore, but I could see that he was reluctant. McKinley offered but as I was the slightest in frame, I insisted and would brook no disagreement. At length they conceded because they knew that the three of them could haul me out should the need arise.

As I began sliding my feet and legs into that dreadful hole, I felt little fear except some shudder at the pale thing I had seen enter it before me. What if it was a spirit and we had disturbed its resting place? The air was cool and smelled of soil and mould. There was no movement, but all was silent and still. At about ten feet down I touched the floor of the crypt, informed my comrades, and prepared to light the candle.

As the tinderbox struck there was a terrifying screech and I dropped the candle. The men called down in alarm and I was stricken with fear for a few seconds so that I could neither move nor utter a sound. Then I gathered my wits and dropped to my knees to search for the candle with unwilling fingers amongst the awful debris. I half expected my hand to be grasped by something cold and long dead but resisting the temptation to shrink from every bony object, I searched blindly until I found it and prepared to strike the flint again.

This time I managed to light the candle and almost dropped it, for I saw glinting eyes and fangs in the darkness. As my eyes adjusted, I saw that it was a large cat, and it confirmed the identification by hissing a warning at me. I called to the others that the graveyard cat had caused the earth slide and revealed the entrance to the room we had been seeking.

I was almost hysterical with relief and forced myself to relax and look around and was amazed at the huge stones built into the walls of the room which was largely comprised of flint and mortar. I had expected to find the charnel house but there was only one set of bones in this room, and they lay huddled in a corner, the apparently complete skeleton of a man. The remnants of what might once have been a bed and a table were nearby, although these were crumbling away, and a pile of dust that might at one time have been a bucket. Some pieces of leather remained intact.

I examined the skeleton in the light of my candle. It seemed to be a man in scraps of garment and had long hair and a beard. I was interested in the leather strap that encompassed his neck and then shocked to see that it had a long lead. My first thought was that he might have been a prisoner and tethered, but the strap was drawn tight and although it was no longer attached to a fixed point I had the deepest suspicion that it had once been attached to something high.

As I stood looking at that horrid sight, I heard the men behind me asking what I had found, and I shouted back that it was the cell of the anchorite. This sorry creature must be Sir Hugh Critchley of Stansham, and he had been strangled with a leather belt and left to rot, walled up in his cell. Was it possible that his keepers had become his jailors and then his executioners; or had he ended his own life like Judas? Would they not have removed him and buried him somewhere?

Why had he killed William? And what had induced him to

then kill his entire family? If indeed he had.

I conveyed this to Gibson and McKinley and was about to ask them to haul me back out when my light fell on a difference in the surface of one of the walls to the left of the window. It might be a door and after I had brushed away webs and mould, I could see that it was the rotten remains of a wooden door with metal bars that had rusted through. Joyously I pushed it and after a few attempts it crumbled and caved in and I glimpsed another larger room beyond. My rope impeded me, so I untied it, picked up my candle and started through into the room beyond, glad to be away from the skeleton.

As I went through the door the cat leapt past me up towards the window and began to climb the shifting surface in an attempt to get out of the cell the way it had got in. The velocity of its jump and the desperate scrabbling gave it the impetus to almost reach the window and the lights of my friends at the surface. They shouted and I heard much noise as the animal paddled in a frantic attempt to escape. McKinley must have grabbed it for I heard him cry when the beast clawed at him and made its getaway. Then all was noise and confusion because a mass of earth fell down and blocked the window and filled the cell which I had so lately vacated.

The dust and pressure extinguished my light and once again I was plunged choking into absolute blackness and eventually, silence. This is how I find myself – alone and in despair. My reckless ambition to be the first into the long-lost crypt brought me here and now it is likely to be my tomb. I have relit my candle; but there is not much of it left. The doorway is filled with soil and the anchorite again is alone in his cell and I am in the charnel house. For that is what this is; there are not many bones to be sure and some are neatly stacked on shelves between the same type of great stones that were to be found in the other room. The ceiling is domed, and I can stand upright.

I have had time to think, and it seems to me that the great stones, planted deep in the ground, are the same as the ancient stones found at various places on the South Downs. There is such a stone on the opposite side of the village of Stansham, called the Devil's Finger and these are similar, though not covered in the patina of moss and algae. There are scribblings on them, most of which I cannot understand but suspect might be runic, and I recognized the Latin inscriptions of the Roman occupier.

When the Saxons decided to build their church on this hill, perhaps in celebration of the victory against the Viking marauders, they seem to have filled in the space between the stones and built their wooden church on top. Then they planted the yew trees to shelter or to conceal it.

I decided to carry out an examination of the room and in doing so I found a flat stone with a dip and a channel. With horror I recognised it was a slaughter stone, and one that had not been out of use for long. Perhaps some twenty years before, a man had killed a child here. And perhaps this was where Little William had met his end.

I listened to the noises in the church above and I knew that they would soon find me, so I examined the bones in the shelves expecting them to be men, women and children moved here when the graves were full. I was surprised to find that they were all men and full-grown ones at that, with terrible wounds that suggested they had been hacked down by blades or axes. Each man had been beheaded as the vertebrae were severed just below the skull.

The length of the long bones and the hair that remained on some of them caused me to conclude that these were the remains of Vikings, thrown into the pit and buried under the wooden Anglo-Saxon church and discovered when the stone church was constructed by the Normans. The builders had treated them with respect, created a small crypt and stacked them in the shelves. A few people had been added over the subsequent years and, at some point, the crypt had fallen out of use.

Seeing the blood stains on the stone I realized that there must be another way in. Hugh's remains had not been disturbed so someone had found a way into this part of the underground room within living memory. I searched every inch of the floor and walls until I found steps. They were partly hidden by tree roots and masonry, but they showed that there had been access, until it was bricked up. I just needed to make sufficient noise that they would know where to dig. I looked for something to strike the stone and mortar that blocked the way. I could not use a bone, it would crumble away, so I have used my tinderbox to bang on the wall and hope to draw their attention so they might free me.

With so little candle left I determined to write the last of my journal and here now I must finish as the light runs out. May God have mercy on my soul.

Chapter Twelve

When Sarah finished reading Macey's journal, she was upset and felt bereft.

'I don't know why I feel so concerned. He lived a long time ago, of course I knew he was dead. But how did he die?' she told the others.

Eleanor watched her closely.

'Don't worry Sarah, we've been in the crypt and his body would have been obvious if he had been trapped there. It's more likely he escaped and, in his haste, forgot to take the journal with him. Perhaps he was unconscious when they found him,' she said.

Chris squeezed her hand. A simple gesture she found reassuring.

'He might have been dead when they found him,' Sarah said, 'or worse. Being in that place after the haunting and the laudanum might have driven him insane, and he might have encountered something worse. He was not strong either physically or mentally.'

Eleanor reminded her that they had more documents to read. 'Anything sensational would have been picked up by the press. If he had died in the crypt, it was unlikely that the newspapers would fail to report something so exciting and salacious.'

'The crypt was probably bricked up again because it wasn't safe. The earth-slide described by Dr Macey might have completely filled the anchorite's cell,' suggested Chris.

'I'm particularly especially interested in the vicar. It looks as though this cottage may have been the vicarage. It has been extensively modified since 1848 but the views and the basic framework must be the same. I know that it was built originally in the early nineteenth century and then extended in the Edwardian period when it had been acquired by my family.'

'They strangled Sir Hugh,' said Chris. 'They must have thought he was guilty, so they finished him off and sealed the cell from prying eyes.'

'Or he hanged himself.' The more Sarah thought about it the more likely it seemed. The mechanism was unlikely to be still in place after five hundred years. Dr Macey didn't have long to examine it. Critchley took his thirty pieces of silver from his child's murder, he had betrayed and possibly poisoned his own brother. 'He was an embarrassment to the Church and the village. I doubt anyone wept for Sir Hugh Critchley.'

They sat in silence. Then Chris said 'I think he weeps for himself. I think he's still there in that church lamenting what he caused. Dwelling in his sins.'

'He deserves his punishment. It's what he should have expected, living as he did,' said Sarah, and the others agreed. 'But it's frightening to think that such evil still exists, condemned to an undead existence for centuries contemplating his sin. He should have been consumed in hell by now.'

Eleanor said, 'That is the curse of St Jude's hill and its ancient inhuman power.'

Chris said, 'Hugh might deserve it but why should his victim William also be doomed to repeat this suffering. It's unbearable. If we can find a way to make it stop then we should.'

'It's nearly 5.00 am if you want to grab some sleep you could take those drinks upstairs and relax,' said Eleanor 'I must go and meet the ambulance on the farm road.'

Sarah felt so grateful for the suggestion, she could not wait to lie down and rest, so she and Chris went to their rooms while Eleanor put on her waterproofs and boots and left the cottage.

'I don't know how long I'll be. Just make yourselves at home.' They went upstairs and heard the front door slam.

Sarah washed, then lay on the bed with the duvet wrapped over her and sipped her tea. She tried to remember all that they had found out tonight. She took out George Macey's journal and began to read again the last few pages. They were dirty and scrappy, smelt of mould, written with a soft pencil and slightly smudged. What had happened to him? Her eyes closed and she slept.

It seemed as though she immediately woke. Chris was in the room, shouting and shaking her. She was aware of him but could not move, her eyes would barely open. She wanted to tell him to go away so she could slip back into the sweet oblivion. He grabbed and shook her. What the hell was the matter with him? He opened the window and let cold air into the room and fetched water from the bathroom to splash into her face.

'Wake up Sarah, it's ten past six. You've been asleep for an hour. She's drugged you. She tried to drug me too, but I fell asleep before drinking it. Then I woke with a chill in the room and saw figures standing at the end of the bed. My first thought was that she had family staying here that she hadn't told us about. I was trying to think what to say when I realised: they were spirits!

'Sarah, it was the boy William and a woman in a veil. I was terrified but without speaking she indicated that I should not drink the tea, and she was right. I could barely wake you.' He pulled her to her feet with an effort. 'You must come and see them. They might still be in my room.'

He helped her to stand and as she was barely awake, half carried her out to the corridor that led to the bedrooms, the stairs dropped away to the front door and she saw that there was a window directly above the front door and the stairs had been changed around so that they faced the opposite direction, and the original landing and window were inaccessible.

Little William and Licoricia were on the landing. Their forms were grey and misty, shifting subtly in the electric light in its absurdly flowery shade. He looked more like a boy than a skeleton, but he was obviously crippled and dressed in a long robe. He held the veiled woman's hand.

Chris saw them and stopped. He told Sarah to wait and went into her room, brought out a chair and placed her in it. She was unsteady, her head was still foggy and she blinked to clear her eyes as she looked at the hazy shapes that struggled to keep their form, but she knew them from their stories, and they were long dead. What did they have in common that they could appear so many years after their deaths?

Chris spoke first. 'Tell us why you are here and what it is you want. We will do all in our power to help you.' The boy looked up at the woman and she down at him. 'Please trust us.'

The child looked back at Chris, and then he let go of Licoricia's hand. He stepped off the landing and made his painful way through the air towards them. Sarah was afraid that he was coming to her and was about to stand and flee but to her horror he approached Chris and lifted his bony arms as though he wanted to be picked up. Chris reached down and gently embraced the pale and shifting creature in his dirty robe, lifting him to head height. The child kissed him on the mouth and slowly evaporated as Chris sank to his knees next to Sarah.

With the thought that the woman might now come for her, she looked in terror at the spirit on the landing opposite. The veiled figure was impassive. To Sarah's relief she turned and walked through the wall out of sight.

'Chris, Chris – are you alright? Can you hear me?' She felt entirely clear headed with shock after that encounter, though her legs were shaking and weak when she helped him into her room and sat him on the bed. 'Speak to me.'

He turned a wide innocent gaze on her, so that she was reminded of a child. Then Chris reappeared as though through his own eyes and smiled broadly while tears coursed down his face. She found tissues for him and waited until he was more in control. They sat cross legged opposite each other on the bed.

'I feel it Sarah and I know what happened' he struggled to express it. 'His dad killed him. In his parents' house William was usually kept indoors and dressed in a robe like a cleric, but it was so that no one would see his disability. He was made to study most of the day and had one body servant to care for him, and she was a deaf mute. But on this day, he had been allowed out and he was playing with his brothers near the stables, they'd found a sheet, rigged it like a sail and he was telling his little brothers a story of a great sea battle at the beginning of King Henry's reign. They were playing at being sailors capturing the rebel pirate Eustace the Monk. William could read and had memorised the story, he was the captain and they were about to storm Eustace's ship when the kitchen maid called them for dinner and they hurried to the hall.

Geoffrey ran on ahead and John carried Simon who was not much more than a baby. I followed them but being lame I …' he stopped and a sob escaped him. 'Sorry, he was slow and was left behind. He's filling my head, Sarah.'

'You're doing really well, Chris. If you don't want to carry on you don't have to, but the memory may not be long-lasting.'

'As he limped past the end of the stables someone grabbed him and put a sack over his head. It smelled of rotten fruit. He clamped a hand over his mouth and lifted him onto a horse. The man mounted behind him and they galloped away from his home. It wasn't a long journey, but down and then up a hill and trotted through cool trees. It was only a few minutes before he was dropped onto the ground and the man dismounted and ripped the sack off.

'They were at the church of St Jude's, and the man was his father, the knight Sir Hugh Critchley, son and brother of a traitor who looked down on his crippled eldest son with stubborn determination in his face. William knew at that moment that he meant to kill him. His father's face was dark and resolute. He was not angry at William. He was angry because fate had given him a cripple before three healthy sons.

'He picked the child up under one arm and carried him towards the empty church. It was late morning, and everyone would be having their dinner, the main meal of the day. He took the path to the Norman tower and opened the door. William began to struggle, he didn't want to go down to the crypt where the bones were, not there. But his father was determined, and his weak cries were lost as they descended the stairs.

'The crypt was much larger then, with small windows and the strange standing stones encircling the space like sentinels.

When he dropped William the boy's legs were shot through with pain. He said 'Papa, my legs'.' Chris began weeping again and Sarah cried too. After a few minutes Chris said 'It's what I heard him say Sarah, I don't want to continue, but he really wants me to tell you, so that we know what we must face when we go back to the church.' She nodded

'Sir Hugh pushed the boy onto the slaughter stone without looking at him even when he said, 'Papa please'. But his father took out a knife. Then he said 'I make this gift to the ancient gods of Albion, to the gods of my forefathers, to the great serpent, for the atonement of my sins and the sins of my blood. Accept this blood of mine as a gift and give me what I desire.''

Chris paused. 'He killed him Sarah, he held down his head and cut his throat even as he said 'Papa no!' The blood filled the slaughter stone and after he had stopped struggling, Hugh Critchley stamped on him so that the marks of the cripple would not be obvious to the village people who had been kept away from him. Then he carried him to the well and dropped him into it.' Chris stopped and looked at her.

'Dear God, you experienced that from Little William embracing you?' Sarah thought how much it was like a dream in which so much can be conveyed in a tiny capsule of time.

'Yes, and he knows that he was found by the villagers and that the Jews were blamed and that is why the Jewish lady looks after him.'

'Licoricia looks after him in death?'

'Yes. Her death is connected to his. We know that she died in trying to shed light on his and they are bound together in death.' Chris paused and then continued in a worried voice 'She is afraid that there is going to be another sacrifice; tonight. She wants to communicate through you.'

Sarah stood up and looked nervously around the room. 'Is she here, now?'

'I can't see her, and I assume you can't, but William told me that we need to find out more about Eleanor before we go back to the church. She's not what she seems. She drugged you and tried to drug me, I'm guessing. She has something in mind for Adam. He's an adulterer.'

As am I thought Sarah and Chris said as if reading her mind, 'Your baby has saved you. I'm not supposed to be here so whatever happens to me is collateral damage. Adam is a worthy sacrifice. A leading academic at the height of his power, on the cusp of a second career in the media, with a harem of women...'

'What? Come on, that's ridiculous.' The tension broke a little and Chris continued.

'Yes, well we know that, but Eleanor's perception is different. Her husband left her and precipitated a tragic series of events. She believes in ancient powers and that an evil beyond our understanding exists on that hill under that church and only the power of Christian faith has kept in imprisoned or tamed these last fourteen hundred years. Now it wants what it came to expect over millennia and still hungers for.'

'But it can't be true surely?' Sarah still baulked at the idea of a formless and ancient power.

'Well, I didn't believe in ghosts until tonight but now I am certain they exist. The important thing is that Eleanor believes in it and currently she has the upper hand.'

Sarah thought for short while and then said 'There does seem to be a curse – Hugh Critchley's wealth increased for a short while but then his luck abandoned him. He lost a child in an accident, then had a huge row with his youngest son who left home.'

'But Simon survived.'

'Yes, survived but came back to accuse him of murder, and he had changed his name. And before that his entire family died or was killed, and the house he had built with his blood-money burnt down.'

Chris paused for a moment and then said 'From what Eleanor and Adam were saying earlier, the sacrifice has to be a valuable thing. William may have been loved by his mother and brothers, but his father didn't value him. It didn't lift his brother's curse, it made matters worse. The family is still cursed and Eleanor is descended from the Critchleys. Her maiden name was Morton.'

'That's similar to Moortmain, the name that Simon took when he went to the crusades and used when he accused Hugh of murder. It also appears in the Book of Hours.' Sarah took George Macey's journal and flicked through it until she could show the relevant page to Chris.

It confirmed what he knew from William's warning. He said, 'She's crazy and hell-bent on reversing the family curse. Another nasty accident at the ex-church of St Jude, the patron saint of hopeless causes.'

'Surely the ambulance and police will be here soon,' said Sarah. There was a pause. 'She didn't call them, did she?'

'I doubt it,' said Chris.

'Do you know what happened to the family? Who caused their deaths and provoked Hugh to become the anchorite?'

Chris nodded and lowered his eyes. 'William feels responsible. It was Geoffrey who set the fire, he overheard Simon and his father arguing and he must have learned that his father had killed William. At the same time he found out that innocent Jews had been murdered for his father's own benefit.

'When Simon left, Geoffrey was alone to bear the full weight of his father's expectations. The family had survived William's death, he was virtually a saint, and they all paid their respects daily. They still loved him you see, he had been a bright, loving, and intelligent child who lit up the lives of those who knew him. It was a love not felt by his father who saw him only as a cripple who would never hunt, fight, or go on crusade, but who stood to inherit the Critchley estate by reason of primogeniture. He killed him so that his second son, healthy, brave John would inherit the title and estates; but, as we know, he died in a climbing accident on the new house.

'So that meant that Geoffrey would inherit, and he was groomed for the role, betrothed to a suitable girl who would bring a good dowry and strategic alliances. When Sir Hugh was called upon to send fighting men at the behest of his liege lord, the king, he would have her tenants or her wealth to satisfy the obligation.'

'So, Geoffrey was sitting pretty?' Sarah was amazed at Chris's grasp of the position.

'You'd think so, and from what I understand from William's embrace, he was a pious young man who would have preferred to have gone into the church but was prepared to do his duty. When he overheard the argument with Simon and became aware of the allegations, he asked his father to tell him the truth but Hugh's reaction was such that Geoffrey must have been confirmed in his suspicions. He had a strong sense of heaven and hell, no doubt preached by the local clergy, and he became terrified that damnation and perpetual torment awaited his father and himself unless there was confession, penance, and absolution. He was desperately unhappy. He had lost two brothers to death and one had just disappeared. He may have suspected his father of another murder.'

Chris stopped and shook his head. Then he continued:

'William is tormented by guilt. He can't rest. He didn't mean to cause the complete destruction of his family but in his childish desperation he reached out to Geoffrey from beyond the grave. He began trying to communicate with Geoffrey, appearing to him in the early hours of the morning when the barrier between life and death is at its thinnest. Geoffrey was haunted by his own murdered little brother.

'In a drunken stupor, one night, Geoffrey set fire to the house. Everyone was asleep and died in their beds, and he also perished in the conflagration. He must have known that his father was mired in sin. No one else had done anything wrong, the whole family and the servants had been to confession that day and were assured of a place in heaven. Perhaps he felt that he had saved them the shame or the shared sin. Either he was insane or drunk. It's not clear which.'

Sarah was astonished 'Geoffrey killed his family?'

'The house burned to the ground and nobody escaped.'

Sarah was shocked at this disclosure. Poor William, a victim of his father's greed, had tragically triggered the destruction of his own family.

'But his father didn't die.'

'No, it appears that Sir Hugh woke in the night and fled when he smelled smoke, leaving his family to perish. It is as though his brother's curse had kept Hugh alive to suffer further and that seems to have been his perception, because having lost everything, for his atonement he caused himself to be cast into the same ground as the son he murdered, and he stayed there until about 1306.'

Sarah said 'Do you know how he died? He either hanged himself or someone else did it, but Macey found the leather strap around his neck.'

Chris closed his eyes and then drew in his breath sharply. A small voice said, 'He hanged himself but it was taking too long, so he cut his throat with the knife they gave him for his meat.' He slumped forward and stopped breathing.

"Chris, Chris, come back" Sarah said and slapped him.

He looked up at her, he was pale and unseeing 'A man took the knife.'

She hugged him. Whether she was hugging Chris or William she didn't know, it seemed to be the same, and he needed it. He was white. His skin was cold and clammy, and his eyes were fluttering. Sarah was afraid that the grave had taken him, and he was slipping from her. She hugged him tighter and rocked him, crooning a nameless song that she found in a distant memory.

After a while, she wasn't sure how long, she felt him grow warmer and then he tentatively hugged her back. She knew he was back when she felt him start wiping his eyes. She let him go.

'Good to have you back' she said.

'He's gone' he said.

They sat side by side on the bed and flicked through George Macey's journal 'The good Judas and the bad Judas' said Sarah.

'What?'

'You know, the Victorian stained-glass window that was going to have St Jude on Jesus's right hand and Judas on his left. They had the same name although St Jude was sometimes called Thaddeus. Judas was depicted in this window as hanging from a tree apparently with his 30 pieces of silver.' They looked through the journal to the discussion with the Reverend Gibson.

'Did they actually put that window in place?' Chris wanted to know. 'It would certainly be a reminder of the wages of sin.'

They read again the final section on Hugh Critchley from Macey's discovery in the anchorite's cell before it collapsed and Simon's accusation when he returned and found that his entire family was dead and their lands given to the Church.

'The Book of Hours. Somebody inscribed the names of the family members into these books and if we can find them then we can trace the family history down to Eleanor, if Morton was her maiden name.' Sarah stretched her legs. 'Let's start in that room to the left of the front door, it looks like a study.'

Chris stood but said 'Shouldn't we try to rescue Adam?'

Sarah shuddered at the memory of his rage in the churchyard and was about to say he deserved it when Chris continued.

'He is the intended victim remember. And his strange behaviour may have been the result of drugs that Eleanor gave him. She gave him something for the migraine and goodness knows what else. Have you ever known him to be violent or so aggressive?'

Sarah knew he was right. She had never known him to behave in such a bizarre manner, and she was grateful to Chris for pointing it out. This was Eleanor's doing.

They set about looking in the house for a telephone to contact the police and ambulance and couldn't find one. There was no TV either. The more they examined it the more it seemed to be a relic of the early part of the twentieth century. Neither of them had their mobile phones.

While they were looking, Chris found a cache of old books in the study. With the Bible and the Book of Hours he found the handwritten recipes Eleanor's grandmother had passed to her. As well as potions there were instructions on knitting with nettles and the spell that would enable the maker to control the person or animal that wore a garment made in this way. The pages were marked in such a way that it was clear what she had been planning.

There were tarot cards placed in the books as markers. Chris pointed out the obvious use of The Lovers as Sarah and Adam and it was used to keep the place in the potion book. The book was open at a recipe for a sleeping draft, but the card was placed in the section on subjugation. It alleged that the liquid rendered the person who drank it suggestible.

She found the Devil, represented as the Green Man was

book-marking the nettle pattern. They were astonished to realise that the nettle gloves were only part of a suit that the victim would wear for the sacrifice. As Sarah looked at it she had a vision of a man covered in green nettle clothing and in thrall to another's willpower. She had a horrifying picture in her mind, with herself as the victim lying naked on the slaughter stone being sacrificed by Adam and then his death, either by his own hand or by Eleanor cutting his throat from behind as he kneeled over her dying body. A powerful gift to a cruel and ruthless god.

It had been planned for today, 31st October, not last night. They had arrived a day early. She asked Chris to look out for calendars and anything that might indicate the timing of the sacrifice that Eleanor had been planning. She had not taken advantage of their ignorance and unwariness to carry out the sacrifice last night when she had the upper hand. Chris must have been a distraction, but perhaps the ghosts had unsettled her. Sarah remembered that Eleanor said that she had never seen a ghost, and she had been shaken to the core by the poltergeist rearranging the pews in the church.

The spirits of William, Licoricia and even Hugh Critchley had reached across the years to try and prevent another tragedy. Eleanor had not expected the intervention of the dead; and it seemed that the presence of both Sarah's unborn baby and Chris had caused Eleanor to deviate from her chosen path. Did she wanted Sarah to escape, or perhaps she had been aware of the fallen tree? Sarah did not know what to believe any more. She had seen the ghosts, they existed and Licoricia seemed to want to communicate with her. Could the dead be trusted? Chris had almost slipped from the world of the living when he was a conduit for William. He was a small child. What power would the ghost of an adult wield?

She turned to Chris and found him looking at her. Immediately she was alert.

'I think that you and Adam were the intended victims of sacrifice and it is obvious that Eleanor's mind has been disturbed by her husband's adultery.'

'And the suffering that caused leading to the tragedy of the death of a man and his innocent children,' Sarah concluded.

'Eleanor is ill, Sarah. She needs treatment, but right now she's dangerous. I think you should let Licoricia enter your mind in the same way that William entered mine.'

Sarah was reluctant but felt she had little choice. 'Don't leave me Chris,' she said.

They returned to the place at the top of the stairs opposite the abandoned window and former landing. They waited for several minutes, focused on summoning her and being open to her presence. Nothing happened. After the terror of being prepared to let this happen to her pregnant body Sarah was tearful with disappointment.

'Perhaps she doesn't consider me worthy' she said to Chris 'I'm an adulteress; didn't they stone them in the bible?'

'Perhaps she's just not here. William has definitely gone. I can't feel his presence at all.'

Sarah thought about the last time they had seen her, when she disappeared into a wall off the old landing. The bedrooms off the corridor were different sizes and several had more than one window. It was clear that an extra room had been created in a small bedroom that appeared to be Eleanor's. It was a severe room, whitewashed and sparsely furnished, with a single bed and a heavy oak chest of drawers. A few books lay on the top and beyond the wall that Licoricia had walked through there seemed to be a closet or en-suite bathroom.

Sarah stopped to examine the books. They were photograph albums and she handed one to Chris and said, 'It might help to know what's in here.'

Among the photos of a smiling Eleanor and her husband, middle aged and bespectacled there were photos of another family with two little girls. Further back she found older snaps of parents and her childhood, and one with Eleanor as a girl holding the hand of a toddler.

Chris grimly held out his album and Sarah could immediately see the problem. Scans of embryos, photos of rooms for a child, baby clothes; then letters from senior midwives, doctors, and consultants. They were meticulously filed in the photograph album, documenting every miscarriage and still birth for a fifteen-year period.

'It's just not fair,' she said. She was more determined than ever to have her child and raise him or her. 'We must save Adam.'

They opened the door to the closet cautiously and then looked with surprise at a metal spiral staircase that led down to the ground floor and came out in a cupboard in the sitting room.

'Is that an emergency exit, do you think?' said Chris.

Sarah was puzzled, until she reached for a light switch. In a shock of incandescent colour, a full-length church window was revealed dropping down alongside the stairs, lit from behind as on a hot summer's day.

'She kept it,' said Chris, his eyes wide open in awe 'it's astonishing.'

'It's certainly breath-taking,' replied Sarah 'but it's the Judas window.'

They stood in silence, taking in the drama of the image which was almost as tall as the cottage. A bright sun shone top right and its rays pierced the branches and leaves of a beautiful tree. Hanging from a branch and casting a dark shadow on the ground was Judas, not sorrowfully in death as normally depicted, but in the very act of dying. His legs kicking and his agonised face lifted to the sun as darkness forever filled his eyes. At the bottom of the picture the pieces of silver lay in shoddy piles among the glowing colourful flowers.

◆   ◆   ◆

Sarah was fascinated by the stained-glass window and would have stayed longer to admire it but Chris grabbed her arm and brought her back to the urgency of the situation.

'We have to find Adam; we can't stay here any longer. Eleanor is descended from a man who betrayed his family, first his brother and then his eldest son. She is obsessed with betrayal. She is going to do something terrible to Adam unless we stop her.'

They went down the staircase and back to the front door where they donned their coats and their boots. The door was locked so they went through the kitchen to the back door, and that was locked too. They split up and began trying to open the windows which were single glazed and made of wood. They were all locked so Sarah brought a knife and a wooden mallet from the kitchen and reluctantly smashed the lock off a sash window and they were able to climb out. She put the knife in her pocket.

Light was beginning to appear in the sky to the east and they listened for any sounds from emergency services or other vehicles. There were none. Cautiously they walked along the path down the valley and up towards the trees at the top of St Jude's hill. Sarah could not get the image of the Judas window out of her mind and she looked back at the cottage where they had left lights burning and wondered if Licoricia and William were still there.

She was reluctant to enter the darkness of the yews circling the church and the graveyard. She stopped at the top of the hill and let Chris walk on. She looked back down into the valley they had crossed and for the first time the henge became apparent as the active particles of dawn threw the shallow ditches in relief.

It's pre-Christian she reminded herself. This isn't just about betrayal, though the Judas window must have meant something to Eleanor during her recent trauma for her to have it installed in Hare Cottage. This is about a sacrifice to something old and pagan, perhaps it is a tithe that has been paid over millennia to a primeval force that defies rational explanation.

Her mind went to one of her favourite folk tales; that of Tam Lin. A human knight fell from his horse when out hunting and was caught by the queen of the faeries. She kept him for a year and a day in luxury until he was to be paid as a sacrifice to hell. Earthly pleasure must be paid for; guilt is as old as mankind. What sort of primitive culture thinks that blood sacrifice is necessary? One that fought blood feuds regularly and sacrificed its young men to increase or retain the tribe's wealth and security? Don't we do that today? All the wars that are waged in the world have similar causes at their roots and involve the sacrifice of a few for the many.

Maybe we should let it be paid, she thought, we should allow the god to have his due. Perhaps then the thing will be satisfied and the slaughter of innocents will cease. She suspected Adam might in some ways be seen as a willing victim, driven by ambition and competitive instincts. He never seemed to be satisfied, and was always comparing himself to others and envying their achievements. He was deeply attracted to St Jude's, perhaps he would be transformed from a mortal man into something more permanent and part of this ancient landscape forever. He would be immortalised through his sacrifice.

With that unholy thought she turned, and then reeled back. Licoricia stood very close. She lifted her grey shimmering veil and revealed a stern pale face. Sarah wanted to pull back, but the other woman put both hands on her face and she dared not move because she could feel the baby react in her womb. She knew from that moment that he was a boy.

'He is your baby's father. If you want to love your child then you will do everything you can to save him. Pay no heed to the glamour of sacrifice, it is the deceit of faery romance and myth; the sacrifice is never truly willing'

Ashamed, Sarah accepted this and knew that she had been beguiled. She breathed deeply the heady scent of the yew trees. She asked the question that had preoccupied her for hours 'What happened to George Macey? Did they find him in time to save him?'

'This is not his story Sarah. You must listen and your actions now will have consequences for the rest of your life.' Sarah fought with an urge to resist but with difficulty she allowed herself to relax into a receptive state and sank to the ground, closing her eyes.

'Through her poisons she has made you hate him so that you are tempted to give him up to his fate. But if you can forgive him and face the trial that awaits you might yet save him.

'This night you have met souls that cannot rest and are drawn to walk upon the earth. William in particular seeks forgiveness from his family for what Geoffrey did, driven mad by his little brother's childish need for revenge on his

206

murdering father. I am bound to him by pity and duty. When he ceases to walk, so will I. You must have faith in love.'

She opened her eyes again. The spirit that was Licoricia had gone. Sarah was kneeling near a graveyard just as it grew light on 31st October. It was cold and damp and she was alone, Chris had gone, and somewhere in the vicinity there was a mad woman who intended to kill someone today and she thought that Adam was the intended victim. She had to stop her, but it would not be simple.

Sarah got up and walked forwards through the yew trees and into the churchyard. The church was glowing slightly as a pink sunrise appeared from the east. Ahead of her was the vestry and she could see that the door was open and lights were on inside. She made her way through the headstones and listened at the door. There were no sounds so she went in and saw that the warm orange room was empty. The door to the church was closed and she was about to open it when she heard it. The sound of something being dragged. Again, she was riven with fear. There was something ominous about that sound and now it seemed to be coming from the tower.

She dared not call for Chris as she did not want to alert Eleanor and she was not sure where he had gone. After a moment's thought she decided that he would have made for the crypt, that was where the slaughter stone lay and that surely was where any sacrifice would take place. She would have to go to the tower and find out what made that sound. Sarah left the vestry and quietly approached the massive yew tree. She saw a mattock they had been using to cut away the yew and she picked it up. After listening for a few seconds, she crept through the gap, straining her ears to hear any sounds that might indicate what was happening in the crypt.

The door was open so that the stairs upwards were visible in the dim light of the early morning. Sarah decided to go up and ensure that there was no one in the tower. She walked as quietly as she could knowing that an assailant from above would have the advantage and was prepared to flee if she was threatened.

She ascended all the way to the bell room without incident and was relieved to find it empty. She could now see from the windows the graveyard and the car park just beyond the lychgate. The white Volvo was parked to one side, as before, and the single-track road lead into the yew trees and she knew that the Land Rover was a few hundred yards further on.

She looked as far round the churchyard as she could see, hoping to spot Chris, but there was no sign of him. She would have to descend and take a look in the crypt. Armed with the mattock she went back down the stairs and tried to close the outer door, to allow access to the stairs down to the crypt. It would not move and using her torch she was able to see that two wedges had been placed at the bottom of the door keeping it in place.

At least this means that Eleanor is outside somewhere, she thought as she removed them and prepared to descend. She closed the outer door and was about to use the wedges to keep it shut when she thought that Chris might have trapped either Adam or Eleanor in the crypt. It might be better to have a means of escape so she put the wedges in her pocket and went down the stairs wielding the mattock against attack.

It was impossible to descend silently as the steps were covered with small stones and mortar. She also needed to light her way as there was no natural light. She made so much noise that she decided to turn her torch on full and face whatever awaited her in the crypt. Sarah stepped into the crypt and placed her back against one of the standing stones. She paused. It was so quiet she expected it to be empty. It wasn't. Chris stood against a stone holding a thigh bone as a weapon.

'Where is she? How did she overcome you?' she said.

'I came to the crypt, I thought that was where she would do the sacrifice, so I opened the door and started down the steps. Somebody was upstairs and kicked me down the stairs so I fell. Then I couldn't open the door. I thought you were behind me. Where were you?'

'Talking to a ghost.'

They both started and turned as the door to the tower closed back over the crypt and a piece of wood was wedged into place. Chris ran up the stairs and tried to move the door but it was firmly stuck.

Sarah swore and said 'I'm so stupid. I should have guessed

she would be around up there. Did you hear a dragging sound just now?' Chris had heard nothing. They knew that Eleanor was planning something hideous and that it looked as though Adam was the chosen victim.

'Do you think it's worth talking to her' asked Sarah.

Chris shook his head 'We are assuming that Eleanor has done this, but it might be Adam. Neither has been behaving normally.'

'Maybe she is possessed?' suggested Sarah.

'By whom? I just think she's mad. Hears voices, perhaps. She's the only one of us who hasn't seen a ghost.'

'So she maintains' said Sarah 'but we don't know if one of her ancestors is telling her to do this to lift the so-called family curse. You must admit, this whole thing has been meticulously planned. She contacted Adam to arrive just before Hallowe'en.' She paused then continued. 'Will she come back here to the stone circle and the slaughter stone, do you think? Or is she going to do it somewhere else.'

'I don't think she knew how to get down here until last night. Your discovery of the crypt door was news to her. She might be planning something quite different.' Chris looked horrified at the thought 'The well. She's going to put him in the well.'

'No. that would be too cruel!' Sarah panicked 'Chris we have to get out of here.' She desperately ran thought all her experiences over the last day, both awake and asleep. There should be another room next to this one. A cell in which the anchorite had lived, and died. Macey had written that the doorway had been blocked when there was a landslide, but perhaps it had not completely filled the cell, and perhaps they could locate the window that allowed Macey to enter.

Sarah emptied her pockets: she had the kitchen knife and the mattock. The earth was soft and easy to dig. They would make good headway with the mattock, otherwise they would have to use their hands.

They began to dig like trapped animals. The knife enabled them to cut away the warp and weft of the root system that held the soil in place. The mattock was invaluable and fine gravel soon tumbled into the crypt. They were sweating with exertion and took it in turns to rest.

Sarah looked at her watch, it was 8.40am and they had been digging for at least an hour. She was resting against the door listening for sounds outside when she heard splintering wood coming from the church. Her imagination worked with dread to think what she might be doing, perhaps with the pews. Was she going to make a bonfire and burn him?

It was quiet again and she had to admit only the loudest noises could be heard from under the tower given the thickness of earth between them. Then Chris said:

'Did you hear that?'

Sarah went to where he was standing knee deep in dirt.

'It came from in there' he said pointing to the earth in front of him.

Sarah took the handle of the mattock and pushed it into the wall of soft earth. It went through easily. Chris joined her and within a few minutes they had created a hole into – blackness.

'I'm not sure we're any better off' said Chris as they made it bigger and prepared to shine a torch through. It was a chamber similar to the crypt but without shelves full of bones. They pushed through until they both stood upright and looked around at the piles of dust and mud that had once been a man's prison.

'It's ghastly' said Chris 'how could anyone live like this, in this space for all those years. He must have atoned for his sins surely in that time?'

They found him as Macey had described, sitting against a wall with a strap around his neck, his skull tipped to one side, his mouth gaping. Sarah felt sorry for him and thought: it's time to end the torment of his unclean spirit walking the earth. She knew that he was only one of many souls that had been drawn here or died here.

'Where's this window Sarah?' Chris brought her back to the real world. She looked at the area described by Macey and it was a steep slope of spilt earth. It might be possible to carefully climb it and the exit would appear somewhere between the vestry and the tower door. She told Chris and he agreed to try, although Sarah was afraid that something heavy may have been placed against it on the outside to ensure that no one fell down it by accident.

While he tunnelled near the roof span, she looked again at the skeleton of Hugh Critchley. She could see that he had attempted to hang himself but she looked for evidence of what might have been a knife. What was it William had said? A man took it? Not George Macey surely? He had made no mention of a knife.

He must have attached that strap to something. She looked above him and saw the shadow of a window and the memory flared of the mullion she had glimpsed next to the path on the south side of the church when she was exploring. There must have been another grilled window when he was anchorite here.

To see it properly she would have to move Hugh. As an archaeologist she had moved skeletons so she overcame an unaccustomed feeling of distaste and revulsion and she took his skull in both her hands and lifted. A disarticulated skeleton would normally come apart easily without its connective tissue, but Hugh's body followed its head and to clung to her clothes. Sarah staggered backwards with the bones and a spidery web material becoming attached to her. She cried out and fell, thrusting him off to one side.

Chris turned and saw Sarah with a tangle of bones stuck to her and a look of terror on her face. He dropped back into the cell and began to pull the clinging bones off her. When they looked at the skeleton laid on the floor they reassured each other that it was web that had made him so sticky.

'Thanks Chris. That wasn't very professional of me.'

'Why did you move him?' asked Chris.

Sarah explained that she thought there might be a way out on the other side of the cell, undiscovered and therefore not blocked. The torch revealed a packed space that looked as though it had been recently disturbed and refilled. It occurred to Sarah that perhaps Peter's colleague had discovered this access when they were exploring the site, had taken what remained of the knife and this was the thing he had not shared with Eleanor's husband, causing the suspicion and mistrust that had ruptured their friendship.

Chris provided a leg up to Sarah who began excavating the half circular shape so hastily refilled and concealed a few years before.

After a few minutes of digging, light came through and they breathed the fresh air of the October morning. Quietly and with caution Sarah made the hole wider until she could see fully into the graveyard and along the church wall on each side, at least as far as the buttresses. This was the most used side of the church so the path was close to the building and the window was only concealed because vegetation and soil had been built up in front of it. There was no gravestone to obstruct them.

With a push from Chris she was able to scramble through it and wriggle onto the path covered in dirt. After establishing that no one was around she covered the window through which she had escaped with dead grasses and tried to make everything look as it had before. Keeping low and slow, she went round the tower and the tree to the crypt door where she let Chris out and replaced the tree branch that had kept them prisoners.

Sarah and Chris crept through the gravestones to the cover of the yew trees and tried to make a plan. It was light and one of them should try to reach outside help.

'You should go Sarah; you have to think of the baby as well as yourself.' Chris insisted. Sarah thought carefully and his reasoning made sense, but she instinctively knew that she had a better chance of thwarting whatever Eleanor was planning. Licoricia had told her that she had to be the one to save Adam from the sacrifice, for the sake of all of them, including their child.

She tried to explain this to Chris, but he did not accept it until she told him that with the flooding there would be physical obstacles to overcome and she was not capable of dealing with them. He reluctantly agreed to go and they decided he would follow the road down to the fallen tree and then make his way to the village.

He gave her a hug and left, skirting the outer edge of yew trees and keeping as low as possible.

Sarah crouched behind the churchyard wall and thought about the last twelve hours. Somehow Adam had been driven into a state of paranoid psychosis by Eleanor, probably with the use of drugs but, she reluctantly admitted, magic might have played a part.

If Eleanor had been expecting to meet Adam and Sarah alone today, she must have devised something to occupy them, rendering them malleable. Perhaps it was to be the combination of an important archaeological find and greed combined with flattery and drugs. That would have been enough, in normal times to render them blind to everything else around them.

Then this evening she would have made the sacrifice. Their early arrival at the church last night and the addition of Chris, had thrown her plans into disarray. She had improvised well, and her use of drugs had turned Adam into a violent paranoid man desperate to save his reputation from perceived threats.

Sarah suspected that the unquiet spirits that had haunted this churchyard were not anchored in time but they had become disturbed more than usual by Eleanor's bloody intentions. Perhaps it was the fact that their blood ran in her veins or the lifting of the fetters that consecration had placed on the primitive hunger of the old gods.

William, a sacrificed child whose rest had been disfigured by other dreadful sacrifices in the nineteenth century was the initiator, she felt sure. His father Hugh was also roused from whatever hell he inhabited by his dead son's agitation and his terrible presence lay like a dark shadow around the hauntings of the last day.

Sarah could see that she was analysing the supernatural occurrences as though they were the layers of soil on the side of a dig. Here were the mysteries of Rudd's death ending a cycle of babies buried dead or killed for sacrificial reasons to placate an imagined power that required sacrifice. Before that there was a lower layer of bloody betrayal and murder in the thirteenth century that destroyed a family and was still unfinished business because Eleanor was descended from them. Below that were the deaths of the Danes who had been slaughtered to a man in the circle of stones, within the neolithic henge of what is now known as St Jude's hill.

After the Danes were slaughtered a church had been built and the neolithic stones hidden. Every week the Christian ritual of the Mass offered up the blood of Christ and the power of the ancient site was suppressed. Now Eleanor thought that she had the power and the right to carry out another atrocity at St Jude's. Did she really think that shedding more blood would stop the chaos?

Overwhelmingly Sarah felt an urge to talk to her. She and Chris had been entirely in her power at Hare Cottage. If she had wanted to kill them, she could have easily poisoned them. She just hoped that the sleeping draught Eleanor had given her had not hurt the baby.

Sarah stood and walked to the church door through the porch. She pushed open the heavy oak door, entered and looked around her. It was no longer dark. The wooden boards that covered the three eastern windows above the altar had been torn down and leaned against the walls. Daylight streamed into the nave and the pews had been stacked to make a staircase up to the windows, like the pyramid created by the poltergeist activity in the night.

Ropes hung from fastenings used to hold the wood panelling in place and Eleanor was hauling a shape into position in the central window. It was a man. His head hung from the rope tied around his neck and he wore green knitted trousers and a medieval surtout and boots. His dead hands stuck out unnaturally, and he was wearing the green gloves that Eleanor had given Adam.

Sarah's heart almost stopped and she stood still to catch her breath. How could she have killed him so quickly, was he dead, or perhaps drugged? Would he wake to strangle slowly on the end of that rope? She had to do something and cut him down. Eleanor hauled and he rose another metre. Then Sarah realised that Eleanor would have to be immensely strong to raise Adam's dead weight that easily. She looked more carefully and saw that it was an effigy made to look like a man and dressed in medieval costume.

Eleanor stopped pulling when Sarah walked down the centre of the church.

'Is that Hugh Critchley?' Sarah asked as she stood in front of the window. Then she said 'the clothes are pretty accurate. His hair was longer and his beard more unkempt.'

The women looked at each other, and Sarah, recovering from the shock of seeing what appeared to be a man being hanged, was torn between compassion for Eleanor's despair and determination that no one else would be hurt.

'How did you get out?' Eleanor was similarly torn between completing her task and dealing with Sarah. She decided to carry on and hauled the dummy figure of Hugh into place above the altar, like a grotesque parody of the father.

'Little William will be easier' said Sarah 'a smaller figure and lighter. You won't need help with him. What made you put Sir Hugh in the place of Christ?'

'It's not about the window' said Eleanor 'but it is a trinity. Father, son and...' she stopped.

'Holy ghost?' Sarah completed it for her. 'I never understood that either. Sometimes represented by a dove I seem to remember.' Sarah decided she had to play for time and hope that Chris could find rescuers. 'The spirit that moves us.'

Eleanor tied off the rope and sat, looking at Sarah.

'There are a lot of spirits that move us, Sarah. One of them is lust.' The accusation hung between them in the still morning air and they held each other's stares to a point where Sarah thought she might falter. It was broken as crows called raucously from the trees.

'Another is bitterness and jealousy' she said. Sarah was going to make a fight out of it. All pretence of female friendship was gone. She felt sorrier than she expected and would have given a lot to turn the clock back to their confidences and comradeship of the previous evening. She thought about her temptation to give up Adam to his fate and the warnings from Licoricia that she had to save him from a curse that was not of his making. Tam Lin she thought. She may turn him into a beast or a serpent but I will hold on to him for the sake of my child.

As though the other was reading her mind Eleanor said 'So you've decided to stick by him even when he was violent and cruel? You know that he would throw you under a bus to ensure that his career progressed and his showcase marriage survived?'

'I know him better than you' Sarah said 'And I'm not going to discuss his human frailty with a poisoner and a potential murderer. What are you going to do to him?'

There was a pause and then Eleanor smiled thinly 'A more relevant question might be: where is he?'

Sarah glanced around the pews that Eleanor had organised into a walkway and steps to the windows. She could see the shape of a child effigy in a white shroud, stained with red blood. There were a lot of crevices and shadows where his body may be hidden, but there was no indication that Adam was here. She could not see how Eleanor could raise him into the Judas window without help.

A worrying suspicion seeped into her mind. What if she had an accomplice? Sarah listened carefully but could hear no one else inside the church. She was standing in the middle of the apse and could be approached from any side. Sarah felt vulnerable and briefly regretted sending Chris for help and for not bringing a weapon; but it was done and she would have to rely on her instincts.

'What do you think this will achieve?' she asked Eleanor, still playing for time. 'It won't bring your husband or those poor children back. You've told us that the thing that resides under the church and thirsts for blood is evil and ancient. Why feed it Adam's blood?'

'Genealogy of course.'

'What? I don't understand. What has Adam to do with St Jude's church and Stansham?' Sarah had been surprised by her answer but she was shocked when Eleanor said:

'Adam Glover is a direct descendant of Hugh Critchley via Simon Moortmain. As, incidentally am I.'

'You can't know that for certain. So many generations have passed.'

'I admit it was a tedious business, cross referencing the generations of antecedents in his family line. But the connection was there in a female member of the family in the eighteenth century, one of eleven girls, got rid of by being married off into the line that produced Glover. There are more than you might think when you look along the distaff lines. Of course, they aren't aware of the curse and probably are not affected by it. My ancestry, being more direct has had to deal with tragedy every step of the way.'

'You can't say that Eleanor. Every family has to deal with tragedy in some form or another.'

'My little brother died in a domestic fire when I was eleven years old. My mum never recovered and battled depression her whole life, which ended prematurely' Eleanor murmured.

'I'm sorry' said Sarah, she was desperately trying to derail the other woman's intentions 'but how can another death end the run of a curse that has presumably been in existence since 1266?'

'I don't expect you to understand. This will be a voluntary act of self-sacrifice by a willing participant who is at the height of his career and power.'

'No. I don't believe he is willing. If you have drugged and brainwashed him into doing this it can't be his own free will. It's coercion.'

Eleanor continued 'I know what happened to Hugh Critchley's sacrifice of William in 1275, and I know why. When you make a sacrifice, it must be with something of value. It's terrible, but to sacrifice a defective child is an insult to the god.'

Sarah said 'William was loved by his brothers. And what about the subsequent deaths? What about John?'

'An accident,' said Eleanor.

'For goodness sake Eleanor, in 1290 the entire family was killed. Surely that is enough atonement?'

Eleanor snapped 'That was probably an accident too. Houses burned easily with no proper chimney, and straw and thatch everywhere.'

Sarah decided to tell her what Chris had discovered from William.

'Chris and I have seen the spirits of William in your cottage Eleanor. He spoke through Chris and according to

Little William's ghost, Geoffrey was haunted by his brother after Simon left and he learned how and why his father had murdered the boy. Geoffrey set fire to the house; it's the sort of crazy thing your friend did to his children. Either he was drunk, or it was deliberate. Surely a sacrifice like that would be enough to lift a curse?'

Eleanor stood and began pacing the platform under the windows.

'No, it's not fair!' she shouted 'Why doesn't he speak to me? Why am I the only one not to see him?' She seemed on the point of tears but this time Sarah felt no sympathy. 'He is my ancestor! My family! You saw him at my cottage?'

'Yes. He was above the stairs Eleanor, after you had left. His hand was held by a veiled woman; she looks after him. They were murdered and they cannot rest. This –' she pointed at the hanging figure 'is not the right way to do it.'

Sarah wanted to draw out the explanation for as long as possible, so she described in detail the order of events after Eleanor had left them at Hare Cottage the previous night. The veiled woman had appeared and they assumed that was Licoricia of Winchester, but she had not spoken to them, just held the boy's hand.

'William wants the killing to stop. Please listen to him.'

Eleanor stopped pacing. 'You mean listen to Chris. Where is your young friend anyway? Where's he hiding?' She looked around and Sarah was too slow in her response, so she continued 'He's gone for help hasn't he? I thought you were trying to talk me out of it but you're just playing for time.' She spat 'Not any longer Sarah!'

She grabbed the rope attached to the Little William effigy and began to raise it into the window space. Sarah considered climbing up to stop her, but she dared not risk the unsteady pile of pews and trestles. If she could knock them down, then Eleanor might fall and that would delay her while she looked for Adam. She grabbed the least stable pew and pulled it out of place. Eleanor's hands were busy with the rope and she was unable to steady herself. With a shriek she overbalanced and disappeared between the pews and the wall. Sarah ran.

Sarah ran back to the porch door and out into the bright morning, through the wet grass and straight to the well-house. She didn't stop to think what she might find but tore open the door and went inside. Sarah searched her pockets for the torch and looked all around the building and then into the well. The grill was in place and there was no trussed-up body there, nor a rope with him dangling at the end of it as she had half expected.

She came out cautiously and looked around, but there was no sign of Eleanor. The tower attracted her attention, and she could just make out where she had scrambled from the cell only an hour earlier. Adam could be anywhere under the dark yew canopy that surrounded the hill, she realised and she would have to carry out a meticulous search if she wanted to find him. Sarah could see that it would make sense for Eleanor to keep him at that end of the churchyard, near the window and where he originally fell. He might be in one of the open graves and that meant searching on the opposite side of the graveyard, to the east and directly in front of the now open windows.

What condition was he in? She decided not to think too much about that but to run as fast as she could along the stone wall on the south side of the church. She passed through the car park, resisting the strong temptation to flee down the road to the village.

Moving on the other side of the wall and staying low as she passed opposite the porch, she heard the door open from the inside. Sarah ducked and found a slit in the coping stones at the top of the wall where she could watch. She saw Eleanor come out of the church. Her face was red and her glasses missing and she limped, but she carried a bag and a pole with a knife bound to the end. She scanned the graveyard. She was obviously able to see reasonably well but she did not see Sarah, who stayed very still and was grateful for the beanie she had borrowed from the Land Rover that covered her bright hair.

It seemed as though Eleanor could not see what she was looking for, and she moved along the church towards the damaged graves and the slope down which Adam had fallen the night before. To Sarah, it seemed like a lifetime ago.

She knew she must stay still until Eleanor had located Adam then attempt to prevent whatever she intended. She obviously wanted to hang him from the rope in the Judas window but to do that she would have to get him into position and then kick out the supports below him. Her blood ran cold at the thought of that but to do it Eleanor must have a weapon. She hoped it was the homemade spear. This was the countryside. What if she had a shotgun? Sarah would not put her life in that much danger and she battled the panic that rose in her throat at the prospect.

Eleanor had disappeared for several minutes and Sarah could not wait any longer. She was about to creep forward when Eleanor appeared and ran to the other side of the church. She reappeared with a shovel and took it to the slope. She must have buried him. What if he was already dead? Would she just hang his body? Sarah thought Eleanor would have let that slip during their conversation. She must have buried him alive and bound in some way so he could not escape.

Sarah crept forward until the collapsed graves were visible. They were cleaner and lighter than most of those in the graveyard and she could hear someone digging. As long as she could hear the sounds of the shovel Sarah could creep closer to it. She looked around a large old gravestone to see Eleanor ten metres away with her back to Sarah. She had found an empty tomb and presumably had managed to put Adam into it bound and gagged or unconscious and left him. More earth had collapsed and covered it so she was now digging it out.

Sarah waited and prayed that he was still alive. Eleanor was muttering something too, but she could not hear what it was. Then she got between the slope and the tomb and using her feet and legs pushed against the lid. It eased forward with a grating sound and then slid off and down the slope. There was an awful moment of tension as Eleanor looked at what was in the coffin.

Then she picked up the spear and prodded the thing in the tomb. To Sarah's relief Adam slowly appeared. His arms were bound to his body and one arm seemed to be damaged. He was covered in mud and when he fell out of the sarcophagus, she heard a muffled cry. Eleanor carefully helped him onto his knees and then poured water into his mouth and over his face. When he had recovered, she told him to get up and move to the church.

It was difficult for him to climb without the use of his hands, but Eleanor persisted until he was on the level. She continued to harangue him.

'You're in big trouble. Don't tell me you can't remember last night and the beating you gave to your own nephew. I have to keep you in the church until the police arrive.'

'What happened? Oh no, what have I done?' Adam spoke hoarsely.

'Chris was seriously injured by you in that fight in the crypt and his life is in danger.'

Adam crumpled and Sarah heard him wail.

'I can't remember anything. I'm sorry, I didn't know. I didn't mean to hurt him. Did you put me in that tomb?'

'Yes. I found you unconscious with a broken arm. It was dark and I panicked, sorry. I thought you'd be safe in that tomb while I took Chris to the cottage. You'll be alright now but I can't let you go. You must do as I tell you until the police get here.'

Eleanor was lying, deceiving him as she did all of us, Sarah thought. She considered approaching them and telling him what was really happening, but he was tied up and Eleanor had a weapon at his back. She would use it on him rather than let him escape. She was not sane.

Eleanor pushed Adam towards the church and only as he approached the windows and looked up did he realise that something was wrong. He stopped walking and looked at the hanging bodies. He turned to Eleanor.

'What's going on? Who are they?' When she didn't respond he turned to them again and after scrutiny saw they were effigies of Hugh Critchley and Little William. 'Did you do that Eleanor? Why? There's an empty window and another rope.'

'That's for you Adam. My dear distant cousin. Can't you see the family resemblance?' She hit him across the head with the pole, cutting his ear, and he fell on his knees. Sarah wanted to intervene, but she felt more strongly than ever that Eleanor would stab him if she thought he might get away. She looked around the churchyard as Sarah ducked out of sight, then made Adam stand again and said, 'Go round the side of the church towards the vestry.'

She's not going to the porch thought Sarah, so she might be able to head them off. When they had disappeared, she moved along the wall and then climbed over it to cross the graveyard and go in through the porch door. She listened but could hear nothing and tried to open it quietly. It creaked and she expected to see them looking at her when she entered. The church was empty, the mannikins hung lifeless against the morning light, the pews had been thrown down and the anchorite brass glowered milkily under the empty Judas window.

Sarah ran to the tower and listened. She could hear them talking as they descended into the crypt and thought she heard Adam asking why she was doing this. Sarah raced through the church and out of the vestry door towards the tree and the tower door. It was wedged shut from the inside. She rattled it and heard Eleanor laugh.

She was going to sacrifice him on the altar stone, she thought, with horror. Why did Sarah have to discover it? Then she remembered there was another way in. Eleanor did not know about the window to the cell. She ran around the tower, pulled aside the grasses, and prepared to slide down into the semi-darkness of Hugh's cell.

She could hear Adam begging for his life in the crypt and Sarah slid feet first through the window landing just as Eleanor shouted, 'Lie on the altar stone or I'll stick you where you stand.'

Adam must have refused because there was a terrible cry and Sarah knew that she had stabbed him. She could see the light beyond the hole in the wall and was reluctant to stick her head through. She picked up Sir Hugh's skull and walked to the hole. She stuck the skeleton into the gap and waited. She could not see and could only hope that Adam would seize the initiative if Eleanor hesitated or baulked at the spectacle of the ghastly sight. A low moan escaped from Eleanor and Sarah peered past his head to see Eleanor kneeling next to Adam's body on the floor.

'Oh God. You've murdered him' Sarah said as she pushed the skeleton through and followed it, filthy with mud and still carrying the thing with its shrouds of sticky web into the crypt.

Eleanor moved away from the body and crept around the walls. Was she so frightened of the skeleton? Sarah knelt by Adam and felt for a pulse whilst keeping her eyes on Eleanor. She had no defence except the skeleton and the other woman was still holding the spear but looked just as terrified. Her eyes were wide, and her jaw hung open.

'This is Sir Hugh. Meet your ancestor and the cause of all this carnage.'

She found a pulse on Adam's neck and glanced quickly to see a wound in his abdomen and cuts on his hands. He needed medical attention and soon.

'It's over Eleanor. Put down the weapon.'

'It was a trick,' Eleanor said taking her eyes off the skeleton. 'It's nothing. You can join your lover in death.' She lowered the spear pointing it at Sarah and moved her arm back to allow a thrust. As she did so a gloved hand closed around her upper arm from the hole in the crypt wall. She gasped and looked to her right as another hand closed over her left arm.

Eleanor locked eyes with Sarah and her look was one of disbelief as whatever was in the cell pulled her slowly through the gap. She dropped the spear and her mouth opened and closed hopelessly as roots from the yew wrapped around her waist and softly drew her into its embrace. When her feet had vanished from sight there was a soft sound of falling earth and soil dropped down into the diminishing space.

No, thought Sarah, not like this. It's too cruel. But she also heard the grinding sound of roots and stone and she knew that she would have to get Adam out of the tower now. The tree was not stable, the door might be closed forever, or the tower might fall.

Eleanor's bag was on the floor and she searched it, finding the bottle of water which she dashed into Adam's face hoping to bring him round. He opened his eyes and Sarah said 'We have to get out of here. It isn't safe. Come on I'll help you.'

He struggled to his feet and they staggered to the steps and up to the tower door. She threw aside the branch that Eleanor had used to wedge it shut and pulled it open.

The yew tree had slipped down away from the tower, its root plate blocked their exit, but the tower was safe and Sarah could hear a chainsaw in the distance.

'That means they are coming to help us Adam. You're going to be alright. Just hold on.' His fleece was soaked in blood and he was white. She sat on the ground next to him and pressed her own jacket over his wound. They would be here soon and everything would be fine.

Chapter Thirteen – Journal of Robert McKinley

December 1863 – Cairo Egypt

It is with great sadness that I must write of the death of my dear friend George Macey. He was an old school friend with whom I had experienced so many adventures. Macey had been suffering from consumption for several years and had left England in 1851 on the advice of his doctors to seek warm dry air. His travels took him through Italy and the Southern Mediterranean until he found the climate and culture of Egypt to be the ideal place for long-term residence.

It is clear that the English ex-patriot community's pursuit of archaeology and their fascination for ancient buried monuments revived his enthusiasm for work. Added to this, his marriage to a lady of the Jewish faith and the birth of three children made his final years probably the most satisfying of his life.

I had not seen him since he set out on his travels and was delighted when he invited me to stay with them almost a year ago. He had uncovered a marvellous site he said, and he required the skills of an artist to depict the most wonderful treasures. The results of my efforts will be published along with George's writings next year and I will soon depart to carry the manuscript and artwork to our British publisher.

Rachel is too upset to discuss the future of the children and herself at present but she will need to decide whether they should travel to England to meet their British family. They are now of an age when education will become important, and I know that Macey was keen that both of his daughters should be educated to the best of their abilities as well as the little boy. He seemed most particular about this point, as though he was afraid that they would be married off or relegated to domestic servitude in some way. They are all bright and delightful children and I hope to see them flourish but I think it will not be easy for Rachel to choose between her own people and those of Macey's family.

The hot climate suited George well and I had hopes for a lengthy remission from tuberculosis. Alas, the energy expended on work during his last year seemed to have drained all the life from him and he died peacefully with his family at his bedside. Before he died, we talked of the events that unfolded during the years 1847 and 1848 when his manservant Rudd died mysteriously.

In truth the seeds of his illness had been sown before that awful time, when he fled from the sorrows of his first wife's death into the arms of laudanum and alcohol. He had been thin and like most Englishmen had a perpetual cough, but I believe it was the hours spent in the suffocating space of the crypt at St Jude's church that began the slow decline resulting in his death.

He had volunteered to explore the crypt that late afternoon as we had finished digging for the day. He followed what turned out to be a wild and savage tom cat through the cell window and found the mortal remains of Hugh Critchley, the anchorite of the late thirteenth century. The cat bolted for the exit causing a landslide that trapped George in the adjacent crypt for almost six hours.

When we had discovered the blocked-up stairs going down into the crypt it took some time to demolish the interior wall, it seemed quite a recent construction. We found Macey unconscious and in a high fever and we carried him by cart to the vicarage to be tended by the Reverend Gibson's housekeeper. I was afraid that he would not regain consciousness.

Gibson and I decided not to publicize the discovery of the crypt and the anchorite's cell. The very day after we had broken it down the wall was rebuilt to ensure that no one could venture into that unholy space. We had seen the slaughter stone and knew that it had been used within living memory.

Macey asked about his journal as he became more rational and I hoped that he would recall enough of the past few days to be able to re-write it. It was lost in the crypt and no one was prepared to search for it. Eventually he stopped asking about it and seemed to spend much time thinking about his experiences. He always refused to discuss the event in any detail, and the death of Rudd remained a mystery, as did the time that Macey had spent underground.

This changed in that last year in Egypt, and I found him prepared to talk about what had happened in the crypt. He had, he said, written his journal until the very last second when the candle expired, using one of my drawing pencils. Then he could do nothing but sit on the floor and await his fate. He wrapped the journal in a linen neckerchief and thrust it to the back of one of the shelves of bone. By this point he had lost any sense of direction in the pitch darkness and was as a blind man, feeling his way among the bones and stones, and the soil and tree roots.

He sat for a little time hoping to hear evidence of our efforts to rescue him. Unfortunately, we had panicked and at that time we were focused on the window to the cell through which he had entered and this was blocked by several feet of earth.

Eventually he heard faint clawing and scraping coming from where he thought the cell was located and hoped we might be about to rescue him. Expecting to see light and hear voices he called to us but received no reply. The sound was getting closer, about to break through into the blackness, and he started to scrape away soil on his side to help the digger.

There were still no replies to his enquiries, and he stopped as fear came upon him that this was no human scraping the earth to rescue him. Before he could withdraw his hand, it was gripped by a bony claw and he smelled the stench of death. Horror rose into his throat, preventing him from screaming.

George tried to prise his hand free and as he wrestled with the slimy stinking fingers, his mind filled with the image of Hugh Critchley sitting in the cell's corner with the leather strap around his neck. He was succumbing to the creature's claws when he saw a pale glow surround them and they relaxed a little. He pulled back and sat heavily on the floor, he thought that it was probably the slaughter stone he rested against.

The light was unearthly, he said, it had no colour and it had only briefly illuminated a bony hand, which was now gone. But it remained and grew until it filled the doorway that had been blocked with earth. I asked if it was Licoricia. He said no, if it had any form it was that of a knight dressed in helm, chain mail hauberk and surtout with the crusader cross. He thought it was Moortmain and that he stood guard over his wicked father's tomb. I remembered then that the Reverend Gibson had written to me some time after our adventure at St Jude's to say that he had deciphered the name on the tombstone that had partially blocked the cell grill. It was that of Simon Moortmain.

Epilogue – a year after the flood

Chris rang the doorbell of a smart townhouse in Oram's Arbour, Winchester and held the bunch of flowers behind his back. When Sarah opened the door, he was a little shy and thrust them at her rather than saying hi and offering a hug. But she brushed aside the formality and dragged him inside.

'Chris, how long has it been? You look so tanned! Go through into the sitting room; the baby is in the bouncy chair and has just finished his rice pudding.'

The sitting room was small and beautifully decorated with so many paintings and sculptures that Chris felt he might be in a museum.

'Aren't you afraid he'll break something or eat something he shouldn't?'

'Not yet Chris. He's only six months old. I'll move them out of the way when he's mobile. I'm just making coffee and I'll put these lovely flowers in water.' She went through into the kitchen and shouted back to him 'Tell me where you've been and what you've been up to.'

He smiled at the gurgling baby and got a matching grin.

'After the enquiry my parents insisted that I go backpacking somewhere like Australia. I was glad to. I still sometimes have nightmares about that place. Do you know how Adam is?'

'Only what I read in the papers or the police liaison woman tells me. He's got enough to worry about, and I don't think babies are really his thing. Have you seen him?'

'Oh yes. My mum insisted that I go to see him and Aunt Jane as soon as I came back, to ensure there was no bad feeling in the family. She was on the phone in her office most of the time, but I did have a long heart-to-heart with Adam, which I couldn't have done if she been sitting taking tea with us.'

She handed him a mug of aromatic coffee 'Still milk and

sugar?'

'Thanks. He is so grateful for what you did for him.'

'He wrote a lovely letter and maybe one day he can meet William.'

Chris nearly dropped his coffee.

'The baby, silly. He's called William George. Well, I could hardly call him Adam, now could I?' she paused 'Have you seen any of the others?' Chris looked puzzled. 'The visitors from the 'other side'. Because I haven't and I'm grateful for that.'

'Not even dreams of George?' asked Chris.

'No. He seems to have abandoned me, and to be honest, what with the enquiry into Eleanor's accident and the all-consuming baby birth and resulting chaos I haven't really missed him. The days slip by without me thinking about Stansham or St Jude's church.'

Chris said, 'Well I'm free from ghosts too, no skeletal children or veiled women or the sonorous tones of a monstrous villain.'

'You sound almost disappointed.'

'No, I'm not. But I have been back to St Jude's.'

Sarah was surprised at this, but curious and wanted to know what it looked like. Had they finished excavations on the stones?

'Funny you should ask that,' said Chris. 'They've stopped work and are talking about re-covering them and keeping the site off limits to the public. Keeping nosy people out has been a problem since it happened, and a man was injured when a piece of masonry fell on him while he was trespassing at night. He almost died.'

'He was bloody lucky,' said Sarah.

'A chap from the community centre board told me that it's been bought by a company that's registered in London and owned by an offshore trust. No one knows who the real owners are, but he said there will be top of the range security so there will be no chance of accidents.'

'But we know there were no accidents, don't we Chris?'

They chatted for a while, munching homemade biscuits. Sarah heard all about his adventures in Australia and she reciprocated with her adventures in the maternity ward until he said, laughing 'Enough, please, don't tell me any more gory details.'

Then Sarah said, 'We should say something about the elephant in the room, shouldn't we Chris?'

He looked around quizzically, then soberly agreed 'Yes. What did happen to Eleanor?'

'What do you know?'

'They found her entangled in tree roots and unable to speak. She was sectioned and is being looked after at a hospital for the criminally insane for her attack on Adam.'

Sarah said 'Yes. She admitted stabbing him, but she didn't know why and they found a lot of incriminating evidence at the cottage. She obviously needed psychiatric help and I hope she's getting it.'

Chris said, 'I hope she never gets out; she scares the shit out of me.'

'There is one other thing,' said Sarah, 'the police haven't been able to trace Peter and Lauren.'

'What? You don't think ....?' He stopped, his mouth open in horror.

'They may have gone abroad, changed their names, started a new life. Perhaps they knew what sort of state Eleanor was in and decided simply not to stick around.'

'Well let's hope they come back, now she's locked up.' He paused seeing the serious look on her face. 'But it's been in all the newspapers and they haven't returned.' He completed his analysis. 'Oh God. Now I really hope she doesn't get out.'

They contemplated that for a while then Chris said 'I wish I could have found my phone. There might have been photos of Little William's spirit.

'I think they probably all ended up in the well.'

'I've been itching to know this: what grabbed Eleanor in the crypt Sarah? What did you see?'

'I saw the gauntleted hand of an armoured knight of the fourteenth century. I saw Simon Moortmain, crusader, and ancestor of Eleanor, drag her through the cell wall.' Sarah had not told anyone this. She felt that only Chris would understand. 'It took them a long time to dig her out and they only found tree roots around her arms.'

'That's interesting' said Chris 'Did you know that the old gravestone that Macey found close to the cell window was that of Simon? The community centre chap told me. He was buried very close to his father's tomb. Perhaps he was determined to prevent more mischief.'

'Well he cut it a bit fine,' said Sarah, 'Adam nearly died.'

'Oh, that reminds me. Adam gave me something for you.' He handed her an envelope. 'It's about Dr George Macey.'

Sarah opened the letter and pulled out a photocopy of a journal by Robert McKinley from December 1863.

Historical Note

This novel is a work of fiction and the names, characters and events portrayed in it are the invention of the author. However some of the historical background is a matter of public record and the character Licoricia did exist in thirteenth century Winchester and she was murdered by person or persons unknown in 1277.

Printed in Great Britain
by Amazon

61113764R00138